The Blood of Toulouse

BY THE SAME AUTHOR

The Marvelous Story of Claire d'Amour
The Call of the Beast
Priscilla of Alexandria
The Angel of Lust
The Mystery of the Tiger
The Poison of Goa
Lucifer
The Albigensian Treasure
Jean de Fodoas
Melusine
The Brothers of the Virgin Gold

The Blood of Toulouse

by
Maurice Magre

Translated, annotated and introduced by
Brian Stableford

A Black Coat Press Book

ISBN 978-1-61227-677-9. First Printing. November 2017. Published by Black Coat Press, an imprint of Hollywood Comics.com, LLC, P.O. Box 17270, Encino, CA 91416. All rights reserved. Except for review purposes, no part of this book may be reproduced or transmitted in any form or by any means, electronic or mechanical, including photocopying, recording, or by any information storage and retrieval system, without permission in writing from the publisher. The stories and characters depicted in this novel are entirely fictional. Printed in the United States of America.

TABLE OF CONTENTS

Introduction 7
THE BLOOD OF TOULOUSE....................................17
  PART ONE 21
  PART TWO 78
  PART THREE...156
THE UNKNOWN MASTER OF THE
ALBIGENSIANS 227

Brian Stableford at Montségur
(2008)

Introduction

This is the eighth volume of a twelve-volume set of translations of Maurice Magre's prose fiction. It contains translations of the novel *Le Sang de Toulouse* (1931), as "The Blood of Toulouse," and the chapter from *Magiciens et illuminés* entitled "Le Maître inconnu des Albigeois," as "The Secret Master of the Albigensians."

Volume One, *The Marvelous Story of Claire d'Amour and Other Stories*, contains translations of early short stories, including the collection *Histoire merveilleuse de Claire d'Amour suivie d'autres contes merveilleux* (1903) and six other stories from various sources published between 1901 and 1913.

Volume Two, *The Call of the Beast and Other Stories*, contains translations of his first three works of prose fiction in volume form, *Les Colombes poignardées* (1917), as "Stabbed Doves," *La Tendre camarade* (1918), as "The Tender Comrade" and *L'Appel de la bête* (1920), as "The Call of the Beast."

Volume Three, *Priscilla of Alexandria and Other Stories* contains translations of the original version of the story collection *Vies des courtisanes*, first published in *Oeuvres Libres* 23 (1923), as "Courtesans' Lives" plus the additional story added to the version published in volume form in 1925, and the novel *Priscilla d'Alexandrie* (1925), as "Priscilla of Alexandria."

Volume Four, *The Angel of Lust*, contains translations of the novella, *La Vie amoureuse de Messaline* (1925), as "The Love Life of Messalina," the novel published as *La Luxure de Grenade* (1926), as "The Angel of Lust," and the chapter from *Magiciens et illuminés* (1930) entitled "Christian Rosenkreutz et les Rose-croix," as "Christian Rosenkreutz and the Rosicrucians."

7

Volume Five, *The Mystery of the Tiger*, contains translations of the novella *Le Roman de Confucius* (1927), as "The Story of Confucius," and the novel *Le Mystère du tigre* (1927), as "The Mystery of the Tiger."

Volume Six, *The Poison of Goa*, contains translations of the novel *Le Poison de Goa* (1928), as "The Poison of Goa," and the prose poems contained in *Le Livre des lotus entr'ouverts* (1926), as "Lotus Blossoms."

Volume Seven, *Lucifer*, contains a translation of the novel originally published under the same title in 1929 and the novella *La Nuit de haschich et de l'opium* (1929), as "The Night of Hashish and Opium."

Volume Nine, *The Albigensian Treasure*, contains translations of the novel *Le Trésor des Albigeois* (1938) as "The Albigensian Treasure," and the collection of vignettes "Communication avec la nature" from *La Beauté invisible* (1937), as "Communication with Nature."

Volume Ten, *Jean de Fodoas*, contains translations of the novel *Jean de Fodoas: aventures d'un Français à la cour de l'empereur Akbar* (1939) as "Jean de Fodoas" and the chapter from *Magiciens et illuminés* entitled "Le Mystère des Templiers," as "The Mystery of the Templars."

Volume Eleven, *Melusine*, contains translations of the novel *Mélusine, ou le secret de solitude* (1941) and the collections of vignettes "Le Côté d'ombre des âmes" and "Révélation des mondes invisibles" from *La Beauté invisible*, as "The Dark Side of Souls" and "The Revelation of Invisible Worlds."

Volume Twelve, *The Brothers of the Virgin Gold*, contains a translation of the novel *Les Frères de l'or vierge*, first published posthumously in 1949.

In the biography *Maurice Magre: Le Lotus perdu* [Maurice Magre: The Lost Lotus] (1999), Jean-Jacques Bedu only offers vague indications as to the early development of Maurice Magre's fascination with the history of the Albigensian heresy—also known as the Cathar heresy—and with the legends associated with the ruins of Montségur. That is understandable, given that Magre was vague about the relevant chronology in his own autobiographical writings. In *Pourquoi je suis Bouddhiste* [Why I am a Buddhist] (1928) he implies that it gripped him in his childhood, but elsewhere he complained about the fact that the "truth" had been hidden from him in that era by conventional historical education. It is, therefore, unclear exactly when he read the three-volume *Histoire des Albigeois: Les Albigeois et l'Inquisition* (1870-1872) written by Napoléon Peyrat (1809-1881), which revealed to him the falsity of the orthodox account and set him firmly in the path to inventing his own interpretation of what had been at stake in the extirpation of the heresy.

Although Magre had certainly begun elaborating his own "secret history" of mysticism and magic by the time he wrote *Priscilla d'Alexandrie* (1925), the incorporation thereinto of the Albigensian heresy as a crucial linchpin probably postdated the writing of *La Luxure de Grenade* (1926), which does not make a connection between Christian Rosenkreutz and the heresy in question. It was probably not long before he produced his idiosyncratic version of the hermetic tradition, as outlined in *Magiciens et illuminés* [Magicians and Illuminati], that he invented the account of the Albigensians beliefs translated as an appendix to the present volume. *Magiciens et illuminés* was published in 1930 by Fasquelle, shortly before his *Confessions sur les femmes, l'opium, l'amour, l'idéal, etc...* [Confessions regarding Women, Opium, Amour and the Ideal, etc.], which was issued in the same year (the latter includes the former in its list of the author's previous works, while the former does not include the latter).

Whenever he read it, however, Peyrat's "history" obviously had a tremendous impact on Magre's imagination, in the same way that reading Madame Blavatsky's account of *The Secret Doctrine* had done, probably a few years earlier. Having written the long chapter on the Albigensians in *Magiciens et illuminés* and completed his *Confessions* he must have begun almost immediately to write a novel in the vein of his previous historical melodramas, based on his own elaboration of Peyrat's scholarly fantasy, with a sense of personal involvement all the greater because he was writing about his own native city and is evolution.

The depiction of the Albigensian crusade presented in the elaborate essay in *Magiciens et illuminés* is largely second-hand, almost entirely derived from Peyrat—as is acknowledged, albeit scantily, in the references appended to the article—although Magre elaborated the borrowed material substantially even there, and he went on to elaborate it even further in *Le Sang de Toulouse* (1931), which presents a first-person account of the entire history of the destruction of the Albigensian heresy, over half a century. The narrator, Dalmas Rochemaure, is ingeniously credited by the author with an active role in all of the key incidents of the history, and although many sections of the narrative are necessarily synoptic, Magre shows great artistry in collapsing such an extensive story into a manageable text, supplying adequate background information without overburdening the story with factual detail.

The notion that his native city and the area surrounding it—of which Magre remained passionately fond even though he had deserted it for Paris in the pursuit of his literary vocation and had only recently returned to live in the Midi in 1930—had a secret history, long-buried by the "official" history that represented the Church's crusade against the Albigensians merely as an incident in the unification of France as a nation, was tailor-made to attract his attention and his affiliation, and he embraced it wholeheartedly. However, Peyrat's work, although highly inventive, was not entirely original either, and the fantasization of the history of Toulouse had already begun, in a work of which Magre was undoubtedly unaware, but the existence of which nevertheless serves to situate *Le Sang de Toulouse* within an eccentric and elaborate long-standing tradition

Although Peyrat's account of the last stand of the surviving Albigensian *perfecti* in the castle of Montségur, allegedly built by Esclarmonde de Foix—of whom little was reliably known save for her name, but whom Peyrat made into a symbolic heroine and a kind of guiding light of Catharism—is a fabulous romantic invention, due almost entirely to his own imagination, the remainder of his history is based in large part on a previous work that was thought at the time to be a reliable history, although twentieth-century investigation has revealed that it too contained a strong dose of scholarly fantasy: Étienne de Lamothe-Langon's three-volume *Histoire de l'Inquisition en France* (1829). Lamothe-Langon claimed to have based much of his account on archives preserved in his native city, Toulouse, and several sets of *Annales de la ville de Toulouse* had, indeed, been published in 1687, 1772 and 1776, but those documents consisted of little more than lists of names of people holding public and religious offices at various times. Lamothe-Langon invented stories to go with many of the names, primarily in order to illustrate the horrors of the Inquisition, although he remained broadly neutral with regard to the supposed substance of Albigensian heresy and treated Simon de Monfort and his genocidal crusaders in a broadly respectful fashion, save for disapproving of the massacres they carried out.

Lamothe-Langon had earlier written 459 articles for the *Biographie Toulousaine* (1823) and had also published a *Biographie des préfets des 87 départements de la France, par un sous-préfet* (1826), but nobody seems to have bothered to investigate the extent to which those texts are polluted by invention. Later in his career, however, he went on to become a prolific writer of fake memories and biographies, beginning with a best-selling six-volume set of the memoirs of the notorious Comtesse Du Barry (1829-30), which recycled material from his historical novel *Le Chancelier et les censeurs* [The Chancellor and the Censors] (1828) as well as material borrowed from earlier fictitious texts concocted as political slanders. In much the same way, his history of the Inquisition recycled some material from his Gothic novel *L'Hermite de la tombe mystérieuse, ou le Fantôme du vieux château* [The

Mysterious Hermit of the Tomb; or, The Phantom of the Old Château] (1822),[1] which had been misrepresented as a translation of a work by the popular English novelist Ann Radcliffe.

The twentieth-century discovery of the invented elements of *Histoire de l'Inquisition en France* (1829) led some historians to begin referring to "the myth of the Inquisition," as if the persecutions of the institution detailed in the text were wholly invented, but that might be taking skepticism too far. Lamothe-Langon's cavalier embroideries did, however, inject a strong dose of melodramatic fiction into the history of the Inquisition's depredations in his native city and the surrounding area, upon which Napoléon Peyrat was only too glad to draw, and which he was eager to augment with further inventions. Magre's additional elaboration, in offering a purely speculative account of the Albigensian's beliefs—of which no reliable historical accounts had survived the persecutions of the Church—and integrating that account into the secret transmission through the ages of a uniquely precious wisdom, was particularly spectacular.

In a curious sense, *Le Sang de Toulouse* brings Lamothe-Langon's project full circle, in producing a text akin is some ways to *L'Hermite de la tombe mystérieuse*, while continuing the labor of his scholarly fantasy by fleshing out and adding further human interest to stories of which only the merest hints were dropped in the actual *Annales de la ville de Toulouse*. For instance, a comparison of the various versions of the story of Pierre Maurand given by Lamothe-Langon, Peyrat and Magre, show an interesting process of gradual expansion. Such high points of Magre's detailed elaboration as the accounts of the horribly bloody massacre of the entire population of Béziers, the escape of the inhabitants of Carcassonne and the final doomed defense of Montségur, are, however, only mentioned by Lamothe-Langon as incidental matters of fact, and owe their fantasization almost entirely to Peyrat.

---

[1] To be available from Black Coat Press in 2018.

The idea invented and popularized by Peyrat that "the Cathar treasure" was smuggled out of Montségur by four knights before the castle fell, and was taken to a cave called the grotto of Ornalhac, where the last Albigensians were walled in and buried alive, became a great inspiration to twentieth-century treasure-hunters. It is also greatly elaborated in the harrowing final chapters of Magre's novel, in which Magre does not hesitate to follow Peyrat in identifying the key element of the treasure in question—here confided to the protagonist's care rather than that of the legendary knights—as the Holy Grail: a hollow emerald containing drops of Christ's blood, collected during the crucifixion.

That notion was to become a highly significant element in subsequent scholarly fantasy and fantastic fiction, encouraged by the creation in 1937 of a *Societé des amis de Montségur et du Saint-Graal*, of which Magre was a founder member, along with the English antiquarian and occultist Francis Rolt-Wheeler (1876-1960). The abundant spinoff of the fascination eventually culminated in the highly successful scholarly fantasy *The Holy Blood and the Holy Grail* (1982) by Michael Baigent, Richard Leigh and Henry Lincoln, whose thesis was adopted by Dan Brown for his best-selling novel *The Da Vinci Code* (2003). That revitalization of interest helped bring the *Le Sang de Toulouse* back into print in 2003 and to maintain its status as Magre's most celebrated book.

The idealist philosophy that Magre designed for attribution to the Albigensians in the relevant chapter of *Magiciens et illuminés*, and transferred, albeit a trifle obliquely, to *Le Sang de Toulouse*, is an idiosyncratic derivative of the Buddhist notion that every individual human life is an element in a chain of reincarnations in which all sins have eventually to be punished and expiated, in future incarnations if not the present one. The ultimate reward of that expiation is to escape the cycle of reincarnation into a carnality that is essentially corrupt and evil by attaining instead a spiritual unity with the divine, Nirvana. That blissful state has to be achieved by finally contriving to lead a pure life free from sin, with all previous moral debts discharged.

Magre observed continually that the imagined state of Nirvana is not a goal to which most people, fatally addicted to the vulgar pleasures of carnality, actually desire, and he was never entirely sure that he could overcome his own lingering addition to carnal pleasure sufficiently to desire it himself. The contest with that doubt is represented in particularly striking terms in some of his later novels, especially *Mélusine*, but it is arguable that Magre's depiction of the allegedly-successful protagonist of that novel is considerably less convincing than his characterization of the hero of *Le Sang du Toulouse*, who eventually has solitude and meditation forced upon him, but whose principal desire throughout the life mapped out in the action-packed plot is to savor carnal pleasures. That characterization was necessary in order to allow Dalmas Rochemaure to play a suitably involved and relentlessly active role in the unsuccessful fight against the extermination of the Albigensians, but it also helped to make the hero sympathetic to a wider range of readers.

There is, however, a further complication to the schema that Magre introduced, perhaps a trifle paradoxically, into his depiction of the Albigensian philosophy, explicitly in *Magiciens et illuminés* and tacitly in *Le Sang de Toulouse*, which is his representation of the *consolamentum*. The *consolamentum* was the Albigensian version of the last rites, administered by *perfecti* to their less accomplished followers, apparently analogous in its meager fourteenth-century documentation to the Catholic Sacraments. In Magre's version, however, the *consolamentum* becomes magic of a powerful kind, which enables those who receive it not only to take a short cut to escaping the cycle of reincarnation, but also enables them to die painlessly and joyfully. *Le Sang de Toulouse* makes much of that joy in annihilation, especially in its description of the siege and capture of Montségur, when the avidity of the Albigensians to find death becomes a central matter of concern for the novel and its protagonist. Although

Dalmas Rochemaure does not understand that hunger for death, because not one of the *perfecti* he consults actually takes the trouble to make it comprehensible to him, he is in no doubt about its sincerity. The reasoning behind it is spelled out more explicitly, if somewhat extravagantly, in the relevant chapter of *Magiciens et illuminés*, but however excessive it might be reckoned by a skeptical observer, it is a very revealing invention.

What Magre was actually seeking in life, and what all his characters in search of spiritual enlightenment are actually seeking in their research in the wisdom of the ancients, is not an awkward and thorny path to the divine but a short cut. The Buddhist message has never been particularly difficult to come by, even in the Occident, but its prescriptions are hard to follow, even for those who find themselves sympathetic to its philosophy, and the attainment of the eventual reward is arduous even for the most committed. In essence, what Magre hoped to find, as a solution to his despair, or as a means of living with it, was a *consolamentum*: a magical formula that would cut out all the crap of life and its undischarged moral burdens, and allow him to make direct contact with the divine, preferably without dying, but, if that were still necessary, doing so painlessly and joyfully.

In regard to that goal, *Le Sang de Toulouse* is more honest than a great many scholarly fantasies, including Magre's own. Fantastic as it is, Magre's fiction is consistently more convincing in its convictions, and perhaps more truthful in its conclusions, than his autobiographical writings and his scholarly fantasies—as can readily be seen in the present volume by comparing the translation of *Le Sang du Toulouse* with the essay on which it is based. The novel is a fine piece of work, dramatic and poignant, and is supplied with a flamboyant final flourish; the article, while certainly interesting, never comes close to plausibility, even in itself, let alone as the keystone of a more elaborate fantasy of history.

The awareness of that distinction must have been a significant element in encouraging Magre to build increasing quantities of fiction—and fantastic fiction in particular—into his supposedly non-fictional writings, converting texts such the series of vignettes assembled in *La Beauté invisible* into curious hybrids. It must also have been a factor encouraging him to produce the experimental fictions *Le Trésor des Albigeois* and *Mélusine* alongside *Jean de Fodoas* and *Les Frères de l'or vierge*, which are primarily action-adventure novels, the former deliberately cast in the same mold as *Le Sang de Toulouse*. It is certainly the case, however, that Magre never fully recovered the verve and intensity of *Le Sang de Toulouse*, surely because he never had another project on which to work that was so dear to his heart. It remains, in consequence, his finest achievement as well as his most celebrated.

The translation of *Le Sang de Toulouse* was made from a copy of the 2003 reprint published in Monaco by Editions du Rocher. The translation of "Le Maître inconnu des Albigeois" was made from the London Library's copy of the 1930 Fasquelle edition of *Magiciens et illuminés*.

Brian Stableford

THE BLOOD OF TOULOUSE

Glory to the sunlit soil that extends to the sea where Moorish galleys sail all the way to the land where pines grow and all the way to the endless ocean! Glory to Toulouse, the city of the twenty-nine gates, which Tholus, grandson of Japhet, founded, the city built in red stones, stones as unshakable as the hearts of heretics!

Glory to the Garonne that springs from the Pyrenean mountains, which keeps a little of the light of Aran in its ensorcelled waves, gives the cep of the vine its appearance of a drunken dwarf, and to the poplar its power of meditation!

Glory to the men of Oc who, in the first years of the thirteenth century of Jesus Christ, knew the truth about the three aspects of God, and the course of souls under the successive doors of the dead, and perished for having known it.[2]

I want to transmit to you orally the unusual scenes to which I was a witness, the joyous or criminal deeds that I accomplished, the laudable prowess in which I glory, and the desolation and beauty that I have contemplated without dying.

In those days the women were more beautiful than they are today, with an impulse of the loins that gave fortunate liberty, the Garonne ran wider in its bed of sand and pink pebbles, and the sun outlined more clearly the ocher Saracen towers on the hills. Toulouse was full of poets and literate men.

---

[2] Author's note: "At the beginning of the thirteenth century, the south of France was ravaged by a crusade that Innocent III preached against the Albigensian heretics, and whose goal was to dispossess Raymond VI, Comte de Toulouse. The Comte de Toulouse was then the most powerful lord of Christianity after the King of France, and his Estates enjoyed an exceptional liberty and a great civilization."

There was a school of Jewish medicine and a college of Arabic philosophy. The great commercial route of the Midi put Saint-Gilles and Fréjus in communication, by means of winged galleys, with the multiform Orient. Caravans brought perfumes and spices from Damascus, carpets from Samarkand and musical instruments that no one knew how to play from mysterious China.

Now, there are no more marvelous silks, there are no more Occitan singers, there are no more Arab philosophers. And by virtue of a just law, nature becomes less magnificent in the profusion of her trees and the color of her suns as men become more wicked.

The things that I am going to say will make you weep, for nothing provokes tears like beauty that is irremediably lost, like intelligence that is extinguished. But tears are more useful to humans than joy, and the salt they contain is an aliment of virility.

If you are astonished that I have been able to traverse such great calamities and have survived, know that I was chosen to transmit this story. My task is to recognize, to the wonder of their eyes, the men who ought to hear me, those who will keep the memory and transmit it in their turn. The accounts written on parchment have been destroyed by those who want to maintain ignorance, but words fall into souls like doves that come from afar and only alight in order to depart again. And that is a form of justice. Evil and hatred cannot look one another in the face, and speech dissolves by virtue of the light it emits, as the sharp blade of a necromancer reduces to nothing the cloud of evil spirits.

I too am going to evoke the dead. They do not sleep in peace, in accordance with the prayer of the Church. There are no sung psalms, there is no ceremony, that can prevent dead creatures from haunting the places where they have done evil.

Montfort, the evil one, is here, more hermetically sealed in hatred than in his breastplate. Foulque, the hypocrite, is here, and it is necessary that he raise eternally to his eyes the fingernails in which he hides pepper in order to shed false

18

tears. Raymond, the uncertain, is here, and he continues to toss a coin in the air to put an end to his absence of decision by heads or tails. Here is the execrable Tancrède, with his donkey's ears and his owl's eyes, who had a taste for causing suffering and was proud of having invented an instrument of torture. Here is Dominic, the bald, and Innocent, with his tiara of peacock plumes. I show the faces that were hidden under the hoods and the leprosies that erupted behind the velvet doublets. The majority among the strong of old are only shivering shades, and come running meekly when I make a sign.

Behold, too, the innumerable victims, those who have suffered patiently, those who have become yellow with rage, those who have fought for their right. The desire to see the punishment enchains them as much as the sin. My memory summons them all with the swords of their wars, the genitalia of their desires and the books of their dead studies. And if there are Perfecti who are liberated by forgiveness and who have escaped the terrestrial circle, may they give measure to my thought, metal to my voice, and breath to my lungs, in order that, in the magical world of syllables, I shall pour the gold of truth.

PART ONE

I

The resonance of a bell is at the origin of my life. I woke up one night with the joyful desire to hear the bronze resound. In those days, my blood flowed with such great force beneath my carnal envelope that I could not prevent myself from realizing that which animated me. I looked at the opening in the form of a cross that cut through the wall of my monastic cell. There was nothing but darkness outside. I could scarcely distinguish the contours of the Roc de Sédour. The waves of the Ariège were beating the stones of the abbey gently. I glimpsed the door that opened to the cloister and cocked an ear. The convent was silent. The file of pillars extended before me, with the regularity of a nocturnal obsession. I took two or three steps and I started to laugh noisily, so much was my soul filled with an uncaused delight.

I had not formed any plan. It would have been easy for me to procure a secular garment and a bag with some nourishment inside, if I had had the least foresight of what I was about to accomplish. I have always thought that the soul meditates during sleep and makes irrevocable decisions that the waking man must obey. I felt so light that I started to run.

Above the porch of the cloister, like a red eye, a window was illuminated. It was that of the chamber of honor, the chamber of frescos, where the papal legate, Pierre de Castelnau,[3] who had arrived at the convent the day before, was

---

[3] Author's note: "A monk of the Abbey of Fontfroide, whom the Pope sent to repress heresy in the Midi. He rapidly rendered himself odious by the violence of his repressions. Ray-

lodged. He was already awake, or perhaps had not yet gone to sleep. I judged that insomnia was the portion of the wicked, those tormented by some remorse. Was the slumber of my innocent soul not as profound as a night charged with clouds? I remembered the anguish that I had experienced before the limpid gaze of that face of wax turned toward me, the scorn with which I had suddenly been enveloped, and that memory redoubled my ardor. I seized the flap of my robe with my left hand in order to traverse the cloister more rapidly and reach the tower where the bell was, with its power of sound.

For almost exactly a year I had been a novice in that abbey of the Order of Cîteaux, founded by a holy man by the name of Martial near the little village of Mercus in the valley of the Ariège. In vain, my father, the celebrated Rochemaure—the cathedral man, as he was commonly called—had begged me not to put on the somber cowl that, according to him, I would rapidly throw into the nettles. He had always given evidence of a profound intuition in speaking of my character and my future. He always punctuated what he said with a gesture that he had retained from his profession as a builder. It seemed to be pointing at the spire of a tower cleaving the sky.

"You never do anything reasonable," he said. And he struck his forehead to make it understood that my intelligence lacked equilibrium.

"It's necessary to construct one's soul," he also said, "as one constructs a cathedral. The spire can only be high if the foundations are deeply sunk in the ground, like roots."

He had wanted me to enter as an apprentice the lay brotherhood of which he was the master, but the ecclesiastical fraternities had just obtained an ordinance from the Comte de Toulouse to prevent laic construction. Then he had made me

---

mond VI, Comte de Toulouse, was the principal object of his hatred. He had undertaken a personal campaign in Provence to detach his vassals from him."

learn the use of weapons with a Florentine master who taught in the open air in the Place des Carmes. I acquired a taste for handling a sword, and rapidly excellent in that, but it did not last. I linked myself in amity with Samuel Manasses, the son of the physician, and was initiated by him into poetry and Greek philosophy. I then perfected my knowledge of that language, and I also learned Arabic in order to read Plato, for the only texts by that great sage that could be found in Toulouse were translations into Arabic brought from Seville by literate Jews.

It was then that I encountered the monk Petrus. He lived by begging and he lived in abundance, thanks to the method that consists of addressing insults in jest to the man from whom one wants to obtain a meal or money. He preached at crossroads against the wealth of bishops and the debauchery of great lords. He pleased me initially because of his thinness, for plumpness in a man has always inspired disgust in me. We debated under the florid arbors that existed in those days near the Tour de Bazacle, but which the wars have caused to disappear, like all beautiful and pleasant things. I was much the more eloquent because of the admirable gift of speech that I had received from nature.

My aptitude in debate was such that at the age of seven I harangued children of my own age at the corner of the Rue de Taur and the Place Saint-Sernin. During our discussions I surprised in Petrus' eyes flashes of an admiration that he disguised with ignorant bluster and sometimes even stammering. He had little knowledge, but his faith was communicative. I thought that I would vanquish him easily in the metaphysical combat that we recommenced every evening, but not at all. It was him who triumphed. This is how.

He thought that by means of an intelligent manner of prayer one could communicate directly with Jesus Christ. It required patience and method, but if one had both, one could have an almost quotidian commerce with him. In spite of his humility, he, Petrus, lived under the surveillance of Jesus. Several times, when he was in the process of drinking too

23

much in ill-famed taverns, a slightly hunchbacked peasant, bearded and simple in appearance, had come to sit down facing him and had gently taken the glass out of his hand.

"Who is that unknown peasant?" he had asked his companions.

They had contented themselves with laughing, because they did not see anyone; and Petrus had known, via the certainty of the heart, that Jesus had appeared to him in person. He continued to drink, but slightly less, because, he said, it is only excess that is reprehensible.

He made me promises of prompt vision if I prayed as he indicated to me and with the desirable fervor. I had the naivety to ask him to set a date and the said, tranquilly: "About a month." And he added: "On condition that you put an end to the insanity of your discourse"—words that he only pronounced with the pious goal of diminishing my pride, for he did not know envy.

There was a great deal of talk in Toulouse about Martial and a vow of silence that he had respected for five years. I immediately set out to walk to his abbey, where I knew that the rule of Saint Benedict was applied rigorously.

That rule required that the vocation of a candidate be tested as soon as he arrived. The door had to close three times before him, with an interval of one day each time. I remained in prayer for three days under the July sun, which was more ardent than usual and under the clear night that became malignly cold when the mountains began to be outlined against the azure. But I did not complain, because hope was resident in my heart. However, as I thought I remarked a certain irony on the doorkeeper's face, I was determined to draw him outside and correct him with my staff.

On the fourth morning, the two battens of the door opened solemnly and it was the prior who came to welcome me, as is customary. I forgot the doorkeeper's punishment and fell to my knees. But it was not the sandal of the revered Martial that I kissed in the dust. He had died some time ago without my having any knowledge of it. I found myself in the presence of a fat abbot from the North sent by the mother abbey, who spoke to me in the harsh and discordant patois that people speak in Paris.

Sympathy and antipathy circulate among men by means of currents almost visible to the eyes. Behind the abbot's smile I perceived a kind of mocking scorn when I told him, albeit with modesty, that I was a resident of Toulouse. And when I added, lowering my eyes, that I was the son of the Rochemaure who was the celebrated master of a fraternity of cathedral-builders, he made a semblance of not knowing the name and he lifted me up in his soft hands, with an unctuous touch, affecting a feigned kindness.

I enclosed myself in my silence as if behind a mute wall, and it was averred by everyone that I kept quiet because I had nothing to say. The most vulgar chores were given to me. I did not complain at being employed in emptying chamber-pots, looking after pigs in the sty or being posted in the fields with weapons in order to fight bands of marauders, but I suffered from not finding silence favorable to the divine presence. In the midst of talkative and argumentative monks I was transported into a world of speech devoid of beauty.

The abbey was at odds with all the local jurisdictions and no one there was occupied with anything but law. Instead of prayers, the novices learned by heart and recited the laws of Justinian, to the rhythm of a ballad. The customs and usages of all times and all lands were copied on parchment. Parliamentary edicts, royal ordinances and the judgments of consular tribunals were discussed.

I took refuge in the interior convent of the thousand cloisters and the thousand sanctuaries of my soul, and I waited for the apparition promised by Petrus. But the only peasants I saw were vulgar mountain men who came to sell their vegetables and fruits, and their form, devoid of all transparency, was made of dense matter visible to all. And I suffered above all from the pitying smile that I saw on the lips of the prior when he considered me, for one becomes stupid among those who consider you to be stupid, and one is only elevated among those who believe you susceptible of elevation.

That lasted until the night of the bell.

The day before, the arrival of Pierre de Castelnau had taken place, with great ostentation. He came from Toulouse, where he had repressed heresy, and before going to Foix he had wanted to converse with his friend, the abbot of Mercus. I had heard such horrible things said about the repressions ordered by him that I had not wanted to believe them. Since I had known that he was in the convent I had experienced a sort of apprehension.

I had been charged with taking care of the horses of his escort in the tables and I had not seen him. As I was traversing the cloister to go to the refectory I suddenly found myself in the presence of the abbot and an imposing individual, albeit of meager stature. He was wearing a crimson dalmatic over a red silk tunic.[4] His belt had a ruby clasp. His gloves and hose were the color of fire. From a broad triangular bonnet a crimson hood fell back over his shoulders that made his dull waxen face and the petrified blue of his extinct eyes stand out.

Was it a presentiment of what was going to happen? My heart began to beat forcefully in my breast. Pierre de Castelnau had stopped and I saw his eyes examining my hands with curiosity, which were soiled up to the elbow by the dung I had just been shifting. He asked me a question, but as he expressed himself in his shrill northern language, I did not understand it. The tone indicated that he was saying no matter what, without attaching any importance to it, with an objective of scornful benevolence.

---

[4] Author's note: "The papal legates were monks, but to reinforce their authority, they traveled in lay vestments and magnificent apparel. It was the man who was to become Saint Dominic who first had the idea of fighting the Albigensians with their own arms, simplicity and poverty, and going to preach barefoot, as mendicants."

Neither of us knew, at that solemn moment, that the first link was being sealed of an unparalleled chain of woes. Between the Pope's envoy in the red costume and that wretched domestic of monks, an occult link was established that was only to be broken by death. And on that link was to depend an inconceivable drama, the destruction of southern cities, the rape of beautiful young women, the death of knights and the silence of singers.

Dusk was descending placidly, and neither the legate nor I had the slightest presentiment of the future events that would be elaborated around us. I blushed, I opened my mouth, and I sensed an expression of stupidity covering my features, while I tried awkwardly to hide my hands behind my back.

Pierre de Castelnau turned to the abbot and said that I was doubtless the monk especially devoted in the kitchen garden to planting and picking the parsley. He was making allusion to an absurd superstition claiming that parsley grows almost visibly if it is sown by someone simple-minded.

The abbot started to laugh in a servile and acquiescent manner, and they both resumed their stroll.

I was saying that I started to run along the cloister. I went past the chapel without stopping. A murmur of prayers emerged from it, because the force of the rule had the chapters relayed there in spite of the juridical preoccupations. The one that had begun at the eighth hour of the night would only be relieved at sunrise.

The bell was in an ancient tower against which the church was built. I crossed its threshold and I climbed the spiral staircase like a shadow deprived of substance, whose passage causes no sound.

A joyful dilatation inflated my breast when I began to ring. I had not premeditated anything, but it was the tocsin that I rang, with hurried, redoubled thrusts, at full tilt.

Fear is the animating element that is the most rapid in propagation. Immediately, doors began banging in all directions. Through a loophole level with my head I distinguished by starlight forms with necks extended in interrogation. There were footfalls in the chapel, and all the monks who were there, those who were praying as well as those who had the faculty of sleeping standing up with their hands joined, rushed outside. They collided with a group that was running into it in search of a refuge. The paved courtyard, the cloister and the corridors filled with clamors. I heard the voice of the bursar crying: "The treasure! Save the treasure! A certain Laurent, of sickly temperament, who was subject to crises, fell to the ground howling. I recognized Brother Robert by his ridiculous obesity; he had found a huge cross, I know not where, and was raising it with a gesture of importance, as if everyone's salvation were subordinate to his gesture.

Suddenly, a voice rang out: a peremptory voice, that of someone who knew.

"It's the Seigneur d'Ussat's soldiers."

The Seigneur d'Ussat, a violent man and a convert to the heresy,[5] had had long quarrels with the jurists of Mercus, and he had recently threatened the abbey with pillage. Now, he had a habit of keeping his promises. A clink of weapons followed. Somewhere, monks were doubtless arming themselves. But those who were distributed in the courtyard and along the cloister believed that Ussat's soldiers had forced the doors.

I was still ringing. And then, far away to the north, a bell responded to mine, and then another to the south, and gradually, I heard them from all sides of the horizon. They were all sounding the tocsin, and their repercussion was profound and infinite, crossing the valleys and the mountains.

I quickly realized, however, that those bells were not sounding in reality. I knew to which crenellated tower and which church belfry they belonged. One was ringing in the tower of San Salvi in Albi, another in the advanced barbican

---

[5] Author's note: "The Albigensian heresy taught that life is evil, that a man is condemned to live again incessantly through successive reincarnations, until he is detached from desire by absolute disinterest."

in an easterly direction, on the ramparts of Carcassonne, another was the bell of the church of Saint-Nazaire in Béziers. There were more distant ones, those of Maguelonne, those of Beaucaire, others that were agitating in towers made of marine stone and had broken Saracen arrows. All of them had a desperate tone, announcing calamities, the sorrow of peoples, and the death of beauty.

Thus, the tocsin that I had set in motion without knowing why was a kind of signal, awakening in all the bells of the south a mysterious life of bronze, whose music was in my heart.

I did not have time to be astonished or sad. I felt myself seized violently around the body and a face almost stuck itself against mine. I respired a noxious odor, by means of which I recognized the brother responsible for ringing the bell. He had a frightful habit, by virtue of malignity or unconsciousness, of exhaling his bad breath in your face at close range.

"Why are you ringing? Who ordered you to ring?"

There was indignation in his voice because of his usurped function. I shoved him away with all my strength, and doubtless something in my gaze frightened him, for he ran down the stairs uttering cries.

I went down behind him, lending an ear to bells that were fading away over silent rivers and unknown landscapes. At the foot of the tower was a group of monks who must have interrogated the ringer and were waiting for an explanation. On seeing me they all cried out together, wanting to know what the danger was that was threatening the convent.

"Why? What's happened?" they said, surrounding me.

Then I started howling: "God has withdrawn from you! God has withdrawn from you!" And at the same time, I wrenched myself out of their hands.

It only took a second for their terror to change into anger and a desire for vengeance. While I ran hither and yon, trying to escape those monks seized by rage, a hundred voices cried that Brother Dalmas had gone mad and that it was necessary to seize him. My loss of reason was announced from cell to cell and proclaimed from the windows, and one monk, who had hoisted himself up as far as the steeple of the chapel in order to escape the peril, even announced that the stars had begun to pale in the sky.

I bumped into Brother Robert's belly and, seizing the cross that he was holding, I threw it at the legs of those who were pursuing me. I launched myself into a corridor, closing the door behind me, traversed the deserted refectory at a run and emerged into the kitchen garden. I suddenly remembered that there was a ladder at the back, standing against the wall.

I scaled it and let myself down gently on to the body of the odorous, vast and indulgent earth. In the distance, in the clover and in the vines, matinal crickets were responding to one another. I saw the Roc de Sédour outlined to my right in the pallor of the dawn. I knew that by following the Ariège I would find a little higher up a fordable place, and would then have only a few steps to take to plunge into the forest, where it would be impossible to catch me. I started to run.

As I ran, I bumped into a hillock that I had not perceived and fell on the ground. My open arms embraced a sort of mound covered with earth, at the summit of which was a little stone cross. Lord! I pressed against myself the clay soil beneath which Martial had wanted to repose without a coffin, in order to become stems, roots and the juice of sap more rapidly.

And during the second in which I made an effort with my hands and knees to get up again, I heard his voice, which said to me:

"Go, my child, into the forest, where you will no longer hear human speech vibrate. Instruct yourself with the howling of wolves, the creaking of branches, the sound of water running over pebbles. For the living speech is born of human silence. Those who, like you, are marked for the perpetuation of the truth with the aid of fleeting words must prepare in solitude the nascence of the Word."

I resumed my course, but I had a power of delight that lifted me up. I knew from then on what my law was.

II

I lived in the mountains like the wild beasts. During the day I watched squirrels leaping from branch to branch, lizards gliding over stones, grasshoppers bounding in the grass like diurnal stars. In the evening I went down toward the farms in the valley and women sometimes gave me a bowl full of soup made of detritus, like that given to dogs. I heard men growling inside the houses and I glimpsed their angry gazes, for almost everyone in the vicinity of Foix had converted to the new heresy and hated all those who wore the robe and the tonsure.

Only one, an old man with a goiter, the master of a sheepfold that belonged to the Seigneurs de Lavelanet, took me in amity and made sure that I had my quotidian nourishment. But my destiny was always interrupted by some eccentricity of the course of favorable things. One evening I found the old man with the goiter asleep outside his door, alongside a jug of milk that someone had just extracted and which was fuming. A share of that appetizing milk was probably destined for me. I picked up the jug and poured its contents slowly over the goiter of the master of the sheepfold. He woke up and uttered screams, as if the milk had been his blood flowing. All sorts of rustic creatures emerged from nearby animal sheds, and I only just had time to flee in order to escape their pitchforks.

Without being aware of it, I was drawn to Toulouse as if by a magnet and I left the mountain region for that of the plateaux. It was mid-August. I picked grapes from the vines. I spent the night in barns. Sometimes I bathed, shortly before dawn, in one of those great stone baths like a Roman tomb, which I encountered in the middle of a silent village.

But I was not happy. My tonsure had disappeared under the growth of my hair. My beard had sprung forth on my chin. I sensed a sort of animality twisting my limbs, rendering them more shapeless and more vigorous. I was only clad in rags. An ugliness invaded me, of which I could not render an exact account, but which I sensed to be alive as I passed my hands over my face. I remembered my reading of Plato, the apparitions promised by Petrus, and, confusing them in my mind, I regretted books of philosophy and the presence of Jesus.

One morning, from the top of a hill, I recognized a village near Pamiers that I had once visited in childhood; I had accompanied my father, who had been summoned to repair the church. I went down the slope and headed for the village. It was Sunday, and people were coming out of the mass. I saw, from a distance, peasants who were considering me attentively. They were speaking to one another, and I heard someone say: "That must be the mad monk who escaped from Mercus Abbey."

Immediately, they made a forward movement, and I distinguished on a few faces the glad and savage expression of men about to track a dangerous animal.

My errant life had developed my running speed singularly. In a matter of minutes I was separated from them by ditches, briars and heaths. I kept moving for a long time, knowing the sagacity of which men are capable when pursuing men. I encountered a river that I assumed to be the Ers. I was out of breath and my body was fuming. I threw myself face down on the bank in order to drink. I noticed, to my great surprise, that for the first time I had been tempted, instead of taking water in my hand, to lap it in the fashion of four-footed animals.

When I had satisfied my thirst and rested, I felt full of a wellbeing that was not localized anywhere and with which a confused desire was mingled. I had a desire to sing, to exteriorize my strength in action, and, like a dormant larva beginning to awake, carnal temptation agitated in the mystery of my flesh.

There was a path that followed the river between tall poplars and leafy hazel-trees. I started to follow it. Frogs that were resting in the grass made leaps toward me. I amused myself by crushing them, in spite of the love that I had always testified for those aquatic beings, and the soft sound them

32

made as they burst under my feet procured me a bizarre satisfaction.

Suddenly, I stopped still. The path I was following was obstructed by broom, laurels and the low branches of the hazel-trees. A little further in, however, a luminous bank ended, where the widened Ers formed a calm pool, like a sunlit mirror in a frame of golden sand. And there, at the water's edge, protected by a circular wall of trees inclined around her, a woman was lying.

She had just been bathing, and she must have wrapped herself hastily in the sheet of supple linen embroidered with silver by which her body was enveloped. Droplets of water were still sparkling on her bare arms and at the birth of the shoulder, indolently protruding from the sheet. The oval of her lowered face, the features of which I could not distinguish between the hair knotted in three braids, was supported by a hand so small that I almost started to laugh. The other hand was pressing the linen sheet to her body in order to dry it, and designed a slender and perfect body. The sun gave the golden sand around her a red tint and made her shadow violet. The immobility of the poplars, the silent flight of the water, and the beauty of the light bathed that woman in a mystery of tales of enchantment.

And although I could not see her inclined face, I knew immediately, because of the three braids, who she was. The Chateau de Belpech must raise its unique octagonal tower behind the trees to the right. It was there that the infanta of Foix, the beautiful Esclarmonde, had obtained permission from her father to come to satisfy her eccentric love of solitude.

Esclarmonde! For any good Christian her name was synonymous with malediction. She wandered alone through the woods in order to find certain fallen deities of paganism whose language she knew and which descended from their mountains for her. She did not fear men because the demon that inhabited her body drove her to give herself to them. Her father, Comte Roger, uniquely possessed by the love of riches, sometimes came to reside in the Castellar of Pamiers in order to extort money by force from the monks of Saint Antonin. The insensate! He then confided Esclarmonde to his steward Roaix and allowed her to reside alone in the little tower of Belpech. It was the aged Roaix, from a Toulousan family, who had converted her to the Albigensian heresy in her early childhood. Nicetas, the man from the Orient who was known as the accursed pope, had even come in secret to Belpech to accomplish there some unknown magical ceremony whose execrable rite enchained the young woman forever to the new church.

That is what I had heard reported by the talkative monks of Mercus, especially by Brother Robert. I did not know yet that almost all the words of a fat man are dictated by evil thoughts. Brother Robert was a slanderous man of base soul, who was reputed to know everything and who pretended, when he could not support what he said with evidence, to know it by virtue of direct divine communication. When he talked about Esclarmonde he crossed himself and made a semblance of fearing certain evil spells because of what he had said. I remembered clearly what he claimed to have seen.

Returning to the Abbey of Saint Antonin one night, to which he had been sent from Mercus to carry a precious pyx, he had heard strange noises. In the middle of the immense avenue between oaks that ends at the porch of Saint Antonin, a naked young woman with a miter on her head and three golden braids along her shoulders was playing the harp. Beside her stood a bearded old man wearing a turban in a Persian or Egyptian costume. Behind them, in a long file, all the wolves of the forest were marching slowly, as if for a ceremony. Their blazing eyes emitted little flames that lit up and were extinguished by turns. And there were serpents slithering, toads hopping bizarrely and birds flying overhead whose heads had a vaguely human expression in spite of their beak and plumage. Brother Robert added that he only owed his salvation to the presence of a host that was still stuck to the bottom of the pyx.

I had only added a dubious credence to such stories at the time. I had even laughed often with monks saner than me—who were, in truth, quite numerous at Mercus. But the name of Esclarmonde retained a mysterious resonance. I only had to pronounce it to evoke images of sin and magic. And now the sorceress with the beautiful face, aureoled by the legend of her damnation, was lying before me on a bed of sand, illuminated by the reflection of the sun and the water, in the voluptuousness of midday!

I ought to have fled out of natural shame. It is a sin to look in the face those who have vowed their souls to evil. Fear ought to have made my teeth chatter. But blood flowed to my temples and an unknown force warmed by blood. I knew little about women. Before my novitiate, I had sometimes gone to prowl the back streets of Toulouse that extend from Saint Sernin to the ramparts. In the evening they were full of songs and the music of the instruments know as darbukas, which come to us from the Arabs and are so melancholy when they play for joy. There were the street of the Jews and the street of the Moors. It was a Mooress that I had pleased. I had heard mention of amour in a low-ceilinged ground floor room where there was nothing but a sordid mat, a chest for clothes and an earthenware vase for ablutions. I heard rustling behind the wall, the cries of women fighting one another and drunken soldiers hammering with their fists in the streets shouting that it was their turn. I had conserved therefrom the memory of a tenebrous voyage on a ship of perdition, amid waves of stone, in a tempest of ignominy.

And now memories returned to me of guitars and ballads sung by winy voices; I respired a carnal warmth and there was the music of a darbuka somewhere, as sad as the prescience of an evil deed that one is on the point of accomplishing.

I parted the branches of wild laurels cautiously and I sensed a bestial expression invade the features of my face as I advanced.

The young woman did not see me. She was motionless, and that immobility stopped me. But she made a movement of her head and a kind of undulation departed from her milky neck, which slid over her shoulder and was lost in the linen creases, like a living radiation of flesh.

Then I launched myself forward. A blind beast trampled branches, caused the sand to creak and threw itself on the extended prey. She was light and devoid of strength. I seized her around the loins and I started running straight ahead, moved by the instinct that drives a savage beast to seek an isolated spot.

I had heard a feeble groan and delicate arms had attempted to repel me, but that movement of a body against mine redoubled my furious intoxication. I bounded amid the cracking of wood and the fluttering of foliage. I only slowed down for a second in order to prevent the marvelous tresses from being caught by bushes. When the path turned and quit the river, I perceived some way ahead of me the profound mass of a forest looming up with its shade and its propitious solitude.

Had some servant raced forward too late to help his mistress? Had the villagers who were pursuing me picked up my trail? It seemed to me that I heard clamors resounding behind me and that there was the whistle of an arrow in the air, but I was already respiring the freshness of tall trees close at hand, the breath of the abode of wolves and birds of prey.

Suddenly, lowering my head, I perceived for the first time the face of the woman I was carrying. The open mouth allowed the gleam of the teeth to be seen. The features had an almost infantile youth, but they did not express the bewildered terror I might have expected. My hirsute and sweating face and my human breath did not overwhelm the young woman in her light linen veil with horror. While running, I was struck with astonishment. I leaned over her further. Then I perceived a singular geometry in the regular oval of her face, in the correspondence of the raised eyebrows with the hairline and the creases of the mouth, a superior calculation whose total escaped fear and desire.

To the metaphysical problem posed by the contours of that flesh, which I sensed to be above my intelligence, I sought a solution in her gaze, but that gaze was blue and immense, like those avenues one sees in dreams bordered with hieroglyphic columns, the indefinite perspective of which ends at the phantom of a temple. It was a gaze as devoid of hatred as it was of forgiveness, as cold as the sword of the Last Judgment.

A new sensation took possession of me with an imperious violence. I was a man who was running, carrying not a woman but the tabernacle of the spirit. I had stolen the Holy of Holies of an unknown religion. I could not measure the mysterious extent of my sacrilege, its consequences in the realm of the angels, the penalties that had fallen to me. The spiritual light had made the election of a creature, it had chosen the most perfect in which to become incarnate, and immediately, the beast had pounced in order to satisfy the primordial law of pollution. And that symbolic beast was me. I was bearing the primitive powers to their culmination. I represented the extreme point of materiality. I was contamination avid to communicate itself, a living leprosy, a bounding lesion.

I lifted in my arms the suave form of election, and I placed her on the ground, surprised within myself that I had not been consumed by the contact. She stood there like a statue, still piercing me with the cold sword of her eyes. With her two clasped hands she held her veil over her breasts, but it was translucent. There was nothing beneath the veil but pure light. She stood before the somber mass of the forest, clad in the splendor with which one imagines the gods to be surrounded, foreign to the forms of the trees, the color of the air and the earth that did not soil her feet.

From all directions I heard human voices that were drawing nearer. I had a desire to fall to my knees and weep. But the instinct of survival was stronger. In a few bounds, I reached the nearby thickets, and I lost myself therein.

III

The setting sun caused the helmets of the watchers at the top of the barbicans to glitter like steel lamps. I saw looming up before me the Babylonian accumulation of Toulousan roofs and turrets, and perceived the city huddled within its circle of ruddy ramparts like a knight in the crimson of his body-stocking.

I went through the Montolieu Gate at the moment when four men were beginning to maneuver the iron-studded battens in order to close them. Afraid of having been identified by the soldiers of the guard, or mistaken for one of the *cagots* to whom entry to the city was forbidden,[6] I slipped into a group of peasants and beggars who were going over the drawbridge at the same time. And as I had lost the habit long ago of contemplating the animation of capitals, my feet bore me naturally toward the Rue de la Pourpointerie, in order to enjoy its splendor.

Toulouse, in the time of its Comtes, could only be compared to Byzantium or ancient Alexandria. Knights returning from the crusades had brought back Oriental fashions, the taste for sumptuous colored fabrics. Via Aigues-Mortes and Narbonne, boucrans arrived from Tripoli, haïks from Gerba and ivory and ostrich-plumes from the Mahgreb. There were shops filled with multicolored parrots in aviaries, dazzling

---

[6] "Cagots" were a Medieval European population analogous to the "untouchables" of India, not distinguished from the majority population by religion, ethnicity or any external feature, but nevertheless loathed, despised and cruelly persecuted throughout western France and northern Spain, for reasons that are profoundly unclear, as they left no writings of their own and references to them tend to be obliquely unhelpful. Active discrimination was not officially halted in France until 1789, and muted popular prejudice continued even thereafter.

goldfinches on perches of precious wood, ibises from the Nile standing on one thin leg; others in which lapis-lazuli from the land of Ketama steamed in metal caskets, and whose walls were hung with coral branches of all hues; and others so stuffed with musk and aloes, amber and rose, that merely by passing along the street one could retain the perfume in one's garments for months. One crossed paths with negroes from Barbary, reminiscent of joyful demons, Moors from Seville or Granada with green silk turbans, Byzantine merchants with cunning eyes, and the Toulousan noblewomen glimpsed behind the muslin of litters gave the impression of princesses of Bagdad.

But the shutters were banging and the lamps were being blown out. People were wishing one another goodnight before shutting themselves in their houses. The magnificence of the dazzling Rue de la Pourpointerie was extinguished, like a jewel-box whose lid is closed. I recognized a few familiar silhouettes in passing, a few faces of young women with whom I had once exchanged smiles; I lowered my head and avoided their gaze.

I turned into the Rue des Augustins and reached the outlying district. It was in going along the street of the Jews that I perceived that someone was following me. A mendicant from the group with which I had mingled as I came through the Montolieu gate was marching behind me obstinately. I made a long detour in order to lose him, going as far as the Rue des Trois-Piliers; but the hour had already come when, in the quarters of the center, chains were being extended at the extremities of the streets. I would be obliged to wait until the next day to knock on my father's door.

I headed toward Saint Sernin. In the shadow of the sacred basilica, the pavement on which I would sleep would be like a feather bed to me. It was a mild September night. The church reposed on its naves in the form of a cross like an immense stone bird settled for eternity. The five octagonal stages of its tower seemed to be launching themselves toward the starry sky, and there was an ardor in that movement of superimposed architectures that was communicated to my human heart. Alongside the church, like its brother, the ancient oak of Toulouse deployed its branches over the sleep of thousands of birds.

As I wandered through the garden full of tombs and cypresses that surrounds Saint Sernin, I heard footsteps, and saw a man advancing toward me. It was an exceedingly ugly old man, as wretched in appearance as myself. I recognized the beggar who had been following me obstinately since the Montolieu gate.

I have always inspired a spontaneous sympathy in many people. I was not extremely surprised to learn that that old man experienced one for me.

"I recognized you immediately," he said to me. "You're among the believers of the Church of the Paraclete, the one to whom the heavy task has devolved. And here you are, arrived faithfully at the appointed hour. For know this: the time is now imminent. The reign of the Antichrist is about to end."

It was thus that the heretics designated our Holy Father Pope Innocent. I tried to explain to him that, quite recently, I was a novice in the Order of Cîteaux, but he was not listening to me. He was speaking incoherently, sometimes darting a glance at me full of pity.

"Poor child! You are young and you are strong, but your shoulders will buckle and your heart will break because of the blood that you will have to shed."

I thought that the miseries of an errant life had deranged the man's brain. I told him that I was looking for a comfortable place in which to sleep.

"Yes, sleep while you can," he replied. "It is easier to escape a furious wolf in the mountains than the actions one must accomplish. We both have our mission, but you are commencing and I am about terminate."

I had headed for the old dwelling of Pierre Maurand, in order that his entrance porch would shelter me from the nocturnal dew while I slept. I lay down on the ground. The old man sat down beside me. Suddenly, he pointed with his finger at the cross that, at the extreme summit of the steeple of Saint Sernin, gave the impression of cleaving the blue-tinted accumulations of the constellations.

"You see that cross," he said. "It's necessary that, before I die, I wrench it from that steeple, where I placed it myself fifty years ago. I was then the boldest of apprentice masons, and on the day of the inauguration of the bell-tower, before the Comte, the Capitouls and the Bishop of Toulouse, I received the perilous mission of going to plant the cross in the sky at the moment when mass was celebrated. It was necessary not to be afraid of the immense space and the internal funnel that vertigo creates in the soul. At the place where the fifth stage finishes there was nothing more than a few shaky planks in the void. I climbed up with the cross at the end of my raised right arm. At the extremity of the spire I lifted a trap and, clinging on with my hands and feet, I plunged the cross into an iron groove. Then, full of pride, I looked around.

"I found myself in the middle of the sky, in a perfect solitude, and the verity of the world appeared to me. There was no basilica beneath my feet. The murmur of the people in the streets, the liturgical chants that resounded: all of that had no reality. It was above me that the true basilica was deployed, so beautiful with its transparent stones, its altars and its Christs of dream. For we only see the appearance, the material double of the ideal reality. I heard songs in the clouds, I saw a prodigious mass celebrated there, under the luminous curvature of arches, between columns that split the sky, of which the host was the sun. I was tempted to launch myself toward that divine world, but my destiny was to live and yet to support many woes. It is since that day that I have had the power of distinguishing in the atmosphere of every man the future actions that he must accomplish."

I had a desire to drive that insensate away from my presence, but there was a sort of inspiration in his voice that made me reflect. He started talking to me about the sadness of the times and the misfortunes that were in preparation. He attributed them to a single cause: the presence in the world of gold. At the same time as gold had penetrated into the churches, God had emerged from them. A gilded Christ, a tableau in the painting of which there as a parcel of gold, became symbols of evil, like a very pure wine into which a drop of deadly poison had been poured. The church of Saint Sernin was full of gold; there was gold in its crypts, in the ornaments of its altars, in the reliquaries of its saints. It was no longer worthy to bear a cross on the spire of its tower. It was up to him who had placed the cross, to remove it.

The heretic's discourse ended up interesting me in spite of the blasphemies with which it was mingled. It was at the moment when I resolved to listen to him that I fell into a profound sleep.

I must have slept for a long time. The sound of a trumpet woke me up. I thought immediately about death and the trumpet of the Last Judgment, but this one did not make a noise loud enough to have originated from the breath of an angel. I observed that the old man was no longer beside me and that the door of Pierre Maurand's house was wide open. Furniture and objects of every sort were heaped up around me. They must have been carried out while I was asleep. There were oak dressers, Roman seats, damascened tabled, copper standard lamps, silver cups and vases in Pyrenean stone. Brocade cloth, fabrics laminated with gold, belts and weapons made enormous sparkling piles. A marble goddess, half reclining, was smiling at me in an enigmatic fashion.

A tall, thin man was standing on the threshold. He was the one that had blown the trumpet. He stopped, and as I stood up he advanced toward me. He had long white hair and an expression of such great mildness on his face that I did not recognize him at first. It was the former Capitoul Pierre Maurand.[7] I was still a child when Toulouse had been thrown

---

[7] Author's note: "The Capitouls were the municipal magistrates of Toulouse, elected by the people. There were twelve for the city and twelve for the outlying districts. They enjoyed

42

into upheaval by his condemnation as a heretic. The Papal Legate had only left him his life on condition that he departed on a pilgrimage to Jerusalem. In spite of his eighty years he had gone on foot to embark at Aigues-Mortes. It had been thought that he would not return. I remembered his harsh, irritated face when I had seen him going along the Rue du Taur surrounded by soldiers. He was another man now, who seemed stripped of all passion, like a tree that no longer has leaves and yet remains charged with sap.

"Take what you please," he said to me. "Everything is as much yours as mine."

He must have considered the wretched state of my garments, for he picked up a robe with a fur collar and sleeves and held it out to me.

I perceived behind him a group of servants who were whispering, and seemed consternated. Their eyes were fixed on the robe. One of them made a movement to throw himself at his master's knees, but Pierre Maurand stopped him.

Heads had appeared at windows. I saw forms running from the streets behind Saint Sernin. There were debauched women, and those people with astonishingly pale and monstrous faces that one only sees by night in the hovels of cities. They were questioning one another. I heard one shout that there must have been a fire. A young woman with sagging breasts and a cunning smile, seeing my sumptuous robe, thought that I was an important seigneur and came to circle around me, simpering.

Pierre Maurand had seized some of the objects distributed on the ground at random, and he was striving to distribute them to the audience.

"Take away this furniture, take these clothes," he said. "I no longer want to possess anything, I give them to you."

At first there was a moment of stupor. In the light pallor of the morning, which was about to appear, I saw suspicious

---

considerable power. In the absence of the Comte they sometimes even declared war without consulting him."

gazes and fearful grimace on the faces of the wretches who were forming a circle. The poor always think that generosity conceals a trap.

But Pierre Maurand did not cease to exclaim: "Take, take!"

As there was a slight eccentricity in the tone of his voice and the gesticulation of his thin arms, they thought it was an act of folly from which it was necessary to take rapid advantage. Abruptly, they rushed forward. I saw arms opening to seize, silhouettes that gave the impression of breaking and falling on to all fours. Furniture rolled on the pavement with a sound like carts. A sort of dwarf was almost crushed by a bed with an awning that he was dragging. A man who had thrown a carpet over his head fled with a candlestick in each hand. Everyone gave the impression of having stolen what had been given to them.

Stupefied, I was still standing still in my splendid robe. Pierre Maurand doubtless thought that I was retained by my timidity, for he placed a silk bonnet on my hirsute head and then picked up a necklace of precious stones and threw it around my neck.

At that moment, a partly-dressed man who seemed to have been woken up by the noise people were making emerged from his house and stated running back and forth shouting: "My God! My God!"

I understood that he was the steward of the house. He criticized the servants, reproaching them for not having warned him, and not having gone to fetch the soldiers of the watch to disperse that rabble.

"You have no heir," he said to Pierre Maurand, severely, "but you might live a long time yet. At least let me save something, for the time when you become more reasonable."

Pierre Maurand shook his head gently.

I saw, like little flames on my breast, the stones of the necklace that he had placed there. I had a burning sensation there and a sentiment in which anguish was mingled with delight. It was the first time that a precious object had been in my possession. And as if that object communicated to me an abrupt appetite for greater riches, I threw myself to the ground to dispute with prostitutes and prowlers what remained on the pavement.

I had seized a Cordovan leather belt with diamond buckles, which I pulled toward me. An old woman had taken possession of the other extremity, proffering threats. And as I was there, like a dog pulling a bone from the remains of a dead animal, I heard Pierre Maurand reply to his steward: "Yes, wealth is bad for everyone, even for these wretches"—and he extended his hand in my direction, with a gesture of pity. "But everyone must undergo a proof. It is in the putrescence of gold that humans find their purity."

Another Albigensian heretic had said something similar to me at the commencement of the night.

"And this? Is it also necessary to give them this?"

As if it were an irresistible argument, the steward placed before his master's eyes an object that he had kept under his arm. It was a painting in which a skillful artist had reproduced a woman's face, in the manner of the ancient painters of Greece.

Pierre Maurand made an avid gesture to seize the painting and to tilt it in the direction of the sky in order to see the image more clearly. The slightly crazed expression of his face gave way, for a second, to the unconsolable sadness that beauty lost forever produces. He raised the portrait of a woman toward the crimson that bathed Saint Sernin, as if to steep it in the eternal light. Then, turning his head, he threw it away.

"All material attachment distances us from the spirit," he said, softly, as if to himself, but with an alteration in his voice.

In the distance, the sound of chains being lifted in the streets was audible. The bells began to ring. A file of monks emerged from the convent of Saint Sernin and walked through the cypresses. The ancient tombstones had tints of gilded ivory.

I let go of the belt that my hand had continued to grip. I got up and I let the furred robe fall from my shoulders. I snatched the necklace of drops of fire from around my neck and threw it on the ground. It suddenly seemed to me that I could see Esclarmonde standing before me such as she had appeared to me on the threshold of the Ariégois forest. I experienced beside Pierre Maurand the same sentiment of an inexplicable and superior presence that I had experienced before her. But as it is dolorous not to understand what is above you, I preferred not to think about it any longer and I headed toward my father's house with a rapid stride.

IV

My father and my mother experienced a great joy in seeing me again. I understood that the joy in question was tempered by the fear of seeing me devote myself to some insensate action, but I reassured them rapidly be the rationality of
all my words. I learned that during my absence, my sister
Aude, who was five years old, had returned to Blagnac, where
she had been confided to peasants because the country air was
necessary to her delicate health. I only paid her scant attention;
at that time children only inspired me with surprise because of
the smallness of their proportions.

When I was suitably dressed, my father's first concern
was to accompany me to the Arab steam-baths that the architect Bernard Paraire had just constructed in the Rue Saint-
Laurent, on the model of those in Granada. He left me on the
threshold and headed toward Saint Cyprien. He was going to
inform the charcoal-burners who brought charcoal twice a
month from Ariège to Toulouse of my return. In order to avoid
my being killed by the Comte de Foix's men-at-arms, he had
charged them with finding me and taking possession of me.

He had a hesitation in quitting me. He retraced his steps
to tell me that he would wait for me at the gate when I left. It
was not the pursuits of the ecclesiastical authority that he
feared. He assured me that the Capitouls and the Comte de
Toulouse would be able to protect me against the bishop. I
thought that he feared a danger of another order.

The steam-baths were full of people. One could not arrive there in a litter, the threshold was so crowded. Under the
porch I passed women of an extraordinary beauty. They glided
with a supple gait and gave the impression of having no other
garment than the fur robe that covered them. I could not tell
whether they were great ladies or the low-born prostitutes that
our lords maintain in the most beautiful house of the city.

There were two swimming-baths, one for men and the other for women, but they communicated by means of a small stone staircase and a gallery bordered with sculpted arcades. I was astonished by the familiarity with which people called to one another and the words they exchanged. How had mores become so licentious in a matter of months? Was I really in the same city where, a few hours before, Pierre Maurand had distributed his property to beggars for the sake of a mystical love of poverty?

When I was dressed again, curiosity impelled me to climb the stairs and lean over between the arcades. I had only been there for two minutes when I sensed someone beside me. I turned my head ad saw a young woman whose face reflected a marvelous gaiety. I recognized her as the impudent woman who, when I had emerged from the water, had let ironic laughter fall from the height of the gallery like drops of cold crystal. I had thought that she was mocking my gaucherie, for God had modeled the form of my body with irreproachable care. Instead of being semi-naked under a light veil with a silver net to retain her wet hair, she now had a head enveloped in a vast amaranth turban that brought out the violet color of her gaze. She was wearing a tunic laminated with silver and a purple robe, above bouffant trousers. That particularity made me think that she was a Saracen, or one of the captives that the crusaders had brought back from Jerusalem.

"Walk behind me," she said to me, "but above all, don't give the impression of knowing me while we're in the street."

Her foreign accent would have made me laugh in my turn if I had not been so confused. I was not sure that she was speaking seriously. I replied, with embarrassment, that my father was waiting for me in the Rue Saint-Laurent.

That redoubled her gaiety. She seized me by the sleeve, giving me a sign to follow her with a movement of the head and a wink. We passed alongside the women's swimming-bath and my confusion redoubled at the spectacle of the general immodesty. The young stranger turned round and, in order to prevent me from seeing, she placed her hand playfully over my eyes.

She took me to another exit that led to a side-street. There she was awaited by a matron of jovial aspect and another creature with a bronzed complexion, carrying a large package from which sashes and linen for the baths protruded. All three started walking with further laughter, and I followed them.

I had only taken a few steps when I saw an assembly in a little square. A monk was speaking, standing on a stool. His face was menacing. He pointed a finger in the direction of the steam-baths and a few words reached my ears.

"They please themselves in the putrescence of their bodies... They are like beasts avid for coupling... They have lost the shame that is the commencement of purity..."

In the monk who was thus scourging the usage of the baths I recognized Petrus. I was only half-surprised, remembering the scant care he had for his person and the amicable reproaches I had made him on that subject. I would have liked to make myself known to him, but the amaranth turban was about to turn the street corner.

We walked as far as the Bazacle quarter, where the streets, behind high stone walls, hid ancient gardens. Abruptly, the three women disappeared. I saw an open door. It gave access to a garden where I took a few hesitant steps. Large sculpted box-trees framed a pool tiled with mosaics. Yews loomed over clumps of hyacinths and jasmines like lofty thoughts above women's smiles. The sand of the pathways was mixed with gold powder.

Invisible birds were singing amid giant rose bushes.

The house at the back of the garden was in the Moorish style, and verses from the Koran could be read above lacy arcades, between thin colonnettes.

As I stood, bewildered by what I saw, I heard the laughter of the unknown woman again. I recognized her melodious voice, to which the foreign accent added something pleasant. She was annoyed because someone had forgotten to put nutmeg in the wine with the hyssop and honey, and because the snow sorbets had not been brought rapidly enough. Then she suddenly appeared in the midst of the roses and asked me why I was standing there like a simpleton, yawning in the middle of the garden.

I was confounded by so much impudence and so much grace. *How different the women of the Orient are from those of Toulouse!* I thought. This one was more so than I would have believed.

She told me that Sézelia was the ridiculous name that she had been given since she had landed among the Christian barbarians at Marseille. Venetians had stolen her from an island whose name I did not recognize and brought her to sell in Provence. It was there that she had been baptized and taken to mass for the first time. I understood from the gleam in her eyes that her conversion was only apparent. But experience must have informed her that religion is the one thing that it is necessary not to talk about frankly. She had been bought by a Genoese, a man of a certain age, who did everything she wanted and had brought her to Toulouse. The crystal of her laughter cracked when she talked about him and took on a resonance of hatred. She remembered her homeland, where the arts were loved, with regret, and she considered Christians as demi-savages solely moved by their lustful appetites.

She made me eat and drink so frequently that I was soon befuddled. Then she played the darbuka and wept. Afterwards, she laughed more loudly than before and took off some of her garments in order to dance.

The afternoon declined. I was lying on animal skins. The hyacinth and rose perfumes of the garden mingled with that of a resin that she sometimes threw on a cassolette where charcoal was burning. I was overtaken by a strange intoxication. Although I had shaved off my beard that morning, in accordance with the custom of clerics, Sézelia told me that I was as hirsute as a peasant; she approached her cheek to mind and then took it away, saying that I had scratched it. I savored the beauty of the hour with the vague apprehension of being the vim of an enchantment

As Sézelia, lying beside me, spoke at hazard, a name struck me. It was that of the Genoese who had fitted out this house for her. His name was Foulque.

Now, Foulque was the name of the new Bishop of Toulouse, whose scandalous election the Pope had just ratified. He was notorious in Provence and Languedoc for his immoderate liking for women and the bad poetry he wrote for them. He had only had amorous disappointments, because of his ugliness and coarse habits. After years of a dissolute life he had entered into the ecclesiastical career as that in which one enriched oneself most rapidly. A bitter and active hatred had come to him for the race whose daughters had refused themselves to him. He was one of the rare men capable of doing evil in a disinterested fashion.

"Bishop, that is indeed the title of which he prides himself incessantly," said Sézelia, shrugging her shoulders.

I did not have time to reflect on the danger I might be running. My expression must have darkened at the name of Foulque, for Sézelia went on in order to reassure me: "He won't come today. He's celebrating a mass at Saint Sernin. It's today that the famous tree is to be felled."

She had not finished when I was on my feet, I had seized her by her slender neck and was already shaking her.

"Are you sure? The tree of Saint Sernin?"

She replied that she was sure of it and that the thing must have been done by now. It was necessary that the Toulousans were deprived of common sense to attach importance to the life or death of a tree.

That was a drama that had been going on for a year. An age-old oak filled with innumerable birds rose up before the great door of Saint Sernin. It obstructed it with its branches and bathed it with its shadow. It was older than the church, older than the city itself. It had seen the Romans, the Goths and the Saracens pass. The cantors complained that in spring, during vespers, their canticles could not be heard because of the noise of the sparrows and the swallows. It was claimed that a nightingale came to sing there, but only on the night of Saint John. The soul of Toulouse lived in the profundity of its roots and the wings of its birds.

Now, the prior of Saint Sernin, a jaundiced old man embittered by a disease of the liver, had resolved to cut down the tree. He had the right, the tree being on the terrain of his convent. The consuls had opposed it. Comte Raymond had said that he washed his hands of the matter. It had been remitted to the justice of the new bishop whose election was imminent, and the love of the people for the tree had only increased.

I felt that love vividly. Still holding Sézelia by the top of her laminated tunic, I made her tell me what she knew. Foulque had given orders for the tree to be felled before nightfall. He had said the day before that the Toulousans were no better Christians than her, a Saracen. He counted on humiliating them in the pagan cult that they rendered to the oak.

Sézelia's tunic had torn in my hands and her naked upper body protruded from it like a living flower from a vase. As I headed for the door she ordered me imperiously not to leave. I took no account of her and sketched a gesture of adieu.

Rapidly, she took a little dagger from a casket and followed me into the garden, trying to strike me with it. Her tunic had split entirely and she tore it off. Standing between two yews, as if between two somber guardians, she gave the impression of a golden statue with violet eyes. She shouted insults at me in an unknown language, and as she threw herself at me, I was obliged to twist her wrist. She fell on to the sand, a vanquished bronze fury, bathed in her loose hair. I saw her, as I looked back, throwing a handful of sand and rose-petals at me.

Outside, I started running in the direction of Saint Sernin. I felt light and full of ardor.

There were people on the doorsteps. Others were running and calling to one another. A fat man shouted to his wife to come and lace his corset. A pike thrown from a window nearly fell on my head. In the Rue Saint-Rome I mingled with a group that was going in the same direction as me and I heard the news that was being exchanged.

The Capitouls had come to see Comte Raymond. After remaining silent in their presence for a long time, he had tossed a coin in the air, saying that if it came down tails he would prevent the Bishop from cutting down the oak. As it came down heads, his face had brightened and he had said that he could not do anything more. Arnaud Bernard wanted him to send the city militia to defend the tree, but the other Capitouls had been afraid.

Soldiers were blocking the streets around Saint Sernin. In the crowd, I shouted that it was necessary to advance regardless, and I perceived that my voice had an unaccustomed resonance, carrying a long way. The people surrounding me looked at me with surprise and admiration; and when I explained that the people of Toulouse could not be contained by a few soldiers, that explanation traversed the square and was heard throughout the city.

A human tide lifted me up and carried me to the first rank, directly in front of the sergeant-at-arms, the disagreeable cold of whose breastplate my hand perceived, like the chill caused by a snake.

Then, like the multiplication of the sound of my voice, there was an unexpected multiplication of my strength. I threw the armored man in front of me with such force that a joyous clamor resounded on all sides and the crowd, imitating my example, rushed into the square.

It was at that precise moment that the first blows of the ax attained the trunk of the ancient tree. And as the bishop had thought of imposing silence on the city by celebrating a solemn mass, the song of the organs rang out at the same time.

In order to cut down the tree, the executioner and his aides had been requisitioned. I saw their execrable faces fill with terror, and the monks of Saint Sernin, who were standing in two rows, scattered like leaves.

The disorder was indescribable. The soldiers, reformed in small groups, sheltered from stones behind their shields.

Cavaliers ran hither and yon, striking at random and leaving a trail of groans behind them.

Many courageous young men had recognized me and had gathered around me, I heard them shouting: "Dalmas! It's Dalmas!" We had formed a human chain around the tree and everyone swore to die rather than retreat.

But then, between the Hôpital Saint-Raymond and the convent, a mass of cavaliers appeared like a wall of iron. Those cavaliers, with the shafts of their lances, struck all around them as if scything wheat. Another wall of iron was advancing along the Rue du Taur and was about to emerge on to the square. The Capitoul Arnaud Gilabert, paler than the chalk-white façade of his palace, his arms widespread, like an obese Christ, begged us to abandon the defense of the oak. I saw the red doublets of the executioners to the right, behind the silver of breastplates.

I understood that the tree was condemned. Then, with that splendid voice that God had just given me, I shouted: "Let's rather set fire to it!"

I had no firm plan, but a few seconds later, someone had put a bundle of lighted straw in my hand, and I heard voices crying: "Yes, let's burn the tree!"

The oak had profound cavities in its structure, and they were full of vegetable debris rendered flammable by long dryness. Scarcely had my torch fallen into one of them than a high flame rose up, crackling, and was communicated to the high branches of dead wood. A great light trembled over the square, causing the armor to sparkle and terrifying he gaping faces at the windows.

Within the church, the firelit stained-glass windows doubtless spread an abrupt light of catastrophe. It was the moment of the elevation. Either to ward off the peril, or to satisfy his theatrical taste of a former troubadour, Bishop Foulque interrupted the celebration of the mass. He traversed the nave and, standing on the portal of the church, full of pride in his sacerdotal garb, he extended the host toward the people.

With an immense clatter of wings, the ten thousand birds that had made their habitation in the foliage of the oak, rose up together like a cloud, which the fire tinted crimson. And while the tree blazed, the birds rose up, and as the evil bishop raised the body of Christ, I saw all eyes fix themselves in another direction, in the air.

I looked in my turn. At the extremity of the steeple, a man was standing with his arms around the spire, and, as his feet were unsupported by anything and the spire could not be seen, he appeared to be standing in the void, with a cross over his head. There was a vast, unique sigh of anguish among the entire audience. The man's arms rose up, snatched the cross away, and hurled it into the void.

For a minuscule fraction of a second, everyone was able to see that the man made a movement to rise higher, to fly into the sky. He fell back, rebounding from the stages of the tower and came to flatten himself near a lateral door on a tombstone.

A howl of horror followed. And as I fled, I went past the man. The skull had burst but the face was recognizable. There was an ecstatic light in the depth of the eyes. I thought I saw there the reflection of the phantom basilica with the flameless candles and the silent organs, the splendor of which he had described to me the previous evening, and toward which he had departed.

I lost myself in the crowd. I walked for a long time at random, striving to calm down. I felt remorse because of my father, whom I had forgotten, because of the sin into which I had plunged myself. And tears flowed down my face when I thought of the calcined oak, and Saint Sernin, who had lost his cross.

V

A long time before it was accomplished, the act began to live in the depths of my soul. For an act does not surge forth without reason; it is like a plant that has a seed and roots, and it rises slowly toward the light of its realization.

I do not know exactly when the first design of my act was sketched in the great tableau on which God paints mad and terrible mages. Doubtless it was during the period when I was obliged to hide in order to escape the pursuits of ecclesiastical justice. For some time I only went out at nightfall, and my father accompanied me, and brought me back to the house when the chains were extended in the streets.

It was then that I saw once again the papal legate, Pierre de Castelnau, whom I had glimpsed at Mercus. The Albigensian heresy was growing in the city and he had all those identified to him by cowards and informers thrown into prison. He employed the Templars and the Knights of Saint John of Jerusalem installed in the Rue de la Dalbade in two fortresses facing one another. Those knights escaped the authority of Comte Raymond and that of the Capitouls, and were only responsible to the Pope and his legate.

That day, Pierre de Castelnau emerged from the Château Narbonnais and went alongside the Garonne on horseback. Doubtless he had come to obtain approval from the Comte for some further arrests. He had only one servant behind him and yet he carried neither a sword not a spear. An object of execration in the city, he affected to traverse it disarmed, sensing behind him the shadow of the Latran, which protected him. I saw his blue bulging eyes, his parchment face and the two red patches put on his cheeks by the perpetual anger in which he lived. When his cloak brushed me in passing, like a wing, something obscure rose up within me, in which there was already the seed of a future act.

Several months passed and I was not disturbed. I found my friends again, and observed that a great change had taken place in them. An element of hatred had been introduced into souls. Everyone was suffering injustice, and that injustice had various effects.

The monk Petrus had resumed his habits of intemperance and had become fanatical.

"Have you seen Jesus?" he asked me, with severity, as one demands whether a habitual event has not happened. And when I replied in the negative he insulted me and told me that it must be because of the perfume of heresy that my person gave off.

My friend Samuel Manasses was increasingly anxious and agitated. He lived with the presentiment of misfortunes, which, according to him, were going to strike his family and himself. He was so thin and pale that when he went past them in the outlying district, children shouted: "A ghost!" He helped his father care for the sick and read Plato. He dreamed of going to the Orient to find the Jewish philosopher Maimonides, convinced that he could learn from him the wisdom of life, the secret hidden behind visible forms.

One morning, when I had gone out early and was going along the ramparts, I saw a group of Templars on horseback passing under the arch of the Villeneuve gate. In their midst I thought I recognized the thin silhouette of the legate in the monk's robe that he only put on for ceremonies. A trumpeter preceded them and caused an appeal to resound at intervals. They were riding rapidly, and I emerged from the city behind them.

To my great surprise, I saw them ride past the gallows and head toward the cemetery where cagots and plague-victims were buried. When I arrived, in the midst of people impelled by the same curiosity, I saw that a grave had been dug up, and I recognized the jovial face of Tancrède, the Bishop's executioner. He was kicking away bunches of flowers while his aides dragged a coffin out of the ground. It was at the place where Marie, the draper nicknamed in Toulouse "the illuminate," had been buried the previous year.

Marie had been reputed during her lifetime to be a saint. All day long she ironed doublets in her father's little shop in the Rue Saint-Rome, murmuring prayers. Sometimes, she put down her iron and invited a spirit invisible to everyone else, which she had perceived in the street, to come in, or she announced an impending event that never failed to come to pass. My mother, who liked her a lot, had taken me to see her. I remembered her icy hands on my forehead and the shiver of fear she had experienced on touching me. Under the influence of Pierre Maurand, she had converted to the Albigensian heresy.

The last of her prophecies, which had been the most widely reported, had announced that the spirit of evil would be manifest in Toulouse by three detestable creatures: a man who would wear a miter, a man who would be dressed in red, and another barded in armor. Bishop Foulque had been designated as the first, the legate Pierre de Castelnau was the second; the advent of the third was dreaded. When Marie the draper had died, at the age of twenty-five, she had asked to be buried in the cemetery of the plague-victims. An immense crowd had accompanied her there, singing canticles.

Now her coffin was broken by the executioner with blows of a pickax. Thus Pope Innocent had ordered.[8] The bodies of heretics had no right to repose in the earth, in the same way that their souls were condemned to eternal suffering. The judgment dated from the previous day. The ashes of Marie the draper were to be thrown to the wind. But it is not ashes that

---

[8] Author's note: "In 1206 Innocent III had excommunicated an abbé, of Faenza, because he had refused to allow a heretic to be disinterred." That datum is reproduced by Lamothe-Langon in the introductory chapters of his history of the Inquisition, where the first version of the story of Pierre Maurand is also found, both copied from there by Napoléon Peyrat, but Marie the draper is entirely Magre's invention.

are found in the coffin in which a dead woman has reposed for more than a year. The rumor was going around that when the planks were opened a sweet odor would spread around, and Marie would be perceived, her eyes closed and her face calm, as at the moment of her death.

I was in the front rank of the audience. The coffin was upright when the lid was detached. I saw an almost black mummy to which the absence of a gaze and singularly long and apparent teeth gave an atrocious aspect. The body could not be seen under the putrescence of the garments and I firmly believe that it no longer existed.

Pierre de Castelnau had unrolled a parchment and he read the sentence of the ecclesiastical tribunal to the phantasmal head. A wretchedly-clad old man tugged my arm then. I recognized Pierre Maurand. He drew me outside the cemetery wall. He seemed neither indignant nor saddened. I only understood much later what he said to me.

"As long as the body subsists, it draws the spirit by its attraction. Fortunate are those whose rapid dissolution permits the soul to launch itself toward the superior regions where one is no longer separated by form. It might be that Marie was still retained to the earth by the link of a memory or an image, perhaps by love of her smoothing-iron. The blows of the executioner's pickax have just liberated her forever."

On the day before Good Friday I accompanied my friend Samuel Manasses to a meeting of notable Jews where he was to replace his father, summoned to a patient in Saint Cyprien. While I waited I paced back and forth outside the door of the rabbi in whose home the meeting was taking place. I noticed when he came out that he was even paler than usual. I asked him the reason.

An old custom dictated that on Good Friday a Jew presented himself during mass at the door of Saint Étienne's Cathedral. He had to knock on the door three times. A priest opened the door to him and asked his name. He replied: "I am a member of the race that crucified Jesus." Then the priest slapped him and the people assembled in the square accompanied the Jew back to his hose, booing him.

Thanks to the enlightened authority of the Comtes of Toulouse, that custom had fallen into desuetude. The priest touched the Jew's cheek lightly and the crowd did not make any demonstration. The day before, the members of the Jewish community met in the rabbi's house and drew lots to determine the name of the man who would knock on the door of Saint Étienne.

"It's my father who has been designated," Manasses told me, with trembling lips.

I replied that I did not see any reason for distress in that.

"My father has none of the faults habitual to men and I often think that God wanted to make him a model of perfection. However, he has allowed himself to become proud. Oh, very rarely, and he repents immediately. I think that he will be humiliated to have to fulfill this mission tomorrow, and I'm suffering for the undeserved punishment that he'll experience."

Isaac Manasses had returned when we arrived at his house. It was agreed that Samuel would read me certain passages from a manuscript of Maimonides that he had received recently. As he took the manuscript from the casket in which it reposed the old physician asked which of his coreligionists had been designated at the rabbi's house. And I heard Samuel reply that it was Lévy, the money-changer of the Rue des Nobles. Then, in a voice that had become calm again, he read me pages of an elevated philosophy, of which I did not understand a word, but which I admired unreservedly in order to give him pleasure.

The following morning, at the hour of the mass, I went to the Place Saint-Étienne. There was an unusual crowd. I asked the reason, and a few bourgeois told me that they had come because of the novelty of what was about to happen. Pierre de Castelnau no longer wanted a priest to soil his hand on Good Friday by touching a Jew. The slap was a punishment that was the prerogative of the executioner.

I leapt on to the rim of the fountain in the middle of the square in order to se, over he heads, what was happening at the door of the church. The door opened slowly and in its frame there was the violet cape and black hat by which notable Jews were recognized. But the cape seemed too large, the hat too low. The silhouette was very paltry. It was suddenly dominated by the broad and beaming face of the executioner. I saw an iron-gloved fist like a thinking mallet rise and fall upon the Jew, who fell to the ground.

When he got up, I recognized Samuel Manasses. The waxen whiteness of his skin was stained by two trickles of blood. He remained unsteady, and for a few seconds I perceived behind him in a stone corridor Christians inclined beneath the capitals of the great nave, candles sparkling like souls in torment, and the Christ of the altar more distant than one of the phantoms glimpsed in the perspectives of dreams.

The door closed behind Samuel and in front of him the ebbing crowd made a space. Within living memory, that Toulousan crowd had never shown hatred for the Jews. In the presence of the livid and bleeding young man, it uttered a clamor of malediction and bristled with extended fists. But the poor fellow did not have to cross the terrible void that separated him from a wall of furious men. He looked in all directions as if in search of a support, to escape the universe of violence into which he had suddenly been projected, and he fell flat on the ground. He was dead.

It was at that moment that I began to be haunted by a obsessive image. I perceived it for the first time at the burial of Samuel Manasses. Jews could only be buried after sunset and their cemetery was in a remote corner of Saint Cyprien. Night was falling when the cortege went along the quays of the Garonne. Four young men were carrying the coffin, in which Isaac Manasses had insisted on placing on his son's breast the incomprehensible manuscript of Maimonides. I was the only Christian there and I was bringing up the rear.

Such as I had seen him pass along the same quay a few days before, Pierre Castelnau went past me on horseback, with his bulging eyes and the red patches on his cheeks. I felt the swish of his cloak, and I saw him, in the crepuscular shadows, place himself at the head of the procession and precede it proudly.

Without reflecting that the horse had made no sound on the paving stones and that no one seemed astonished by the inconceivable impudence of the legate, I ran forward and overtook the cortege in order to seize the silent horseman's bridle and drag him forcibly away from the dead man's route. But I did not find him.

As a door was open near the bridge I thought that he had disappeared through it. Then I perceived him a little further away and I retraced my steps, having thought that I had distinguished that he was now following the cortege instead of preceding it. But beneath their violet capes ad the shadows of their hats, the Jews did not seem scandalized by the presence of the horseman. They followed me with their eyes in consternation, wondering what that Christian, an old friend of the dead man, was doing, gesticulating and running to the right and left, for no reason.

VI

My father thought about establishing me brilliantly and he succeeded in it. One morning, he made me put on my best clothes and announced to me that we were expected at the Château Narbonnais. He was going to introduce me to the Comte de Toulouse, who would do something for me in recognition of the services that he had rendered him.

I was very emotional. I knew, however, that Comte Raymond was a man of perfect simplicity. It was not the effective importance of the great man that impressed me; I was emotional in approaching the man most celebrated in Christendom for his goodness. I believed then, naively, that virtues were manifest physically by some sign and I would not have been surprised, finding myself in the Comte's presence, if I had seen an aureole around his head.

When we were introduced, he was sitting like a schoolboy before a long marble table on which his arms, a golden cross over a black key, were represented in mosaic. He was drinking white wine that had just been brought to him from Guyenne. Without paying any heed to my salutations and neglecting any formula of welcome, he declared to us that the wine was a little too sweet for his taste and he was particularly insistent that we take account of it. He had goblets brought for us.

He was only satisfied when my father and I had declared that the wine was, indeed, too sweet. He rubbed his hands, fixed me with the little eyes of an amicable wolf, and then gave me a tap on the shoulder, uttering a loud bust of laughter, saying: "It was you who sounded the tocsin in the abbey of Mercus on the day when the..."

He did not pronounce the legate's name.

"You're the sort of courageous fellow I need. I'll take you as a squire. You'll start today. I like prompt decisions."

The incapacity to make decisions was almost a malady in him. For small matters he strove to accomplish abrupt actions, thus convincing himself that he was a resolute man.

"Thibaut here," he added, "will teach you your métier." He designated the squire who had poured the wine and gave the impression of being a wily fellow with the appearance of a dullard, of whom there are so many in our country.

"And you'll drink very dry Comminges wine."

I was to remain associated in his mind with a pleasantry relating to wine. For he often call out to me subsequently, winking and repeating: "The poor people of Guyenne, eh? They drink sweet wine!"

In his fortress of the Château Narbonnais, the Comte de Toulouse had his magistrate, his knights and his men-at-arms, but he lived in the Rue des Nobles, in a newly-constructed house surrounded by a vast garden. That house had its legend and its mystery. Many beautiful Toulousan women had come to find him there after curfew. It was said that the King of Aragon, in order to win his amity, had made him a present of Arab captives of a marvelous beauty and that he had a harem modeled on that King's. Songs were heard in the evenings and lights were seen under the trees.

Married five times, Comte Raymond retained amour for all his wives, even those he had repudiated, and even the one who was dead. He wept when the name of Jeanne d'Angleterre was pronounced, because that queen had been so jealous of him that she could not be in Paradise. He sent messages to Comtesse Béatrix, who—on his orders—was imprisoned in a cloister in Béziers. Every liaison, even temporary, with a great lady or a poor girl, procured him anxieties and chagrins. He only consoled himself then in the midst of bizarre animals brought together in the garden in the Rue des Nobles.

It was there that Thibaut took me.

I learned from him that, although newly arrived, I had the full confidence of my seigneur, because I had been at the Saint Sernin affair and I had set fire to the oak. Thibaut was taciturn but he knew how to listen, and I rapidly inspired a great admiration in him by means of my discourse. He completed my education in the handling of weapons, taught me the science of armories, and informed me as to how one tames and unleashes falcons.

I saw Comte Raymond every day, and he seemed increasingly worried. His little eyes only recovered an expression of joy when he went past his aviaries in the midst of the fluttering of wings. The peacocks displayed their tails around him, a yellow and blue macaw perched on his shoulder; his tame stork, to which he referred as the twenty-fifth Capitoul, followed him clicking its beak.

"Do you know," he said to me, one day, "that the Albigensian heretics forbid themselves to kill the smallest animal, even a fly? It's because they profess that respect for living things that I protect them and I love them."

A turtle-dove had come to settle on his hand. He raised it gently in the direction of the sun.

"See how cleverly God has colored that plumage, how he has made it pass from white to iron gray and then to a blue that is not found in any sky. It's certainly a great sin to shed blood."

I knew that the Comte de Toulouse had ceased to go hunting the previous year. Without addressing himself directly to me, he went on: "The heretics are right on many points. But then, what of papal infallibility? There is, however, one thing about them that I don't understand..."

He looked at me and a smile expanded his face.

"No, I can't understand that perfection is in chastity."

I was not to see that smile again for a very long time.

It was on the evening of that same day that the rumor spread in Toulouse that Comte Raymond had just been excommunicated. The ceremony had taken place in Saint Étienne's Cathedral, but only in the presence of a few priests. It was said that when the legate had thrown the candle to the ground and trampled it underfoot, the hem of his robe had caught fire. No one had been found to carry, as was customary, an open coffin to the house of the excommunicate, and the legate and the bishop, fearing the indignation of the Toulousan people, had renounced it.

It was learned at the same time that the legate had left Toulouse and had departed for Rome. That departure, singularly, did not attenuate the sentiment of his occult presence around me. In fact, as he drew away along the roads, the obsession with him that I had became more precise and more frequent. It was multiplied by the similar obsession whose phantom I read in Comte's Raymond's gaze.

At the beginning of the century, in Toulouse, excommunication was not such a terrible thing as it is today. For a great number of people, the Church was synonymous with debauchery and simony. The rumor was accredited that in the time of the first Christians, the mysteries had been lost, error had taken possession of the clergy and, as a poison slowly ravages an organism, it had changed the living flesh into putrescence. Wealth and enjoyment had replaced the vow of poverty. Satan now inhabited the cathedrals, flowed in the water of baptism and was condensed in the bread of the eucharist; priests officiated in his name. Distant Rome was like a Babel in which was enthroned, beneath the accursed cross, an Antichrist with a heart of stone.

On the first day, the Comte refused to see anyone. He stayed with his birds. Thibaut and I frequently heard him talking to his favorite stork, as the only confidant capable of giving him useful advice. On the second day he summoned his constable, his magistrate and the Capitoul Arnaud Bernard, renowned for his wisdom and his courage. They remained enclosed together for a long time. Then he gave Thibaut the order to prepare his arms and his fastest horse. We knew that all the armed men in the Château Narbonnais were on foot and ready to leave.

In the vestibule of his house, swinging his baldric in his right hand, he marched back and forth, questioning me directly:

"If I refused to recognize the Pope's orders henceforth, if I sent the legate's severed head to Rome in a casket sealed with my arms, would the whole Midi not be behind me? That's what Arnaud Bernard advises me to do, and he's right. But why does he advise me to do it so forcefully? Who knows? Who knows? In spite of his years, perhaps he hasn't forgotten the story of his wife."

Arnaud Bernaud's wife, who was now old, was said to have loved the Comte in her youth, and to have told him so.

The next day, at first light, were took the road to Carcassonne. The Comte had resolved to take possession of the legate and to keep him as a hostage until the excommunication was lifted. He had only taken fifty cavaliers with him, but a small army, under the orders of the constable, was to join us if the legate took refuge in Montpellier or some fortified abbey.

As the towers of Carcassonne were outlined before us, the Comte called an abrupt halt. His face had brightened. A messenger returned in all haste in the direction of Toulouse. The army was unnecessary. The constable could go back, with his soldiers.

"There's only one way to act," the Comte repeated. "Conciliation, promises, cunning."

But it was better to catch up with the Comte before he quit the Comte's Estates.

We stayed overnight in Carcassonne, only to depart again immediately. We learned in Béziers that he had stopped for a day to confer with the bishop of the city. Perhaps he was meditating having the ceremony of excommunication repeated in all the cathedrals of the Midi. In Montpellier he had left the city two hours before, but he had talked to the bishop for a long time.

My horse, faster than the others, had carried me on ahead. I had the sensation of realizing a dream, of pursuing an obsession that my brain had created long before.

Finally, we arrived in Saint Gilles on the bank of the Rhône, where we were told that the legate had just gone into the abbey to spend the night.[9]

Saint Gilles was a personal fief of the Comte de Toulouse and he had a château there with soldiers, but for a long time the abbey, in revolt against him, had only recognized the authority of the Pope.

"And what if I profit from that," the Comte said to us, "in order not to leave a stone of that accursed dwelling on top of another?" He designated the walls backed up against the hill, as high as those of a fortress.

But the following morning, at sunrise, he presented himself alone, bare-headed and barefoot, at the door of the abbey and asked humbly to see the legate. The legate replied to him that the foot of an excommunicate could not tread the stone of an abbey. He intimated to the Comte the order to wait for him in the château, where he would come to see him."

"I'll receive him with my helmet on, sword in hand," he told us. "We shall see!"

And he did indeed arm himself, and he placed his naked sword in front of him. But the hours passed and the legate did not come to the château. The Comte had only eaten a few mouthfuls in haste. He was still exhausted by the long journey on horseback. He summoned Thibaut and me in order for us to unlace his breastplate and bring him something to drink.

"Fetch goblets for yourself," he added.

Scarcely had we served the Ales wine that he had demanded when a bell rang, doors banged, and without anyone hearing the friction of his sandals, the legate was standing before the Comte.

---

[9] Author's note: "At the beginning of the thirteenth century, Saint Gilles was a port on the Rhône, where pilgrims embarked for Jerusalem. There was an immense abbey there, and the city had at least thirty thousand inhabitants. Consequent to displacements of the Rhône, it is now a town surrounded by land."

The papal legate had the right to enter anywhere without being announced, but out of courtesy, he normally did not use it. He was clad in his monk's robe, which he only wore very rarely, using the authorization that legates had to wear lay garments, for the Pope's envoy had to surpass in magnificence that ostentation of the greatest lords. We were accustomed to see Pierre de Castelnau in his scarlet hood and his crimson dalmatic. He appeared to us to be very small and almost insignificant. He remained silent, looking at the naked sword on the table, the bottle and the three goblets that betrayed the familiarity of the Comte with common people. There was a crushing scorn in his immobility and the fixity of his gaze.

The Comte gave us an imperious signal to leave.

Neither Thibaut nor I ever knew exactly what the two men said. According to what the Comte told his intimates later, he talked to the legate arrogantly, and it was that attitude that caused the conversation to break off. It is more probable that he threatened him and implored him by turns, without result.

After quite a long time, we saw the silent silhouette of the monk descending the steps of the château and heading in the direction of the abbey. I followed him with my eyes. He drew himself up to the full height of his petty stature, and I understood by the fashion in which he turned his head involuntarily that he expected to receive a crossbow bolt between his shoulder-blades.

No sound came from the room where the Comte remained. When night fell, Thibaut and I decided to light a candle and go in. The bottle was overturned and the wine had run over the stone. The Comte's head was leaning forward and his forehead was touching the blade of the sword, perhaps to draw wellbeing from its coldness. When he raised it, we saw that he was weeping. Immediately, however, he blew out the candle in the hope that we would not distinguish those tears. Then he asked us in a low voice to leave him until the next day.

As we closed the door we heard him murmur: "I'm a doomed man! Doomed forever!"

Thibaut and I emerged from the château and went as far as the balustrade constructed above the Rhône, which overlooked the port. The wind was making the rigging and sails of the galleys groan slightly. I distinguished the river beyond and, beyond the ramparts, the bleak extent of the lagoons of Hermitane, where the evening light struck reflections from the masses of salt, and created mists and mirages. Pilgrims, recognizable by the crosses they bore on their breasts, were heading toward the city, and looked at us as they went by. It seemed to me that I had seen everything that struck my eyes before, and that the events that were about to happen were already traced somewhere, even in their smallest details.

Suddenly, I said to Thibaut: "I understood just now, when the legate looked at the wine and the goblets on the table, that Marie the draper had prophesied accurately. We've just seen a living incarnation of the spirit of evil.

Thibaut contented himself with lowering his head.

I went on: "I've often asked myself how men can support the evils of injustice without revolting."

"It's because they're afraid," he replied. "They're all cowards. They're all afraid for their precious lives."

Then I started laughing, without being able to stop myself, and I was conscious that my bursts of laughter were too loud, and an echo, in reverberating them, gave them a bizarre and immense inflection.

"What's the matter?" asked Thibaut.

"I'm not afraid for my life."

At that moment, the action that I was about to accomplish emerged from myself and stood between myself and my companion like a living phantom. Thibaut saw it with as much clarity as one sees a man standing in front of you. When I headed at a rapid stride toward the château Thibaut followed me, asking me what I was going to do. I did not reply, but he knew. I was acting as if in a dream.

I went into the squires' room, which was deserted at that hour, and I armed myself rapidly. Thibaut did the same, although I told him several times that he would do better to go to the refectory, for it was time for the meal and he would not be served if he arrived late. He did not listen to me and followed me to the stables. He mounted his horse and galloped behind me.

I headed for the abbey with the confused intention of knocking on the door, knocking down the porter and penetrating by force or otherwise. I was only a hundred meters from the threshold when Thibaut seized my arm and stopped me. We had just seen, by the light of the stars, that the door was wide open.

A lantern illuminated armories, and a group of cavaliers emerged slowly. They were not speaking to one another, their weapons were not clinking and it was visible that they had been instructed to be silent.

"It's him," said Thibaut, pointing to the last of them.

Apart from a few valets, the legate's escort consisted of twenty men-at-arms, all Romans belonging to the Pope's personal guard, but they did not head in our direction. They took a small road to the left that went along the Rhône, and we followed them. We did not have to wonder where they might be going for long. A few hundred meters away there was a ferry that served the people of Beaucaire and a wretched inn. The group stopped there and we saw everyone dismount. Fearful of some nocturnal enterprise on the part of the Comte, the legate had doubtless decided to pass over the Rhône upstream of Saint Gilles.

"The night brings counsel," Thibaut said, looking at me fixedly.

We presented ourselves at the inn an hour later when we saw the lights go out. It was necessary to negotiate first. We did not want to make use of our title as the Comte's squires, but Thibaut was from Beaucaire and was recognized by the landlord.

"The whole inn has been rented this afternoon by the prior of the abbey of Saint Gilles," the man explained to us. "There are Italians everywhere, even in the stables with the horses. My valets have gone to sleep in the pig sty."

Nevertheless, he had not been able to send away pilgrims who had been waiting for the opportunity to embark for Jerusalem for a week. They were occupying the grain loft and, strictly speaking, we could join them in order to spend the night.

There was a stifling heat, and a human odor poisoned the atmosphere. Thibaut was very preoccupied with knowing where they had been able to hide the prostitutes who were found in all the inns in Provence, and made the renown of that one.

"They must have gone to ground in some nearby barn," he told me several times, with regret in his voice.

We had kept our leg-guards and our chain-mail tunics. We lay down in silence for a long time. In the end, as we could not sleep, the idea occurred to us to light the candle that the innkeeper had given us, but the heat had softened the tallow and it only gave off a vague light. We saw our livid faces without joy, and snuffed it out. From time to time a sleeping pilgrim uttered an exclamation or a grunt as he scratched the vermin on his body. It seemed to me that there were muffled footfalls below us marching back and forth. Late in the night the moon rose, gilded the straw and illumined the sleepers like cadavers.

And with the rhythm of silent footfalls, thoughts came to me. What was there is the soul of that man who did not know sleep? He was a monk who had dedicated himself in his youth to spiritual matters. In the abbey of Fontfroide he was the most studious and the most pious. He had read and meditated on all the manuscripts, discussed Plato and perhaps Maimonides. It was because of his great intelligence that the Pope had chosen him—because of his intelligence, but not because of his love. He had lived in Rome and it was there that the spirit of evil had taken possession of him in the form of pride. Mild previously, he had become violent to the point of sometimes losing his reason. He loved jewels and dressed magnificently. Condemnations caused him a visible joy. He did not hide, in repeating with Bishop Foulque that half the inhabitants of Toulouse ought to be burned as heretics.

What was a human life, in sum? Was it worth so much reflection? He, the legate, all the great lords, all the bishops and the Pope made men die without remorse und the pretext of justice. At the time of the first crusade, when they had taken Jerusalem, the crusaders, although commanded by a saint, Godefroy de Bouillon, had deliberated for three days as to whether or not to exterminate the seventy thousand inhabitants of the city, and after three days of reflection, they had decided to exterminate them. Raymond Saint-Gilles, Comte de Toulouse, was the only one to protest, and he saved as many as he could, aided by my brother Toulousans. So? So human life has no value and there are other invisible stakes above it.

I could recover from my memory every second of that night. There was no hatred in my heart. I was an instrument of God, a cog in an immense machine. To evil as to good, God gave the same power of expansion, permission to create and to destroy. For the just and the unjust he had the same love, there seemed to be no difference. The unjust man was fatally the stronger, since he was not limited by any interior law. What would happen if the just man lacked courage, thinking of his life, when the equilibrium ought to be reestablished by action?

Yes, God wanted evil, he protected the wicked, gave them material power, went so far as to place on their heads, incomprehensibly, the crown of intelligence. But at the moment that he had chosen, he thwarted them by provoking an unexpected action in an obscure man. And he proceeded in the spiritual as in the material. First he planted a seed. That seed, whether fecundated by the juices of the earth or the essences of thought, always expanded slowly.

I rediscovered the proof of that in the substance of my memories. The action had germinated in me like a plant. I was the depository of a divine seed that was now about to be realized in the physical world. It was very little to pay for it with my life. I was consumed by a desire for sacrifice, as if a brand had been placed on my breast.

Even so, I ended up going to sleep. I woke up with a start and it seemed to me that a century had gone by. It was not yet daylight. Thibaut was standing up and trying to look outside through a skylight. I perceived the whinny of a horse.

"Are they leaving?" I asked him, in a low voice, and he nodded his head.

I bounded to my feet. At the same time, we saw a large spider moving along the crack of the window, trying to get out. Thibaut made a movement to crush it. I grabbed his arm swiftly. He looked at me in surprise.

"Have you changed opinion?" he asked me.

I shook my head and took off my chain mail tunic silently. He considered me again without comprehension. I explained to him that I was not expecting to escape and that those who struck me would kill me more rapidly. Then he picked up my helmet and held it out to me, insisting that I lower the visor over my face.

"One never knows what will happen. If you do escape, it's better that you're not recognized as one of the Comte's squires."

As we left the grain-loft, I saw a red-headed man sitting up and smoothing his beard, looking at me with wide eyes. With my helmet closed and my cotton shirt poorly retained by my baldric, I realized that I must resemble a nightmarish caricature.

A valet was opening the stable door when we arrived there. Thibaut remarked to me that we had a chance to recover our horses. I replied, shrugging my shoulders, that I would get to Heaven or Hell as easily on foot as on horseback. With meticulous care, he removed the pennants from our pikes, which were attached to our saddles.

A sloping path descended to the place where the boats were. It was bordered by rushes and tamarinds. The river was calmer than usual. Dogs were barking in the distance. The nascent light was so delightful that it made one want to weep.

The majority of the cavaliers had dismounted, and one of them called out in Italian to a bare-legged boatman who was calmly pulling his boat on to the bank. A few paces away, solitary, I recognized the silhouette of Pierre de Castelnau. He was upright on his horse, his head forward, and he suddenly seemed to me so paltry that if my heart had been accessible to pity, it would have been engendered on seeing him.

Tucking my lance under my arm I drove my horse toward him. Human life is much less than one might believe. Almost without resistance, the weapon sunk into the soft substance of the body and penetrated it. I had often heard it said that to be sure of striking a mortal blow it is necessary to twist the iron while withdrawing it, and I had resolved to do that. But the face of the man I had just struck changed suddenly into the mask of a frightened child, and I heard him say: "Mother!" as he tottered in the saddle. I let go of the weapon and I gazed at the scarlet patch of blood that appeared between his lips.

I had the sensation of remaining thus for an indefinite duration, in the midst of a universe immobilized by the enchantment of death.

At the same time as the legate tumbled from his horse, a clamor rose up on all sides. I saw the faces of Italians turned toward me with an expression of horror, but it was as if I were detached from the time and the place. I remarked how different they were in the form of the face from the men of my own land, and I regretted not having the time to study the differences of race. Like a runaway machine, my thoughts went at hazard, settling on strange problems.

How is it that there is only one among them wearing a full beard? So many horses could never fit on to such narrow boats!

Events never happen as one has imagined them. The men of the legate's escort must have believed that they were being attacked by a numerous troop. The majority, seized by panic, remounted their horses to flee. A few formed a circle around the legate. I perceived that Thibaut had come to place himself beside me and that we were suddenly almost alone on the sand, where the rising sun was stretching out our shadows immeasurably, like the shadows of giants.

I had promised myself not to defend myself once I had struck, but when I emerged from the dream that immobilized me, I drew my sword and sensing my bare breast, asked Thibaut precipitately to lend me a round buckler that was suspended from his saddle, in which the globe of the sun was reflected like a red-gold coin in the depths of a mirror.

He held it out to me. No one attacked us. Then he showed me the road to Beaucaire behind a few clumps of tamarinds, and made me a sign to follow him. We reached it, without hurrying, amazed not to have to fight. When we had taken a few steps we departed at a gallop. We turned round frequently, but no one was following us.

"We've had a narrow escape," Thibaut said to me. "I counted about twenty-five of them. We'll hide in Beaucaire in my parents' house."

And he manifested a great satisfaction.

But as he replaced his sword in its scabbard, I stopped him and placed myself in front of him. I gesticulated; I wanted to go back and fight. I was gripped by a folly of extermination.

"We're cowards to flee. Let's go put all the Italians to death."

Thibaut had a great deal of difficulty calming me down and making me set off again.

Shortly before arriving in Beaucaire I descended abruptly from my horse. The morning air had refreshed my blood. I could do no more. I begged my companion to abandon me, to leave me to sleep under a poplar that was extending its shadow by the roadside.

He was obliged to show me a little tower that emerged above the rampart, swearing to me that it was his uncle's dwelling and that we were almost there. In the end, I decided to go with him.

I have never had any remorse. On certain nights, I have heard a muffled voice crying: "Mother! and seen a frightened face from which blood as flowing between livid lips, but I immediately thought about my comrade Marcayrou, hanged as a heretic from the gallows outside the city. I thought of the great bird of prey that punctured his eyes with its beak, at which I threw stones to no avail on the evening when I went to prowl around the gibbets to see what remained of my friend.

I thought about young Rosamonde Colomiès, the daughter of the armorer who had received from God, like me, the faculty of expressing herself in fine words. I thought that she was twenty years old, was good and very beautiful when it reached the legate's ears that she had preached among the heretics to glorify chastity. I thought of the subterranean prison of the Château Narbonnais, which enclosed, without distinction of sex, the worst criminals, madmen and even lepers escaped from leprosaria and found within the city walls. They lived there in darkness, in the most abject mixture, struggling cruelly against the rats. There were other prisons in Toulouse less frightful, but I thought that the legate had decided personally that Rosamonde Colomiès should be plunged into that living putrescence, saying that the more beautiful the image of crime is, the greater is the risk to God, and the more exemplary the punishment must be.

I have had remorse for many evil deeds accomplished in the course of my long life against men who defended themselves in combat, against innocent beasts that looked at me sadly as I struck them, but for that action, no, I have never had any remorse.

PART TWO

I

I left Thibaut in Beaucaire and I went back to Toulouse on my own, in small stages and taking roundabout roads. I found my parents in great anxiety. Seigneur Elzéar d'Aubays, the Comte's magistrate, had come to enquire about my return several times. It emerged from the conversation that he had had with my father that I should have been in Toulouse long ago, Comte Raymond having advised him by letter that I had quite Saint Gilles on the tenth of January. It was on the morning of the fifteenth that I had killed Pierre de Castelnau. I understood without difficulty that the Comte had immediately attributed the death of the legate to his faithful squires and that in order to deflect the suspicion that might fall upon me he had given a false date to my departure. My political sight was short. I did not realize then what a great interest he had in ensuring that one of his men was not convicted of the legate's murder. I was moved to tears by that mark of paternal benevolence.

When I saw the magistrate at the Château Narbonnais he did not ask me whether the Comte had charged me with any oral message and manifested no astonishment at the duration of my journey. He examined me with an extreme curiosity but without manifesting the ill humor and arrogance that rendered him redoubtable to everyone. The rumor was going around that he had adhered to the heresy, but that it had not given him a mild character.

As I was about to quit him he told me that I was a worthy servant of the Comte, and abruptly asked me a strange question: "How can you see when it is dark?"

Nonplussed, I replied that I did not have the gift of certain animals, like the cat, and that if the night was completely obscure, I was incapable of finding my way.

He bit his lip and dismissed me, repeating that I was a worthy servant and that, in sum, that was quite sufficient.

I realized that the death of Pierre de Castelnau had caused great joy throughout the city. I was surprised to hear many people expressing fears n the subject of that death and considering it as the commencement of great calamities. Although people held forth at length on the identity of the murderer, no one thought of me. Because of the urge to talk that every man has within him, and which I possessed to a high degree, I was obliged to make a great effort within myself not to tell the truth. I succeeded, and did not confide in anyone, even my father. I did not know yet that the truth, more fluid than water, filters through without the help of language.

It seemed to me that in that epoch, because of the action I had accomplished, forces hidden within me were suddenly liberated. I began to eat and drink more. My voice, already singularly developed, augmented its extent further.

I began to have a secret desire for quarrels in which I could make use of my strength. A sensual desire for women overtook me that I had never experienced before. I went to the baths in the Rue Saint-Laurent and I saw Sézelia again, for events have a tendency to reproduce themselves in the same fashion. She greeted me with the same gaiety and engaged me to go and see her, which I did.

And, mysteriously, a face was resuscitated in my soul. With an extraordinary clarity, I saw in the evening, before going to sleep, the face of Esclarmonde de Foix as it had appeared to me when I had contemplated it on a little beach of the Ers. She remained in the background of my dreams and she illuminated them confusedly, like an image of the goddess Minerva above a city of phantoms and larvae.

I had ended up no longer considering her as human, but immaterial and of supraterrestrial essence. So, when I learned from my father that Comte Roger Bernard de Foix had just marred her to the Vicomte de Gimoez, I experienced a painful sentiment and a sorrow that I could not explain. That sorrow augmented further on the day when I encountered Esclarmonde de Foix, Vicomtese de Gimoez.

It was dark and I was about to go back to my father's house at the end of the Rue de Taur when I was approached by a little old man with a face as wrinkled as an apple long fallen from the tree. All his wrinkles were set in motion and he had a cheerful and friendly expression as he turned toward me. He gripped the sleeve of my doublet and said: "How can you see when it is dark?"

For the moment I did not make any connection between the terms of that question and those in which the Comte's magistrate had interrogated me in an identical fashion. I thought it was some mania. The night was very clear. I raised my head and said to him in a natural tone: "I can see because I'm illuminated the light..." I was about to say *of the stars* and I don't know why I said; "by the light from above."

That response caused the little old man a great jubilation. He took me by the arm in a familiar manner.

"I knew it! I knew it! But why don't you come among us? I'll take you this evening. There are many who desire to know you."

I followed him without resistance because I had always had as a principle that it is necessary to obey destiny when it summons us. The course of my ideas at that time as such that I thought at first that I was dealing with some go-between, of whom there were so many in the city. Mores were relaxed and there was talk of nocturnal gatherings in which people belonging to the best families in the city met for orgiastic purposes. The lovely Guillemet, widow of the Seigneur de Lezat, as well as several other great ladies, went to them, it was said, with their faces masked, under the pretext of reconstituting pagan festivals and satisfying their lascivious penchants. The poet Pierre Raymond claimed to attend those gatherings frequently. The austere Capitoul Arnaud Bernard had promised a reward of ten melgorians to anyone who denounced one of those places to the perdition of his police.

On the way, my companion's discourse cast doubt within me.

"If one receives a slap on the cheek, is it necessary to offer the other, as Christ says? You have shown, my child, in a striking fashion, that not all the Albigensians are disposed to die without defending themselves. Many of our brothers think that you have committed a great sin. I must say that, personally, I don't share their sentiment."

He had leaned toward me, in a confidential manner. We had reached the La Dalbade quarter. He went on: "A superior view of things is slow to come to us. Everything depends, obviously, on the number of lives on has behind one. Do you know that Saint Paul passed through thirty-two existences before entering into the bosom of the Father?"

I replied that I did not know the exact figure and asked him how he had come by the knowledge.

"The figure is certain," he was content to affirm. "You're young! What a long journey you still have to make! How many existences you have to live!"

I did not know whether there was pity in his voice or admiration. Those words seemed to me to be a poor preparation for the scenes of pleasure that my imagination was representing."

"It's here," said my companion, designating the ancient dwelling of the Roaix.

And I thought that I was dealing with Frédéric de Roaix, the brother of the celebrated Capitoul.

Several people, among whom there were two or three women, were passing through the open door at the moment when we arrived. By the withering of their faces and the long striped dresses in which prostitutes are obliged to dress I saw that they were daughters of the outlying district. I even recognized one of them, who was nicknamed "the Fleshless" because of her frightful thinness. She was a wretched whore, always haggard and of bad character, with whom I had had occasion to quarrel several times.

I started to laugh, judging by her the milieu in which I was about to find myself.

After having traversed a courtyard, I was pushed into a large bare room illuminated by torches. People who belonged to all classes were gathered here, talking in low voices. Something grave and religious suggested by the attitude of all of them gave me to understand that the meeting had a character very different from the one I had initially imagined.

As I was standing there, arms dangling, a lateral door opened and, agape with astonishment, I saw Esclarmonde de Foix appear.

She was wearing a black robe buttoned in front and a violet veil covered her shoulders. No gold or jewelry glittered about her person, but her hair was retained by a silver headband in which a sapphire shone. That glaucous and marvelous stone in the middle of her immaculate forehead had something supernatural about it. I was struck by the sadness that the young woman radiated. She was looking straight ahead, a little higher than the heads of the audience, as if she were able to follow the scenes of an invisible universe.

The old man that had brought me, cleaving through the crowd, approached her and spoke to her in a low voice, in a familiar fashion. He pointed his finger in my direction and doubtless said something of scant interest, because she did not seem to pay any heed to it.

Such surprise was painted on my features that a young man nearby, whose face was simultaneously naïve and intelligent, leaned over my shoulder benevolently and said: "I can see that you're a neophyte. That woman over there is, for the believers, the symbol of pure spirit, incarnate in form. You must have heard mention of Simon's Helen?"

As I remained silent he gave me a little pat on the shoulder. Then I made him understand, with a gesture that I knew nothing about that Helen. My eyes remained fixed on Esclarmonde, who was now sitting in the middle of the assembly.

"We're human," the young man went on, "we need our concepts to take on substance in the sensible world. When you think about the descent of the Holy Spirit to earth, think about the beauty of Esclarmonde de Foix."

"Eh! I have no need of the Holy Spirit to think about that," I replied to the fool, rather brusquely.

But the Holy Spirit, on which my reflections had never dwelt, was to play a capital role in that evening. I perceived that all the members of the audience were thinking of nothing but the Holy Spirit, dreaming of being penetrated by it. Various orators spoke by turns to announce its advent. The Holy Spirit came from the Orient, breathing over the world in order to fecundate it. Toulouse was the terrestrial capital of which it had made election. Everyone would receive the Holy Spirit in the secret tabernacle contained in the depths of the soul.

I was enveloped by the mystery of incomprehensible words. Around me, faces were radiant. I sensed a joyous and pure exaltation rose up like smoke above a fire. It seemed to me that a bark was covering my soul and preventing me from taking part in the general intoxication. There was something ineffable and mysterious in the air that gave me a desire to weep.

"What is the Holy Spirit, in sum?" I asked my neighbor, for I sensed clearly that it was not a matter of that of the Christian mysteries.

Before he had replied to me I stood up, adding: "I also want to offer my opinion of the Holy Spirit, because I've never been able to hear people talk without also speaking."

The young man took me gently by the arm, smiling. "Words have several meanings, according to a person's degree of intelligence. For me, the Holy Spirit is the force that permits abstraction from the material world, the current that flows back to the divine source."

I shrugged my shoulders, and I was about to head any-way, having absolutely nothing precise to develop, toward the little platform on which the orators stood when I saw Esclarmonde de Foix stand up. She advanced, her arms advanced slightly forwards.

Frédéric de Roaix pushed a woman toward her and I recognized the wretched haggard creature nicknamed the Fleshless. She was almost on her knees, and trembling. Esclarmonde made her stand up with a gesture, and took her head in her hands. I saw with amazement long ivory fingers in the midst of bushy tresses, and the woman that I compared to Minerva placed her lips on the prostitute's forehead.[10] A long murmur followed. Several groups were formed in which people debated animatedly. An old man raised his voice in order to explain the beauty and attraction of death and how everyone ought to desire it.

A bald and entirely clean-shaven man had started walking rapidly, describing a circle around the room in a bizarre fashion, and repeated it with increasing speed.

"What's the matter with him?" I asked my neighbor.

"It's because only circular movement is perfect. He wants to imitate now the pure spirits that only move in a circle."

The voice of the old man who was speaking became imperative. "Extract yourself from this life, which is evil; escape this putrescence in order to launch yourselves lightly toward the essence of being."

"That's going too far," cried someone who had bow legs and a square head, like people of common sense. "Or in that case, the man who killed Pierre de Castelnau was doing him a favor."

That name unleashed contradictions. Everyone started talking animatedly. Everyone was passionate about that sub-

---

[10] Author's note: "The Albigensians practiced absolute fraternity. Many young men of noble families married humble prostitutes as a symbol of their love for all beings."

ject. I noticed that Frédéric de Roaix was going this way and that, speaking in a low voice to various people and pointing at me.

"It was one of the Comte de Toulouse's squires! It was one of us!"

I drew myself up to my full height. For a minute I experienced an extreme pride. In truth, I had not understood anything of what had been said about the Holy Spirit, but what did it matter? My role was different. I was the man of action, the liberator of heretics.

A void had gradually formed around me. Then my eyes encountered Esclarmonde's. She was looking at me. She was looking at the man who had killed Pierre de Castelnau. It was impossible for her to recognize in him the savage creature who had once seized her and carried her away in his arms. Her gaze traversed me like a blade sharper than that of the lance with which I had struck. And suddenly I could read it like a book in which living images were pointed. I read there horror of my action, disgust for my coarse and sanguinary soul. She turned away and disappeared through the door by which she had entered.

I searched around me for a benevolent face. But the young man who had been standing by my side until then had moved away rather abruptly. Heads turned away. What I had mistaken for admiration was a scornful curiosity. Only old Roaix, whose back I could see, his arms open, seemed still to be defending me.

"We need such men! They are despicable, so be it! But all the same..."

I made a movement toward the door. I found myself face to face with the Fleshless and I was humiliated to sense how precious an amicable word on her part would be to me. The prostitute's features were filled with ecstasy and she was holding her forehead high, as if the Holy Sacrament had been placed upon it and she was fearful of letting it fall.

Perhaps my doublet brushed her robe? I must have sketched a hand gesture toward her. A savage, hysterical cry resounded, and she leapt backwards, clutching the folds of her robe, seeking to flee, as if to escape the most irremediable pollution.

The strangeness of the cry immobilized everyone. Seeing me facing her, many thought that the cry had been uttered because of some gesture on my part, or some vulgar pleasantry. I heard angry words. A tall man who appeared to be a knight declared in a loud voice that if I needed to be punished, they had only to tell him, and he would take charge of it. With his arms outspread, he pushed side those who were round him and marched toward me.

I took a step forward, measuring the fashion in which I ought to leap at his throat and try to knock him down. I felt an unbearable suffering, which I hoped to escape by bring my own violence into play.

Then an unknown force, analogous to a living sob, agitated in my breast, rising up therefrom and descending therein only to rise again. So I was in the world of the wicked! My vanity was ripped in two like a garment and it seemed to me that I was naked, as naked and wretched as the first creature when it contemplated the first sunset in a universe charged with darkness. I fell to my knees, crying: "I ask forgiveness from all! I have done evil, I have only done evil, and I do not understand good. Enlighten me, you who know! Do not leave me in the darkness. Extend helpful hands to me, my brethren!"

And with my forehead I touched the paving stones where Esclarmonde had placed her feet, the dust that her robe had stirred in passing.

Much later in the night, a sergeant-at-arms who was carrying a lantern on the tip of a pike and who belonged to the Capitouls' police, demanded brutally why I was gazing with so much attention at the flowing waters of the Garonne.

I could have replied to him that I was one of the Comte de Toulouse's squires, the son of the celebrated Rochemaure, and he would have gone on his way without occupying himself with me. But I replied to him politely that, having encountered good and pure men, I would no longer stop before having discovered the veritable nature of the Holy Spirit.

II

Comte Raymond returned to Toulouse, and I was the first person that he wanted to see. He received me at the Château Narbonnais in the Eagle Tower, the one facing north. He was in warrior costume and as I was about to kneel before him he took my hands in his, which were soft and slightly moist, and he pressed them for a long time, fixing me with his eyes, which were always slightly sticky. We remained thus for a few minutes, and in that silence words were pronounced that could not be spoken.

He started marching back and forth, and I noticed that he was affecting a martial attitude and a stride full of determination.

"How do you think Pope Innocent has greeted the news of the death of his legate? He held his chin in his hand or more than a quarter of an hour, and then he involved Saint Jacques de Compostelle. And what do you think Saint Jacques de Compostelle has inspired him to do? He made him preach a crusade against the Midi, against me, against the grandson of Raymond Saint-Gilles who was in Jerusalem. But he doesn't suspect that his crusaders will be scattered like dust before the wall of stone and iron that I will raise up before them. My nephew Trencavel cannot contain his joy at the idea of fighting against the knights of the North; he is sending for five hundred Aragonese mercenaries, whom he will pay with his personal treasure, and as for me..."

His projects were immense. He had written to the King of England and sent messages to his vassals in Albi, Narbonnais and Provence. The armorers of Toulouse were working non-stop to forge sword blades and spear-heads. Under the direction of the Capitoul Arnaud Bernard, laborers were working in relays to repair and erect new towers. New militias were being organized. The order had even been given to leave the shops closed until ten o'clock in the morning to permit those who were occupied there to exercise in the métier of arms. The women were prettier, commerce was more prosperous and joy was circulating in the streets at the prospect of the imminent war, like a wine giving the intoxication of life.

I went almost every evening to the public dance-hall that had been built on waste ground neighboring the Montolieu Gate. But a state of mind so bellicose reigned there that it became fashionable to dance with a sword by one's side. Robes were ripped by the points of weapons and the brawls that resulted were so numerous that dancing lost its attraction.

At first I had found pleasure in being the center of attention of all eyes, but it soon embarrassed me. The young people who surrounded me had a visible anxious determination not to quarrel with me; I read apprehension in many faces, and when I danced, a void immediately formed around me.

I took a great pleasure in frequenting poets. Pierre Raymond took me to gatherings in which they recited their poems to one another. They lasted until and advanced hour of the night. My pleasure was then combated by the strange facility in sleeping that I had always had. I often abandoned myself to it. There was the stout Guilhem de Figueiras, who was always accompanied by some prostitute or other. He could not go an hour without drinking, and the whore carried a bottle of wine under her robe, which she slipped to him when the audience was acclaiming the beauty of poems. There was Gérard le Roux, celebrated for his success with women and the large size of his feet. I once saw Pierre Vidal.[11] He was old and sad, but preceded by such a reputation for gaiety that it was suffi-

---

[11] Author's note: "Pierre Vidal was one of the most celebrated troubadours of the Midi. His humorous adventures in the Orient were legendary." A number of songs attributed to the widely-traveled Toulousan troubadour Peire Vidal (Peire is the Occitan form of Pierre) are still extant; the brief biographies that exist date from fifty years after his death and are probably fictitious.

cient for him to open his mouth and show his shaky teeth for everyone to laugh.

It was, however, me who obtained the greatest success of laughter on the evening when I read the first poem of my composition. The sadness of the subject did not motivate that laughter at all, and from that day on I renounced the company of poets.

I had neglected Sézelia somewhat. When I went to see her again, instead of the reproaches I expected, she asked me abruptly: "When are you leaving Toulouse?"

I responded that I was attached to the person of Comte Raymond, and that he was not thinking of going far from Toulouse at the moment."

"It's necessary that you leave Toulouse without delay."

"Why?"

"The city will be completely destroyed, destroyed from top to bottom."

And she repeated the certainty of that redoubtable event.

I thought at first that it was one of those follies common enough among women. But she insisted so many times, even proposing to depart for the Orient with me, under the pretext of a pilgrimage, that I ended up becoming anxious. I pressed her to tell me what made her believe in the destruction of Toulouse, a city whose origin was lost in the obscurity of time and was probably as immortal as the planet itself."

She ended up admitting to me that she had it from Foulque, the Bishop of Toulouse.

He hated the city because of the heresy of its inhabitants. Gradually, he had identified the heresy with the houses and the monuments. The corruption had been introduced into the stones, flowed in the gutters and sheltered in the shadow of the streets. He dreamed of an exemplary punishment. The churches above all were accursed. They would be demolished stone by stone. The spire of Saint Sernin would no longer rise into the sky. The bells would lose their concavity and become ingots again.

As I did not lend credence to such an abominable project, she gave me precise details. Bishop Foulque had written to the Pope to explain the necessity of destroying the heretic capital. He had an understanding with the Bishops of Foix, Albi and Béziers. Furthermore, he was kept informed by clerics who arrived every day from the North. The crusade against the Midi had been preached with the same ardor as the crusade against the Infidels. An immense army from France and Germany was about to assemble in Lyon and invade Occitania.

I resolved to report those assertions to my master the Comte de Toulouse. But I did not have the possibility. When I presented myself before him the next day he looked at me severely and almost angrily, and told me that he was leaving for Saint Gilles that very day but that he was taking other squires than Thibaut and me, for we were not men with whom one could go to such a place with security. He quit Toulouse precipitately, and almost without escort.

He only came back a month later. I saw him again on the day of his return in the hall of knights in the Château Narbonnais. He was exhausted, with an expression that was almost haggard. I understood by the fashion in which he winked at me in passing that his sentiments were still benevolent in my regard. In the evening, Thibaut and I received an order to be ready to accompany him.

"We're to be armed, it appears," Thibaut told me. "And yet it's to the Chapter that we're going."

The Comte de Toulouse had convened a meeting of the Capitouls. Custom dictated that it was him who went to the house of the Chapter in order to mark the precedence of the city magistrates over their seigneur.

As we left the Rue des Nobles on horseback, we were joined by an individual who was wearing a sword beneath a black robe and resembled a cleric rater than a soldier. I was getting ready to move him aside rudely when the Comte turned round and said to me: "This is Brother Laurent Guillaume. He's attached to my person henceforth."

We found out subsequently that he was a spy that Pope Innocent had placed next to him.

The capitulary house was behind Saint Sernin adjacent to the outlying district. It was an ancient Roman edifice, perhaps a temple which had been reconstructed. On the façade, twelve columns resembled immobile magistrates of stone. The streets were encumbered by the horses of consuls.

The Comte was already climbing the steps of the threshold when I saw the man he had named as Laurent Guillaume cross himself several times. He approached me with a sly expression and said to me in a low voice: "I've received from God the faculty of perceiving with my sensibility the effluvia of pagan or heretical thoughts. This is a place where idols were once worshiped."

I enjoined him rather brutally to stay on the threshold with the servants and the horses in order to avoid those excessively dolorous perceptions. I must have been mistaken about the rank he occupied, for he made no reply and marched behind me, lowering my eyes, but with a tranquil tread.

The twenty-four Capitouls, those of the city and those of the outlying district, were already occupying their sculpted wooden seats. I noticed an unaccustomed stiffness in the line of their backs. Arnaud Bernard's face, with its square jaw, seemed a geometric puzzle. Some were clad in sumptuous robes. Bernard de Colomiès was making the rings on his fingers sparkle ostentatiously. Raymond Astre was shivering under heaped-up furs. I saw eyes rendered bright by the cunning of merchants, the broad shoulders of large farmers, the long and twisted hands of money-handlers. The hollow features and pallor of more than one face revealed the practices of Albigensian asceticism. The flames of torches agitated by an air current gave bright light followed by penumbras. At the back, a wooden Christ, covered with mildew because of the dampness of the hall, gave the impression of falling into decomposition.

I had scarcely taken my place alongside a few scribes and servants behind a balustrade facing the Christ when an angry rumor rose up. Bishop Foulque had just come in. He traversed the hall theatrically and went to sit down in the armchair opposite the Comte's. The Capitouls, at first mute with surprise, had stood up and were questioning one another. Several made as if to leave. Others, turned toward the Comte, were saying things to him that I could not hear.

Finally, the voice of Arnaud Bernard dominated the noise.

"The members of the Chapter desire to know who summoned the Bishop to their meeting."

The Comte stood up and replied, with embarrassment. It was him. Ought not every decision to be approved by the representative of God? He had just been reconciled with the Church. He hoped at all Toulousans would rejoice in that.

The story of what had happened in Saint Gilles had been running around the city since the morning. The Comte de Toulouse, naked above the waist, had been beaten with rods in the cathedral by the papal legate Milon. Then the latter had led him to one of the crypts of the basilica and made him prostrate himself before the stone where the remains of Pierre de Castelnau reposed.

No, the Toulousans did not rejoice because their seigneur had been humiliated. Étienne Cerabordes, the dealer in fruits and vegetables, and Pons Barbadal, the wine merchant, had the same idea and spat in order to express their scorn.

"Is Toulouse not the most powerful city in the world?" cried Pierre Guitard.

Comte Raymond, pale and resigned, attempted to explain himself. "I believed myself obliged to incline before the will of Pope Innocent."

Clamors interrupted him.

"Why?"

"Why obey the Antichrist?"

"It's the Pope who ought to explain himself on his knees here."

Bishop Foulque had stood up. His face was covered by a mask of hypocritical sadness but he had difficulty dissimulating a detestable joy. Clasping his bosom with his hands he adjured his children to reenter the fold of the Church. He knew full well that they were being devoured by the serpent of heresy. For a long time he had seen that symbolic serpent biting the heart of the people of Toulouse, but he, Foulque, would crush the head of the serpent under his foot.

"You remember the foot of Barral de Baux!" cried Arnaud d'Escalquens, a fat jovial man who had the faculty of expressing his thoughts as soon as they were conceived. Before taking holy orders, Foulque had courted Alazaïs de Marseille, and. in the wake of a gross attempt at seduction, the latter had had her husband expel him with kicks.

The voice of Arnaud Bernad resounded again. It was loud and vibrant. The quadrilateral of his bearded face was turned toward the Comte.

"To what else have you consented?"

I saw my master lower his head, and then he made a great effort. Rapidly, he began to talk.

The army gathered at Lyon was immense and it was expecting further reinforcements. All the Barons of the North were there, Eudes, Duc de Bourgogne, Hervé, Comte de Nevers, the Comte de Bar: cruel and unscrupulous men commanded by a half-English adventurer, Simon de Montfort, of the Leicester family, chosen as leader because of his absence of pity. Faithful Provençals had traveled up the Rhône and had brought him news of the state of mind of that army. It had gathered purely for pillage. The crusaders were talking about Béziers, Carcassonne and Toulouse as the companions of Godefroy de Bouillon had once talked about Jerusalem. It was the wealth of those cities that they wanted and the beauty of their women. He had believed that he was doing his duty in sacrificing his pride to save them.

"What about our soldiers and our ramparts?" cried Arnaud Bernard, who still had the dust of stones sawn on the towers whose repairs he was supervising in his hair.

The richest among the Capitouls consulted one another with their gazes, feeling the same anxiety at the evocation of pillage.

Then Bishop Foulque spoke.

How merciful God had been to enlighten the soul of Comte Raymond! He had permitted him to repent. The Comte de Toulouse repented of the scandalous support that he had so far lent to the heretics. He had become a beloved son of the Holy Church. And what the Holy Church asked of him as a pledge of his repentance? Almost nothing, for it was magnanimous to sinners. The Comte de Toulouse would deliver six fortified places to the crusaders. He would give full power to religious tribunals to render justice on his lands. He would take part in the crusade himself with his cavaliers.

A long silence followed. Every one believed that he had misunderstood. Suddenly, a loud burst of laughter was heard. It was Arnaud d'Escalquens, who was pretending to take the Bishop's speech as a joke.

"So the Comte de Toulouse is going to guide his enemies through his own domains himself!"

Suddenly, everyone burst forth in protests. So their ancient right of rendering justice themselves was abolished! Ecclesiastical justice would henceforth be the only justice. If the Northern crusaders came as far as Toulouse they would find the drawbridges raised and the Toulousans on the ramparts even if the Comte was among them!

"Only the heretics can fear the crusade," shouted Foulque, "and if there are any among you who fear..."

"So what? What if there are heretics among us?" said Pierre de Roaix, turning his marble face, framed by a crown of white hair, toward the Bishop.

"They will die, even if they are Capitouls like you! Ecclesiastical justice does not recognize the inviolability of Capitouls."

I thought that several were about to launch themselves at the Bishop. I sensed a hand that seized my arm. Beside me, Laurent Guillaume had drawn his sword.

"The moment has come," he said, "to throw ourselves upon these accursed Toulousans."

I replied that he was in the presence of the most illustrious men in the city, and that if he did not sheath his sword again, it would be me with whom he would have to deal.

I heard the low voice of the Comte, who was trying to legitimate his conduct. He had reflected, measured the forces in presence. Defeat, in case of conflict, would be certain. He was sacrificing the Albigensians, it was true, but Toulouse would be saved.

"Better that Toulouse perish!"

"We will never surrender the Albigensians!"

"We'll take the bishops and monks as hostages!"

Foulque had quit his chair and retreated to the back of the room, where I was. A few men who composed his personal guard were there. When he was among them, he raised his open arms above his head, making the gesture of repelling an invisible image in the air.

"Toulouse is like Sodom and Gomorrah! Horses will make use of your beds as troughs! Lots will be drawn in the soldiers' camps for your wives and your daughters, with chains around their necks. Colomiès the jeweler, your coffers of pearls will be disemboweled! Astre, sensitive to cold, the mercenaries will put on your furs and you will run naked in the fields to warm yourself! You will labor, Arnaud Bernard, builder of walls, in the places where you have erected stone barbicans! You can invoke your invisible Pope then!"

A wooden stool was stopped in flight by a pike at the moment when it was about to fall on the Bishop's head. All the Capitouls, fists raised, had launched themselves toward him. He retreated to the door, framed by his men-at-arms. The wind, blowing with more force, curbed the flames of the torches so much that the room was plunged momentarily into darkness. Then was heard:

"In the name of the Father, the Son and the Holy Spirit, I curse the heretic race of Toulousans!"

When the palpitation of the light ceased, the Bishop had left the hall.

But the Capitouls were already at odds. Pierre Carabordes and Pons Barbadal cried that they were good Christians and did not care about the Albigensian heresy. Others summoned the Comte to have the Bishop arrested, to break with the Pope and to raise armies against the Northern Barons. The Comte, his arms folded and his eyes staring, stamped his foot, swearing that his decision was irrevocable, but I understood by a certain gleam beneath his eyelids that he was prey to uncertainty and envisaging internally the consequences of a change of mind.

Perhaps there was still time. If, at that moment, the Comte de Toulouse had cried: "Men of my homeland, let us unite against the common enemy, even if that enemy is the Pope of Rome!" perhaps the Midi would have been saved. An obscure witness of that scene, I was tempted to bound into the middle of the hall to adjure the Comte to turn back, and the Toulousans to unite with their seigneur. But what would the word of a young squire have been worth?

I sensed that one man understood, as I did, the value of that moment, and measured the possibility of bringing the Comte de Toulouse back to his true destiny by means of a splendid speech. That was Arnaud Bernard. I saw distinctly on his features the sincere desire to stifle an ancient rancor. Raising his hand to impose silence on everyone, he took a step forward.

By what aberration did the Comte misinterpret that gesture? Did he suppose that the Capitoul whose wife he had once taken was advancing toward him to strike him? Or, weary of the cries of protest, did he want to put an end to them by an irreparable gesture of menace? He recoiled slightly and half-drew his sword. For a few seconds, Arnaud Bernard and he stood face to face, and there was between them the force of a dormant hatred, the mystery of a memory of a woman whose amour two men had shared.

Between parted cloaks, the blue-tinted gleam of blades flashed. Thibaut and I ran behind our master. I heard Laurent Guillaume whisper in my ear: "The advantage is to the man who strikes the first blow. And I noticed the hideous character of his face.

"It's your salvation I want!" cried the Comte again, in the tone of a man who is not sure of what he is saying. "You'll thank me later for having saved your houses, for having conserved your wives and daughters."

In the silence that followed that speech, Armand d'Escalquens was heard to exclaim: "Especially our wives!"

Assuredly, he only wanted to make a humorous allusion to the Comte's mores and was not thinking about Arnaud Bernard's wife. But everyone suddenly thought of that; everyone evoked the blonde Alix Bernard, heroine of an unknown drama, who was said to be still alive and mad in a cell in a Toulousan convent. Under the mildewed Christ on the wall I saw, by means of the gaze of the soul, Alix Bernard of the golden hair gazing with dead opal eyes at the lover and the husband forever separated by the phantom of her flesh. There was a kind of occult presence that immobilized arms and chilled furies.

The Comte made us a sign to follow him and we traversed an assembly as motionless as if an enchantment had suddenly turned its members to stone.

We had arrived during the day and I climbed a hill in order to contemplate, in its full extent, the immense camp of the crusaders.

It was tumultuous, multiform and innumerable. It extended as far as the eye could see, gleaming with reflected light, resounding with clamors, bristling with pikes, crosses and banners. The entire left bank of the Rhône was occupied by German mercenaries commanded by the Comte de Bar. They had conical black tents reminiscent of the dwellings of monstrous termites. At that hour, a great number of them were drinking or washing in the river, side by side with their horses. The majority were on all fours, dipping their russet heads, whose dimensions far surpassed the human norm, into the water. I saw their long beards, soaked, and the idiotic rictus of their laughter. They were amusing themselves jostling one another and throwing sand at one another, and they resembled quadrupeds barded with iron, with a vaguely human appearance.

Bretons, Burgundians, Swiss and Italians were staged on the right bank. They formed quarters like those of a city. The setting sun made the backs of their helmets shine like terrestrial stars. In places, circles of light sprang from improvised forges, and I heard the sound of hammers on the steel of arms. The paths between the tents were cluttered with dice players and quarrels broke out, from which insults rose in various languages. Horsemen passed bearing messages. A file of monks in brown robes snaked around an olive grove.

A quadrilateral of fields marked by oriflammes had been reserved for the monks. It surrounded a chapel where the bishops said mass. But the advance guard of the crusaders, unaware of the honor promised to it, had pillaged it on arrival. The battens of the door had been staved in and even the ornaments of the façade had been smashed. And as the bell was cracked, the church had a sinister air and exhaled an atmosphere of malediction even in the ringing of its angelus.

But beyond the place where the Templars and the Knights of Jerusalem were camped, extended a sea of bizarre carriages, dilapidated tents and carts hung with colored fabrics. There resided the parasites of the army, the prostitutes with their go-betweens, the crooks, the gypsies and the beggars. They woke up in the evening and multiplied before my eyes as if they had emerged from a mysterious ant-hill. I heard unfamiliar songs, barbaric music, savage disputes and sometimes the screams of some peasant woman being raped somewhere.

On a pathway, in a matter of minutes, a bazaar had been established. Soldiers were jostling one another around one tent larger than the rest, on the threshold of which stood an enormous woman. Behind ragged draperies, semi-naked women were smiling. Strolling players were doing turns circled by spectators. That moving, howling, multicolored crowd was shifting around a tall gold-painted phallus, like a symbolic hub. It was the emblem of the great Coesre, the King of *Truands*,[12] which, by a privilege of the King of France, he was authorized to transport behind his cart.

From where I was standing, illuminated by the setting sun, that phallus was disproportionate and gigantic; it resembled a monstrous god of a people deprived of reason. Only the metal cross that marked the camp of the legate, a little further on, was as high. It seemed similarly covered, equally rutilant. And I could not take my eyes off those two blind forces, desire and faith, that were rushing upon my homeland in order to enjoy and enslave it.

---

[12] *Truands* were members of a supposed organization of thieves and professional beggars. The role attributed to them here in the taking of Béziers seems to be based on a mistake, the probable origin of which is explained in a footnote to the account of the event in the essay appended to the novel.

To the right, the three hundred cavaliers that the Comte de Toulouse had brought with him, under the banner on which a black key on a golden cross was painted, made a little diamond droplet in a heap of ordure. I was heading with a rapid stride for the place where my countrymen were camped when I received a violent blow in the chest and fell in the dust.

I had been knocked over by the horse of a cavalier who was passing, followed by a few men-at-arms. He turned round, but without stopping, and I saw that he was not wearing a helmet and that his head with short-cropped graying hair was astonishingly round, like a block of marble, and had the curious particularity of being deprived of eyes.

A voice said: "It's a man who belongs to the Comte de Toulouse."

Then I perceived beneath the knight's eyebrows a green-tinted line that had the phosphorescence of a cat's gaze in the darkness, and I heard a scornful snigger. The group disappeared around a bend in the road.

Full of rage, I leapt to my feet. I perceived that I was unarmed. I was clamoring I know not what insults when a soldier passing on foot who must have witnessed the scene approached me.

"Undoubtedly, you don't know who that knight was who knocked you down," he said.

"No, but if I did..."

The man made me a sign to shut up, and murmured: "It's Simon de Montfort."

I had always believed that a liking for theft and the desire for wealth were the origin of wars. I perceived that it was not so. The possession of women is the motive force that drives men to fight. The soldiers talked about nothing but the beauty of the women they were going to take in the vanquished cities, and as we descended the Rhône and advanced toward Occitanian territory, there was a kind of sexual hallucination of which one could see the phantom in the depths of every gaze.

The Comte de Toulouse did not address a word to anyone, and mine was the only presence that he could support. He seemed to hold it against his knights that they had obeyed him and were following him in the crusade against their brothers. In any case, several of them quit us along the road.

It was near Montpellier that we learned that Trencavel, Vicomte de Carcassonne and Béziers, had resolved to close the gates of his cities and defend them against the crusaders.

The Comte de Toulouse did not like his nephew, whose excessive courage dazzled him. When he learned of his decision he took his head in his hands and wept. I could not tell whether it was because of the woes that he glimpsed or whether he regretted not having done likewise.

And army composed by the barons of Périgord and Limousin, led by the Bishop of Bordeaux had joined the army formed at Lyon. Another had descended from the Tarn and the Black Mountain. That great ocean of armor, crosses and horses unfurled around the walls of Béziers.

The city was bristling with fortresses and dominated a steep hill. We knew that before going to enclose himself in Carcassonne, Trencavel had introduced numerous and well-disciplined troops into it. The bourgeoisie of Béziers was known for the good organization of its militias. The nobles of many châteaux in the environs had taken refuge there.

"The siege will last at least a year," I said to Thibaut, as we were sitting in front of our tent on the evening of our arrival. "The inhabitants of Béziers will show the men of the North what virtue there is in Occitan blood."

Thibaut was content to shake his head, as was his habit. I heard a burst of laughter beside me and I perceived Laurent Guillaume. We were obliged to share our tent with him, and, in spite of our efforts to keep away from him, he was almost always by our side.

"I believe that tomorrow, at sunset, the city will be in the crusaders' possession," he said.

It was my turn to laugh at such a ludicrous assertion. But he added with a tranquil certitude that since the army was commanded by the pious Simon de Montfort and the papal legate Arnaud, Abbot of Cîteaux, the walls would fall and the combatants would be dispersed.

I asked him then to pick up his sword and leave the camp with me; we would see whether a servant of the Pope would reckon so easily with a man of Toulouse.

He refused, with an amiable smile, raising the objection of the severe orders that forbade crusaders to fight one another.

"For you bear the cross," he added.

A large red cross was, indeed, sown on to the body-stocking that I wore over my coat of mail.

"Thank God, who will protect you thereby from death."

I was woken up the next morning by Thibaut, who was shaking me.

"Something's happening," he told me.

I heard a great rumor that as coming from all directions at once. Laurent Guillaume was on his feet and armed, but he did not spare us a glance and departed at a run I knew not where. We armed ourselves in our turn and went out.

The sun had scarcely risen.

It was July and the heat was oppressive. Cavaliers went past us, accompanied by foot soldiers, who were following them at a trot, panting. Some still had straps attached to their breastplates. It was evident that they had equipped themselves abruptly. They were all heading in the same direction, toward the Narbonnais Gate, the one that had been identified as the widest and the most accessible for future attacks. Coming from that direction was the confusion of furious cries, the whinnying of horses and the sound of clashing arms that comes from distant battles.

"If it had been decided to attack the city, all the crusaders would have been warned," Thibaut told me, vey judiciously.

We headed toward the Comte de Toulouse's tent in order to take his orders. It was on the other side of a small wheat-field. As we traversed it, I spotted a sergeant-at-arms who had the ruddy face common among the men of the North. He could not run because a fat belly that he carried before him with a kind of pride, and he was advancing full of dignity, parting the wheat with his pike. I asked him what was happening. He was glad to have the opportunity to draw breath.

"One of the gates of Béziers has just been forced," he told me, with an expression of pride, as if it were to himself that the crusaders owed that exploit. "And do you know who forced it? It was the Truands, with their King at their head. To vanquish the southerners there's no need of soldiers. Thieves are sufficient. I believe that it's necessary to hurry in order to arrive in time to grab some booty."

And he drew away slowly.

The knights of Toulouse were flooding around the Comte's tent. He suddenly appeared in their midst. He was half-dressed, and a livid man covered with sweat was extending his hands to him, imploring him. The Comte took his knights as witnesses

"It's too late now! This is a bourgeois from Béziers who is begging me in the name of his fellows to go find the Abbot of Cîteaux and Simon de Montfort to save the city. Have you ever seen anyone beg wolves for mercy at the moment when they're about to hurl themselves on their prey?"

Increasingly numerous men-at-arms were going past, jostling us. The inhabitant of Béziers had fallen to his knees. He raised his arms and his face was bathed in tears. The Comte kicked him.

"Well, it was necessary to do as I did! It's because I foresaw what was going to happen that I'm here. He tells me that he has a daughter of twenty lying ill in bed. But why haven't you fled? Bishop Réginald de Montpeyroux came yesterday to adjure you to leave the city. Haven't the Jews left already? What didn't you do as they did? Men are so attached to their property that they prefer to die rather than abandon it."

In the meantime, Thibaut had gone to fetch the Comte's horse and had brought it to him. Then his perplexity caused him to raise his voice to the point of shouting: "But they both defy me. They do the opposite of what I ask. Montfort would accuse me of treason and summon me to go and fight by his side. And anyway, where are they? The Abbot of Cîteaux's tent is on the far side of the camp."

However, he mounted the horse. The Toulousan knights demanded their horses in order to form an escort for him. But at that moment a deafening noise drowned out all the voices. An immense quantity of pilgrims belonging to the same religious fraternity advanced toward Béziers singing a canticle. Its rhythm was vast and slow; it expressed the power of a redoubtable God, and the obscure fatality of death. Like a tidal wave abruptly surging forth, rising very high and rolling very far, an innumerable, blind and singing crowd unfurled over us and dispersed us. I saw the Comte de Toulouse resisting with difficulty, in the midst of his men. I thought at first of joining him by fraying a passage with the pommel of my sword, but the desire to see suddenly took possession of me and I let myself go with the torrent that was carrying me toward Béziers.

Either because there was still fighting at the Narbonnais Gate or because the bridge had been broken, it was through the Catalans Gate that I entered the city with the pilgrims. On the way, several of them questioned me in a barbaric and incomprehensible language. I was content to point in turn to the huge red cross on my breast and the blade of my naked sword. They replied with bizarre cries; one of them showed me a huge pocket under his jacket, the other a sack on his back. I saw by the expression on their faces that they were rejoicing in pillage and counting on coming back laden with booty. They must have belonged to very distant countries. Almost all of them were frightfully red-haired.

Alongside me, a thin man of immeasurable height was marching with his eyes raised toward the heavens, repeating a woman's name: "Gunnur!" with an intonation so passionate that I thought it must be the name of his fiancée. He had a coarse face full of benevolence and carried a short, broad cutlass of an unusual form. Another, a sort of dwarf, naked to the waist and hairy, with an ax on his shoulder, was reminiscent of one of the kobolds of the mountains mentioned in the tales of Northern poets. They formed little troops of twenty, quite disciplined, obedient to a man redder than the rest, whose pike had a blue pennant with which to rally them.

There was no trace of conflict at the Catalans Gate, which was already guarded by a group of the Comte de Nevers' soldiers. They shouted to us as we passed that they had opened the gate by surprise and without resistance. They advised us to have our arms ready, for there was fighting in all the quarters of the city.

The streets through which we advanced were dead and silent. All the doors were shut. My companions marched at a slow pace, lowering their voices, intimidated. We came out into a little square that had a fountain in the middle shaded by a plane tree. The sound of the water, the shadow of the houses and the freshness of the air evoked memories of peaceful happiness. The place was so calm that a few pilgrims sat down on the rim of the fountain. Others were tempted to retrace their steps.

Then a door opened and a woman came out of a house. I saw that she had the appearance of a prosperous bourgeoise. She took two or three steps, and perceived us. She shouted: "Jésus Marie!" and started to run. No one budged, except the thin man with the benevolent face, who shouted "Gunnur!" and launched himself in pursuit. He caught up with her in three strides and struck her a great blow with his cutlass, which he held exposed. She collapsed, and he fell upon her body, lacerating her robe in order to search her and almost cutting off her fingers in order to tear away her rings. Then he carefully stuffed what he had taken into one of his pockets, shouting something that must have signified that it was really his, and gesticulating proudly.

For a few seconds the pilgrims formed a circle around the woman, whose blood was flowing over the pavement from a large wound in the cranium. They did not say anything. They were surprised. My first impulse was to throw myself on the murderer, but I suppressed it. All those surrounding me had just uttered a savage cry in unison. In their turn, they wanted to kill.

I saw the dwarf attack a door with blows off the ax. Others made a short ladder in order to scale a small wall. Soon, howls were resounding in all the houses. Although silent, they were full of frightened inhabitants. A baby that had been thrown out of a window fell into the fountain with a splash. I collided with a staggering man who was running, trying to pull a dagger out of his breast that had been plunged into it. A little further on, three giants were fighting over a young woman with the face of a Madonna beneath scattered black hair. One of them had put his dagger under her collar in order to cleave her robe, but he must have done so too rudely, for as it split the robe revealed the body, opened from top to bottom by the blade.

The crusaders were arriving more numerously from all directions. The howls of the victims resounded in a heart-rending fashion. Furniture, fabrics and barrels were dragged into the street. A heroic young man perched on a high roof on which he was sitting shot arrows at the crusaders for a long time from a small bow, like a toy, and killed a considerable number around me. He was taking arrows methodically from a quiver that he had placed beside him and shooting as if at a target, without ever missing. As I gazed from a distance at his pale face framed by long black hair he nearly nailed me to the wood of a door, and of all those at whom he took aim, I was the only one who survived. In the end, the street emptied. No one knew how to reach the roof where he was. When his quiver was empty, he darted a glance around him, got up calmly, and disappeared who knows where, doubtless through some skylight. I had a desire to shout my admiration of the marvelous archer, but prudence retained me.

I marched through the streets at random. Everywhere the spectacle was the same. I was knocked over several times by cavaliers. Sometimes, furious men hurled themselves upon me and I was obliged to parry their blows with my sword until they had distinguished the cross on my breast. In the end, I made the decision to smear myself with blood in order to resemble those who were carrying out the massacre and to avoid being killed by them.

In order to do that, I spotted an open door and penetrated into a corridor and then into a room where the odor was frightful. By the light of a small window I perceived mercenaries lying, drunk, alongside a few terrified and half-naked women, whose eyes I saw shining in the gloom. They took me for one of theirs and shouted to me that they had everything in abundance. One of them pushed a bottle in my direction with his foot. As I took a step in the direction where the women were, they recoiled in fear. I bumped into a body covered in blood that did not budge. I distinguished confusedly the shadow of tresses, and the form of a slender torso with a huge hole in the place of the heart. I bent down, steeped my hands in the blood flowing from it and then applied them to my forehead and cheeks.

I heard a savage snigger.

"He prefers blood to wine."

Other bursts of laughter followed. The mercenaries thought that I had just drunk the blood. But that did not fill me with the disgust that I would have felt a few hours earlier. I was gripped by a kind of intoxication. I had respired a wind that transported corruption. A taste for death had passed into me. I would have liked to destroy and kill.

I was dazed, and I went forth without knowing where, feeding on cries of hatred and despair, experiencing in the utmost depths of my flesh a new and monstrous sensuality. I had the sensation that a sort of hydra, a fantastic beast with teeth and tentacles, had been born in the depths of my heart and was growing there. I was possessed by the ambient evil. I could not detach myself from it and I suffered from only being one with that frightful beast.

The wounded had been brought to a large square. It was said that one quarter was being defended. I learned that more than six thousand people had taken refuge in the Church of

Saint Nazaire, but the soldiers had been able to throw torches in through the roof. The dresses of women had caught fire. They had run around, spreading the fire that was consuming them. The pews and the woodwork of the choir had started to burn in their turn, and then the entire church. God had then wrought a miracle. The walls of the cathedral had split without anyone being able to explain how and all the sinners it sheltered had been buried.

I was exhausted by fatigue. I sensed my reason quitting me. At a corner of what must have been the main street of the city, which had been particularly looted, I heard acclamations. The soldiers who were standing fell to their knees. Those who were in the shops and feasting there appeared on the threshold with their red faces, with their helmets suspended around their necks by the visor, and immediately prostrated themselves.

Preceded by a sergeant-at-arms carrying an iron cross and followed at a distant by a group of Templar knights, a man—or, rather, a phantom—had just surged forth within that scene of destruction. He was wearing the white robe of Cistercian monks and mounted on a white horse with a floating mane. I thought of Jesus Christ, and then of the angel Lucifer; but I immediately recognized that handsome regular face with a big nose and frowning eyebrows that made one thing of an ever-irritated Jupiter. It was the papal legate, Arnaud, Abbot of Cîteaux, who commanded the army of crusaders with Simon de Montfort.

He raised his right hand, and with a regular, automatic gesture like that of a man throwing manna, he blessed the murderers, the drunkards and the profaners; he blessed the weapons that had slaughtered; he threw toward everyone the manna of spiritual recompense, the promise of eternal paradise. After his passage, foreheads were raised, illuminated by delight, and the soldiers of Christ measured the merit they had acquired by means of that day of victory.

In the midst of the Templars riding behind the legate I recognized the latter's counselor, the Spanish monk Domi-

nic,[13] to whom miracles were attributed, and who was reckoned to be a saint throughout Christianity. His enormous forehead and his entirely bald cranium made a dull patch in the
midst of the gleam of helmets.

At the street corner where I was standing there was a
heap of corpses piled one atop another, and above which
someone had thrown a leather sheet. But the sheet, being too
narrow, allowed mutilated feet and dislocated heads with
tresses like sinister vegetation to protrude. Dominic's horse
collided with the foot of a dead man and reared up. I followed
the monk's gaze and I understood that he did not see the
corpses over which he had nearly stumbled. He only had the
faculty of seeing the living, those who wore a red cross on
their breasts. He saw me, and my cross, and his jaws clenched
benevolently. He did not turn his head to avoid the sight of the
heaped-up dead. They were invisible for him. I noticed a large
patch of fresh blood soling his robe and causing it to stick to
his knee, but for the same reason, he must not have sensed
either the dampness or the odor.

I do not know exactly what happened to me during the
hours that followed. At a given moment, I must have fallen
down somewhere and fallen asleep with the hydra of evil
stuck to my flesh, so alive within me, identified so closely
with my being, that I would not have been astonished to feel
long claws instead of nails at the tips of my fingers and to see
my teeth elongating over my breast.

When I woke up, the setting sun was singularly low in
the sky. It cast a disquieting fiery light, by means of which I
orientated myself in order to emerge from the city, but in looking toward the east I saw the glare of another sun, which

---

[13] Dominic de Guzman (1170-1221), later Saint Dominic, the
founder of the Dominican Order charged with special responsibility for persecuting heretics. He attempted to convert the
Cathars, but with little success. He is now the patron saint of
astronomers—mass-murderers, of course, have no official
patron saint.

seemed to be setting in the midst of more ardent blazes. A third, flamboyant to the north, and a fourth, to the south, caused formidable sheaves of sparks to rise toward the heavens. There were suns at the four cardinal points.

I started running straight ahead, prey to an unnamable terror. I was witness to cosmological phenomena that, since time immemorial, had been held to be the presages of the end of the world. Four globes of fire were illuminating the wretched planet of human beings, in order to expose the most secret coverts of their souls. They cast a light so vivid that by their clarity I was able to decipher the interior book of my thoughts. There I read my cowardice, my reckless self-esteem and the enjoyment of evil that, hypocritically, I named curiosity. I had taken pleasure in the crime. I had been an impassive witness to the slaughter of the lamb, and I would justly share the punishment of the accursed.

My teeth chattering, I stopped in a square before a little church, the portal of which was smoking. And it seemed to me that from that smoke sprang the rainbow announced by John in the Apocalypse. I thought I saw on his throne the one who is similar to a stone of jasper and sardonyx. The twenty-four old men clad in white emerged slowly from the church. The four mysterious beasts beat their wings and stared at me with their innumerable eyes.

Then an idea occurred to me. Someone had killed me while I slept. I was dead. That church, which was being extinguished, those open dwellings from which death-rattles emerged, and all those streets elongating in sinister fashion, were nothing but he dream of a soul wandering in the afterlife. Hell had taken the form imposed by the final image of my life. I had mingled with the murderers, I was one of them, and now the sword of the archangel was about to drive me somewhere, with reproofs, against the bloody robe of the Spaniard Dominic, against the eyeless cranium of the Englishman Simon de Montfort. I was so frightened that I started screaming.

Other screams responded to mine. Alongside me, other dead souls were running, in fear of the four apocalyptic suns.

And one of them expressed in the language of living men that fires, terrestrial fires lit by human hands, had been set in the four corners of the city.

"It's the Truands!" he cried. "They're fighting with the Italians over the prisoners."

And another said; "They've dragged away three hundred young women with ropes around their necks and are making them walk by pricking them like beasts."

Then I returned to myself. I considered the appearance of the streets. I was still in the city of Béziers and I was navigating as best I could, wanting at any price to escape the funereal circle in which I was turning.

Suddenly, I recognized the place where I was. I recognized the small square, the fountain and the plane tree. I noticed a cadaver sitting up, one of those killed by the admirable archer on the high roof, in the same position where I had left him. In the basin of the fountain, the corpse of the baby that had been thrown from a window was floating in the water, eyes open. It was bloated and its face, rendered enormous and black, was like that of a monster. But the location, with the dusk and the silence of death, had recovered the placid calm that had impressed me in the morning.

I was not far from the Catalans Gate. I was about to launch myself into the side-street that led to it when I heard a joyous cry and a name: "Gunnur!" I saw the pilgrim with the cutlass by whose side I had marched. He recognized me and gave me an amicable wave. His face still had an expression of benevolence but its color had become earthen. He was dragging after him a chest attached to him by straps, into which he had put his booty. He showed it to me triumphantly. In the midst of miscellaneous objects, partly wrapped around a golden candlestick, there was a long hank of a woman's hair, which he must have cut off with his cutlass, because the extremity was bloody. He saw the direction of my gaze and picked up the tress proudly in order to show it to me. He made it stir like a snake. Without knowing why, I thought of the divine tresses of Esclarmonde. He must have thought that I envied him such a possession, because he emitted a loud burst of laughter.

Then, with all the strength of my arm, I struck him on the head with my sword, the same blow with which he had struck the fleeing woman. But I delivered it from in front, and I shouted with all my might: "Gunnur!" He fell face down and did not move again. The square had become darker and more silent, and I started running toward the Catalans Gate.

I got through it unhindered, but when I was far enough from the ramparts I took a small path that followed a direction opposite to that of the crusaders' camp, which ought to lead to the road to Carcassonne.

I was hungry, thirsty and exhausted. When I had marched for a long time and night had fallen, I sat down on the roadside. In the distance, the glow of the burning city could be distinguished, and the outline of its calcined skeleton. A continuous, desperate clamor reached me, which must have been the plaint of the young women that the Truands were raping.

A shadow extended before me and I realized that I was at the foot of a cross. I got up, threw my arms around it, and shook it with all my might. But it had been profoundly embedded in the earth and it resisted as if it had had roots. In the end, I finished up extracting it and bringing it down. Then I tore off the body-stocking on which the red cross of the crusaders was sown, and scattered the fragments. Only then did it seem to me that I was liberated from the monstrous beast that I had carried in my heart. And as the guard of my sword was also in the form of a cross, I armed myself with a stone and struck it until it was twisted.

IV

In Narbonne, it was impossible for me to buy a horse. The number of people who were fleeing was so great that I would not have been able to find one even if I had wanted to pay a fortune. A Jew sold me a donkey and with that equipment I set forth for Carcassonne.

At the foot of the mountain of Alaric, two days later, I was stopped by a group of the Vicomte's soldiers. They were not letting anyone into Carcassonne except combatants. They saw solely by the color of my gaze that I was one, and they let me pass.

It was very hot and I had dismounted in order to relieve my donkey. When I reached the ramparts I saw that there were watchmen on all the towers and that the posterns were closed. Carcassonne, dating within its walls from the Visigoths, was enclosed like a warrior in stone armor.

As I prepared to cross the drawbridge I crossed the path of a few cavaliers who were emerging from the city. By the pennants that floated from their lances I recognized that they belonged to the Comté de Foix. Behind them was a woman covered from head to foot in a long back cloak. She turned round to make an amicable sign to a bare-headed young man of short stature who was watching her draw away, motionless, leaning on his sword. I recognized the impassive features and dreamlike eyes of Esclarmonde de Foix, Vicomtesse de Gimoez.

With my unkempt beard, covered with dust, and drawing my donkey by the bridle, I had such a wretched aspect that my first thought was to hide. But Esclarmonde rejoined a cavalier with the head of a peasant who must be her husband, the Vicomte de Gimoez, and passed by without letting her gaze fall on me.

I followed her with my eyes as she drew away. I envied the men of her escort for breathing the same air as her and raising the same dust. I would gladly have paid with my life for the joy of holding her horse or carrying a message written by her hand.

A voice questioned me rudely.

"Where are you going? Where have you come from? I'm wondering why a beggar was allowed to pass."

I was in the presence of a short, stout man who had unlaced his breastplate, doubtless because of the heat. He had to be a person of some importance for, at a sign from him, two soldiers got ready to seize me.

Doubtless my attitude lacked respect, for he shouted at me again.

"I'm the Seigneur d'Espinouse, do you hear?"

I hastened to reply that I was Dalmas Rochemaure, squire of the Comte de Toulouse, and that I had just done battle with the men of my homeland.

He shook his head dubiously and murmured a phrase that included the word "spy" and also "prison."

But at that moment the young man to whom Esclarmonde had made a sign of adieu came forward. He wore a soldier's hauberk with thick mesh. His movements were lively. He had a cheerful attitude full of enthusiasm. By the marks of respect with which he was surrounded, I recognized Roger Trencavel, Vicomte de Béziers and Carcassonne.

"Why not? Perhaps my uncle has a servant more courageous than he is," he said, turning to an old knight with a long gray moustache whose costume was singular and whose gaze was full of malice. I discovered subsequently that he was the celebrated Pierre de Cabaret, who had retained from his sojourn in the Orient the habit of wearing a red turban and a striped silk surcoat, and carrying a large Moorish scimitar.

Roger Trencavel made me a sign to follow him beyond the second enclosure, all the way to the foot of the Tour Narbonnais. There he asked me to tell him what I knew about the crusaders' army and the destruction of Béziers.

I recounted all the scenes that I had witnessed, and while I was speaking he tapped a flagstone with the point of his sword, with blows that became increasingly forceful.

When I had finished he remained silent for a long time, sometimes darting a severe glance at me, as if I had unleashed such great calamities personally. Then he said to Pierre de Cabaret: "They'll be here within a week."

The old warrior in the turban leaned toward him and murmured something in a low voice, pointing at me.

"You think so?" said Trencavel. And I sensed benevolence radiating from him.

"He can come with me," said Pierre de Cabaret. "I'll utilize him for the defense of the Samson Tower."

Roger Trencavel had charged each of his Barons with the defense of a tower, and Pierre de Cabaret commanded the Samson Tower. He had brought men-at-arms from his château, who numbered scarcely more than thirty. In order for them to be instructed in the art of war, he had also brought workmen from the workshops of the Mint, who formed a proud corporation that affected to scorn the obligatory handling of arms. I received the command of ten of them.

It was on the ninth day after my arrival that we perceived the advance guard of the crusaders from the height of the ramparts. For an entire day the immense army flowed round the city like a swarm of iron insects and surrounded it completely. The waves that divided it had the appearance of a blue blade thrown across an anthill.

The crusaders had left a wide empty space between their front lines and our ramparts. No one knew exactly how the death came about of the Seigneur d'Espinouse, who was commanding the Narbonnais Gate. As he was fat, he had the habit of taking off his breastplate in order to breathe more easily. He was watching the sunset from behind a crenellation when an arrow launched with infernal skill pierced his belly clean through.

Roger Trencavel immediately gave strict orders that no one was to expose himself needlessly. The Mint workers took advantage of that to give evidence of a ridiculous pusillanimity while patrolling the round-path. Those I had under my orders often laughed at me behind my back, making insulting remarks about my master, the Comte de Toulouse and speaking scornfully about the Toulousans, who—out of cowardice, according to them—had made a pact with the crusaders. I wanted to show those metal-founders that the soul of a Toulousan might surpass fear.

I knew that they were great lovers of music and songs. I borrowed a viol from one of them and on the evening after the death of the Seigneur d'Espinouse, as they were all gathered in the guard-room of the Samson Tower, I told them that I was going to sing but that I needed celestial space before me and the light of the stars above my head. I went out and went to sit down on a crenellation, in the open, with my legs dangling over the void.

Accompanying myself on the viol, I sand the ancient Song of the Violet, which I had learned from a wandering singer under an elm tree in the Place Saint-Sernin. Among the talents I had received at birth that remained latent in me, for want of being developed, was that of singing with a moving intonation and an incomparable force. My voice expanded into the distance, traversing the extent, reaching as far as the camp where the men of the North were sleeping heavily like oxen. Many of them, marveling, advanced silently in order to hear me better. When I finished, I could see blurred human silhouettes beyond the ditches, in the ecstatic pose that reverie and music produce.

Then, lifting up my seven-stringed viol I stood up on a crenellation, expressing with a gesture of my arms my delight at having created, but virtue of my singing, a few minutes of truce consecrated to beauty.

And as the poltroons of the Mint shouted to me to beware, and I lifted my viol again, I received a violent impact in the breast that projected me on to the stone. An arrow, perhaps

117

launched by the same archer who had killed the Seigneur d'Espinouse, had just struck me over the heart. Fortunately, I had put my coat of mail on beneath my body-stocking, because of the prudence from which is customary in Toulouse not to depart, even if one is reckless. I spat over the rampart to express the disgust inspired in me by the savages who, after having profited from the song, had attempted to kill the singer.

We made sorties, and the crusaders attempted to take the city by assault. The two fortified outlying districts that extended along the right bank of the Aude were lost in turn, captured and burned. Many valiant men fell in combat. War machines were seen in the distance looming over the tents like fabulous beasts.

The men who were confided to me were singularly transformed. One was killed, several were wounded, all of them sensed the proximity of death, but gradually, their initial fear was transformed into a courage that almost equaled mine. At first I sensed a secret bitterness at that; but I thought afterwards that it was to my example that the courage in question was due, even though no one admitted it. I reflected also that the men who come from the land that extends from Marseille to the sandy pine forests are like that; they only manifest their courage after an ostentation of poltroonery.

That courage and our common love of music almost cost us our lives. The Mint workers had had the custom, before the siege, of going in a band in the evening to a little wood of laurels and fig trees situated outside the city. There they sat down and listened to the voice of an extraordinary nightingale that had established its domicile in a unique centenarian oak. Now they were deprived of that song because the little wood was situated between the city and the crusaders' camp, closer to the camp than the city.

As soon as night fell they listened, and sometimes claimed to hear a feeble echo of the marvelous song. In the end, a fat man named Samatan, who seemed to have a mind as thick as his body, declared that he would rather die than not hear the song of the nightingale. I proposed, but without believing that he would accept my proposal, so audacious was it, to leave the city when the night was further advanced and go as far as the little wood, hiding ourselves as best we could. To my great surprise, many of those musical founders accepted joyfully, and I could not take it back.

Nights in July are particularly serene. About fifteen of us left, bent double, running from one bush to another, and reached the little wood without attracting the attention of either the sentinels of the camp of those of the city. There we waited for more half an hour, amusing ourselves with Samatan's skill in imitating the croaking of a fog—which, he claimed, would incite the nightingale to sing.

In the end, it sang, and we were all transported by the spell of that extra-human melody into a celestial universe. When, by virtue of an inexplicable whim, the marvelous bird paused, its silence spread around us a melody so great that the war, the Cathar heresy and death seemed to us to be deprived of any importance.

And as I glimpsed that melancholy on the faces of my companions in the gloom, bearing in my throat a gift of song almost equal to that of the nightingale, I could not master the generous impulse that impelled me to return the dream to them that they had savored and lost.

At the top of my voice, I brought forth from my lungs on their behalf the first lines of the Song of the Violet. They threw themselves upon me immediately to stop me. Now, I have no idea how, but our presence had been detected in the camp and we were surrounded. Arrows whistled and men in shining armor rushed us from all sides at once. They shouted savagely without fear of frightening the divine bird in the branches of the oak. My companions, who had come unarmed, fell round me, but thanks to the lamp of prudence that is always aglow in the heart of a man of Toulouse, I had brought my sword. I was able to parry the first thrusts and cause the shadows to recoil around me. I started running as fast as I could toward Carcassonne. Samatan, thanks to my aid, was able to pierce the enemy line. I sustained him with my arm, for he had difficulty running because of his stoutness.

We arrived alone at the Samson Tower and waited in vain for the return of those who had accompanied us.

Pierre de Cabaret appeared, scimitar in hand, awakened by the tumult, and assured me that, for having led that expedition, I would be transferred to the prison tower the following day. But graver events, in precipitating, deflected his attention from that punishment.

The next morning, a knight of gigantic stature mounted on a horse of unaccustomed dimensions cavorted in front of the ramparts on the side of the Narbonnais Tower. He was so extensively barded in iron that no one thought of launching arrows at him. He proffered insults and demanded a single combat with one of the knights of Carcassonne.

The entire city had come to watch from the ramparts. As I arrived myself I heard the Vicomte de Béziers demanding his arms and his horse. But Pierre de Cabaret ran toward him, gesticulating, as well as several the barons, and he renounced going to fight.

I thought immediately that a glorious exploit might perhaps enable me to avoid prison. I was not a knight, but if I emerged suddenly and charged the gigantic cavalier, he could not refuse to fight me. I was about to go back to the Samson Tower to get a horse worthy of combat when I was anticipated by an adolescent so small that he would seem like a dwarf compared to the enemy against whom he wanted to measure himself. A breastplate and a helmet had been handed to him in haste, which were not his own and were too large for him. His lance, by contrast, was short to the point of being ridiculous.

He went past me in the midst of enthused men who were shouting and running. I heard someone say that he was the son of Seigneur d'Espinouse. The drawbridge had just been lowered and I raced to the ramparts in order to see what would happen.

In the distance, the crusaders formed an uninterrupted line, and after emitting clamors they were now standing silently. The combat only lasted a few seconds, and the spectators on either side were scarcely able to take account of what happened.

Young d'Espinouse had launched himself forward as fast as his horse could go. He collided with his enemy, who waited for him without moving and sent his little pike flying into the air at the first thrust. The two horses, nostril to nostril, started to wheel round rapidly, each seeking to bite the other, for animals side with their masters; if they could talk, they would shout much sage advice in the midst of battles, and events would change course in consequence of it. In the dust that the combatants kicked up, it was evident that they were exchanging sword-thrusts.

And suddenly, from all parts of the horizon, coming from the crusaders as well as the inhabitants of Carcassonne, there was an immense clamor of amazement. No one had doubted the victory of the gigantic warrior over the child, and the latter had only been allowed to depart as a propitiatory sacrifice to the mysterious god of war who likes futile heroisms. The crusader knight was seen to be traversed like a flash of lightning by the blade of the admirable d'Espinouse at the place in the throat where the helmet joins the breastplate. It had required an extraordinary hazard for the point of the weapon to find the only millimeter of the body susceptible of being traversed. The knight collapsed and the enormous horse fled, full of shame.

The entire city of Carcassonne, prey to delirium, formed two human ranks behind the drawbridge between the two enclosures, under the arch of the Narbonnais Tower to welcome the hero, who came back slowly. His mother, a woman with white hair, tall and impassive, was standing beside the Vicomte de Béziers, who was getting ready to seize the victorious child.

On all sides people were crying: "It's David who has killed Goliath!"

But how slowly he was coming back, having departed so rapidly! There was something uncertain and unsteady in his bearing. He even let go of the bridle of his horse. When he passed over the drawbridge the acclamations froze on the lips. The faithful horse stopped in front of the mother. It was a dead man that it was carrying.

Goliath had indeed been slain by David, but David was dead too.

Then I regretted bitterly not having been fast enough to get in ahead of the son of d'Espinouse, for I would have come back without a scratch, because of my lucky star.

V

The heat, more intense than usual that year, had dried up the wells. Certain inhabitants took advantage of that only to drink wine, which they had in abundance in the cellars, and they were drunk from the early morning on.

The assaults were continual and the combatants, obliged because of their small number to run from one tower to anther in accordance with the attacks, were eventually exhausted. A bizarre malady spread through the city which cast those afflicted with it into languor and caused them to die in three days, in great mental distress. As the cemetery was situated outside the ramparts, the Vicomte ordered graves to be dug in the courtyards of houses and public squares, with the result that people were walking through a vast necropolis. People said that they would be fortunate if they could get out of the city with nothing but the shirts on their back—an imprudent wish that was to be granted.

That day, at sunrise, a bishop came with canons bearing crosses to the foot of the Narbonnais Tower in order to negotiate. I happened to be there and I was able to count a dozen Christs whose metal was glinting around the bishop's miter. That cortege drew away after a brief interval, and the rumor spread through the whole city that Arnaud, the Abbot of Cîteaux and Simon de Montfort, in command of the crusade, had invited Roger Trencavel to come and negotiate an honorable capitulation with them, under the safeguard of their oath. It was specified that in order to avoid the unfortunate quarrels that the men of an escort might have with the crusaders, he had to go to the camp alone, with a single squire.

Then, the inhabitants were seen running from all points of the city toward the entrance to the château. The knights and the soldiers did the same, and when the Vicomte appeared on horseback, the members of that crowd fell to their knees and begged him not to trust the word of the men who had massacred the sixty thousand inhabitants of Béziers. All of them proclaimed that the bishop, the dozen Christs and the oaths were not a sufficient guarantee. Roger Trencavel, pale and calm, tried to reassure his people and his soldiers by the tranquility of his attitude.

"I shall be back in an hour at the latest," he said.

Bare-headed and without any weapon, cad in an ordinary doublet, he traversed the crowd slowly. When he passed over the drawbridge and started galloping toward the camp he turned round and with his black-gloved hand he gave his city an amicable gesture, like the gesture of adieu that one makes to a mistress that one will not see again.

Pierre de Cabaret, next to whom I was standing, was twisting his white moustache so much that I feared he might rip it out. As no attack was to be feared, the crowd had invaded the ramparts. Toward midday a pauper woman who was said to be a visionary stated uttering frightful howls without apparent reason, and when attempts were made to shut her up she departed at a run along the crenellations, leaping from one to the next. Her hair undone, she passed like a somnambulist along the round-path and went to fall, finally, to the foot of the Tower of Trésau, from which her cries rose up for some time thereafter, chilling all hearts with fear by their impressive tone.

The sun was about to set and people waited in vain. Suddenly, there was a buzz in the distance, which grew. A trail of murmurs ran through the crusaders' army, swelling and rising. It reached the ultimate extremities of the camp, where the laggards were, the improvised stalls of merchants, and the caravans of actors and strolling players. And that rumor, which became immense, was a rumor of joy, something like the delight of an entire people participating in a monstrous farce. We saw men running across the plain making obscene gestures toward Carcassonne. It was the time when fires were being lit for the evening meal. Through the descending shadows, silhouettes could be distinguished in the firelight that were guffawing or sketching grotesque dances. Even the machines of war started trembling like drunken giants.

And it was as if the heart of the heroic city had broken. A sob uttered by all the creatures enclosed within the circle of stone walls, one unique sob, rose up toward the nascent stars. No one doubted the treason, nor the loss of the city deprived of its leader. There were very few who fell to their knees. Everyone wept standing up, and the despair was visible in the depths of the pupils, like a landscape of nothingness with infinite perspectives.

"Come," said Pierre de Cabaret, going past me.

I saw that he was making a sign to the Jew Nathan, who had been chosen, because of his knowledge of mechanics, to organize the mountainous heights. I heard him say in a muffled voice: "We can still save everyone."

We went into the great hall of the château, where the brothers Bellissend, the Seigneurs d'Avignonnet, de Bram and de Beauxhoate, the armorer Sarraut, the butcher Camus and the principal citizens were already gathered. All of them thought that the crusaders, in order to take advantage of their disarray, would attack at dawn. Only the butcher Camus proposed surrender. The others wanted to make a sortie *en masse* in order to perish in combat.

Then Pierre de Cabaret explained that Roger Trencavel's father had once hollowed out a subterranean tunnel going from Carcassonne to the Château de Cabardez, one of Cabaret's fiefs.[14] That subterranean tunnel, which was several leagues

---

[14] Author's note: "The cities and châteaux of the Midi all possessed very extensive networks of subterranean workings. It was Arab engineers who had taught the techniques of their construction." Generally-accepted history has no record of any such tunnel being employed during the siege of Carcassonne, but records that Roger Trencavel was taken prisoner on 7 August, in spite of the guarantee of safe conduct he had been given in order to negotiate, and died nor long afterwards in mysterious circumstances; the city surrendered on 15 August,

long and had collapsed in places, Roger Trencavel had had repaired at the commencement of the crusade. All the inhabitants of the city could escape by that route, but for that, all night would not be too long.

Everyone received the mission to alert a quarter and to direct its inhabitants toward the entrance to the tunnel, which was in one of the château's cellars. The desperate clamor gradually fell silent, to give way to whispers and hopeful sighs. Many who had prepared to die were gripped again by the love of life.

The surroundings of the château were filled after an hour by a silent crowd, but that crowd came laden with luggage of all kinds, bundles of clothes, sacks of provisions, and even items of furniture. A dealer in earthenware pottery presented himself with a donkey laden with his pots. He resisted, begging, saying that he cherished his donkey, a lifelong companion of his existence, as much as himself. I believed that I recognized the animal on which I had made my entrance to Carcassonne a few days before.

It was necessary for everyone to renounce burdens that would have slowed down the general progress. Pierre de Cabaret was obliged to draw his scimitar and to swear that he would put to death anyone who presented himself with any sort of burden on his back. There were some who turned back and went home, preferring to confront the fate of the inhabitants of Béziers rather than renounce their possessions.

Late into the night, a sort of interminable human column had already plunged into the propitious earth. Pierre de Cabaret charged me with going to make appeals in the houses and see whether any invalid or deaf person had been forgotten somewhere.

---

but its inhabitants were not massacred and were allegedly allowed to leave. Pierre de Cabaret attempted to defend his own castles against the crusaders but capitulated after a matter of months, and is said to have escaped with his life, at least for a while.

In the deserted city I encountered an old man who was carrying an enormous packet of arrows under his arm. He was going to barricade the door of his house and he told me that when the crusaders presented themselves, he counted on killing as many of them as he could.

A family in which there were children and old people were sleeping peacefully in a low house. A candle had been lit next to the statue of some saint or other, shriveled and corroded by time. They did not get up in spite of my exhortations, The father shouted to me that he was tranquil. Nothing bad would happen to them. The saint would protect them.

The night ended. The city was abandoned when I returned to the château. Pierre de Cabaret was on the threshold with a few faithful followers and they were all preparing to go into the tunnel in their turn. One of the Belissend brothers arrived at a run and said that the window of the Seigneur de Canacaude was refusing to leave. He added in a scandalized tone that she was even rejoicing at receiving the crusaders, and that she had made preparations for that.

Canacaude was a respected name. The Seigneur de Canacaude had been a friend of Pierre de Cabaret and the old Vicomte Trencavel. He had fought by their side in the Orient and he had died the previous year, I had been told, of an abrupt emotion that his wife had caused him. By the way that everyone raised their arms to the heavens I understood that she was known for her light conduct and her eccentricities.

"You, who are, in sum, a handsome fellow," Pierre de Cabaret said to me, "try to persuade her to come with us. But hurry, because it will be daylight soon and the crusaders will be here within an hour."

The Dame de Canacaude lived in one of the finest dwellings in the city, facing the Church of Saint Nazaire. I ran through the empty streets but as I was unfamiliar with the quarter I was obliged to retrace my steps and I lost a certain amount of time.

Under the light that precedes the dawn, the Church of Saint Nazaire was like an immense livid phantom whose stones were oozing despair. The portal was open and darkness was swirling mysteriously in the choir and at the feet of the twelve apostles in the apse. The square, transformed into a cemetery, was studded with crosses. And on the other side, facing that mortuary landscape, I perceived the Dame de Canacaude behind a narrow stone balcony on the ground floor of her house. A cross taller than all the others rose up very close to her, to the height of her bosom, and her nonchalantly extended hand gave the impression of trying to pick it like a flower of that bizarre garden.

She was covered in powder and carmine; black curls had been stuck artfully to her temples and she was attempting to smile in an engaging manner. With a mechanical gesture, she divided over her throat the veil that was thrown there. Behind her, the matinal twilight illuminated the four columns of an open bed, the gold of brocades and the gleam of wine in carafes.

In a rapid voice I told her about Pierre de Cabaret's order enjoining her to leave. She replied, showing me her teeth, that she had learned from her venerated husband that a Dame de Canacaude ought not to fear anything. I thought momentarily that it was heroism and thought that it was my duty to tell her how the noblest ladies had been treated in Béziers. I did so not without blushing. But she was content to raise her eyes to the heavens and say that God would protect her.

Then I read in her soul, thanks to my native intuition. She was possessed by the appetite that all women have to prostitute herself to conquerors. I wondered whether I ought not to drive that caricature before me by pricking her with my sword. And suddenly, a lassitude took hold of me, as if that womanly treason had caused an interior cup to overflow. I no longer experienced any human passions in movement around me. The destruction of cities, religious furors, and the massacre of innocent creatures became foreign to me. I no longer understood the cause that impelled men against one another. I felt sad and solitary in an incomprehensible desert.

A dog howled mortally not far away. I perceived birds overhead that were flying at a prodigious height. I interested myself in that flight for a few minutes, as if the entire universe were revolving around it. A green-tinted light spread that seemed to decompose the stones of the church and the houses, and the earth itself. I lay down, with my head against a cross, in order to go to sleep as soon as possible. Everything appeared to me to be vain and the coolness of the matter on my cheek gave me a kind of foretaste of desirable death.

Then, in the clarity of the dream that bathed me, like a fantastic beast, the donkey laden with pottery—my donkey—slowly traversed the square covered with graves, sniffed the threshold of the church momentarily, and disappeared through the open portal.

I bounded to my feet. Without my being able to explain why, the passage of that donkey had just reawakened a hidden force within me. I perceived at an infinite distance the clamor of a trumpet that resonated in the silence of the sunrise. I started running toward the château as fast as my legs would carry me.

The surroundings were absolutely deserted. I went in, listening to a dull sound that was coming from underground. I went down a tortuous stairway, precipitately, and found myself in the presence of the Jew Nathan. He was directing the labor of a few men who were in the process of demolishing the masonry of the subterranean vault in order to block its orifice.

"One minute more and it would have been too late," he told me, shaking his head as if it were a matter of scant importance.

I launched myself into the tunnel. The beams sustaining the sides had been wrenched away over a length of at least a hundred meters. Lanterns had been placed at intervals. The crowd that had passed through had left a frightful odor. In certain places water was oozing from the low ceiling. I had never thought that the light of the sun was so desirable and necessary to life.

When I had walked for a long time I found myself in the presence of a stone staircase of interminable length. The steps were often missing and it was necessary to aid myself with my hands. It seemed to me that that lasted for hours, and I thought that the stairway, in order to be so long, must be built within the flanks of a mountain. Suddenly, a pink light vibrated around me. The stairway turned abruptly. I had arrived. I was about to let myself fall to the ground, but I straightened up, brushing away with an instinctive gesture the earth that various collisions had mingled with my hair.

Three women of a resplendent beauty were standing at the entrance to the tunnel, making me a gesture of welcome.

VI

In truth, I had heard talk of them a long time ago. The reputation of their beauty had spread through the army of the crusaders. On evening, on the bank of the Rhône, the deformed knights of Burgundy, along with Hairy Bretons, had spoken freely about them. They had even gambled for their future possession, as if goddesses were not always sheltered from the desire of goats and wild boar.

They were three, in Carbardez of the three towers, which bore their names. Brunissende was the daughter of Pierre de Cabaret, Nova was the daughter of his first marriage and Stéphania had married his eldest son, who had died on the morning of his wedding. Brunissende had hair as dark as the slopes of the Black Mountain in the evening. Nova had the gilded color of heather in the sunlight. Stéphania, the smiling, resembled a fragment of amber sculpted by a sculptor of genius. All three dressed similarly in immaculate linen robes. The rumor was that in the ardor of their Cathar mysticism they had made vows of chastity.

The inhabitants of Carcassonne were dispersed through the vast land of Languedoc. Pierre de Cabaret had only kept a few families in his château and the combatants necessary for the defense of that inaccessible place, which enclosed the torrents of the Orbiel. Naturally, I was one of those.

When one has marched through a desolate region, one suddenly finds behind a crag a cheerful little village with fountains, and inns. Thus, in course of my warrior destiny, I encountered a beautiful image by which I was permanently dazzled.

The room in which I spent the nights, which I shared with a few knights of Carcassonne, was situated near the steam-baths. One morning I came across the three marvelous creatures. They had the languid quality of women who have just emerged from the bath and their wet hair was dangling

131

almost to their feet. Brunissende's lips were tightly closed. Nova's eyelids were fluttering. Stéphania had difficulty not smiling. They passed by. But the sign of amorous predestination had appeared for us. I loved all three of them from that day on, identifying them mysteriously. In my dreams I no longer any but a single face, and by a bizarre illusion it had the features of Esclarmonde de Foix. I carried henceforth in my heart the veneration of a unique beauty that was clad in three human aspects.

I taught peasants how to hurl stones with a sling or to handle a crossbow. With a few men-at-arms I sometimes went as far as a farm in the vicinity and I escorted a cart laden with grains and forage. If I turned round I almost always saw, at the window of a tower or the round-path of a rampart, a form in a linen robe following me with her gaze. I did not know whether it was Brunissende, Nova or Stéphania. I was penetrated by the delight that the prescience of love gives.

Everyone at the Château de Cabardez professed the Albigensian heresy. A beam had been nailed over the château's chapel to forbid entry. That chapel was adjacent to a small platform that overlooked the countryside. I walked there every evening, amusing myself watching the nocturnal birds circle, and listening to the noise of the waters of the Orbiel at the bottom of sheer slopes.

When everything was silent in the château, a white-haired old soldier who had accompanied Pierre de Cabaret in the Orient came to kneel before the chapel door. As immobile as a statue, he prayed for a long time and then withdrew as he had come.

After their evening meal, the three beauties of Cabardez made a tour of the château's walls. Once, they were late, and when they went past the chapel they saw, at the same time, the old soldier kneeling, and me leaning on the balustrade.

They stopped, but without anything appearing of the sentiments that might have been agitating them. I saw them confer for a few seconds. Then, in a voice from which emotion was carefully banished, Brunissende called to me and asked me to help her to remove the beam that barred the door of the chapel. It was poorly fitted and I contrived to dislodge it without too much difficulty. Then they invited the old man to go in, telling him to pray entirely at his ease if such was his faith. I even heard Brunissende add that there, where the Albigensians were the masters, everyone had the right to believe in accordance with his soul, without fear of persecution.

They remained outside the door, similar in their white simarres to angels making a nocturnal round. I experienced a great disturbance and I sensed that it was shared. Then I said to them, purely for the sake of breaking the silence, that I desired to be better instructed in the new religion, for when I was in their presence there were certain things of it that I could no longer reasonably accept. The cheerful Stéphania asked me what those things were.

"I cannot believe," I said, "that life is evil and diabolical, as the pure Albigensians teach, and that it is necessary to detach oneself from it, when I gaze at certain human faces so filled with beauty that they give the desire to live in order to contemplate it." And I stared at them, in order that it should be evident that I was talking about them.

They started to laugh with a great simplicity, and Brunissende told me that there was someone in the château who could explain the mysteries of the truth to me better than them. She assured me that she would ask that exceedingly wise man to speak to me the next day, and all three drew away, continuing to laugh, doubtless to put on a show and to disguise their emotion.

I knew that an Albigensian perfectus of reputedly great sanctity lived in a little chamber in a tower and remained there, plunged in perpetual meditation. It was said that he saw future events by gazing into a mirror of a singular form, as, it appears, certain Arab magicians do. I did not think that Brunissende had taken my words literally, but the next day, at the same hour, finding myself near the chapel in the hope of making the same encounter as the day before, I saw a man of short stature coming toward me, of indeterminate age, whose face was so pale that it seemed transparent, and I was tempted at first to look through his body at the objects that were behind him.

He approached me and said to me in a soft voice, calling me his brother, that if I had a question to ask him, he would gladly reply to me.

I was stammering a few words, pierced by my disappointment at encountering him instead of the admirable creatures I was expecting, when his eyes, posed on mine, became troubled and it seemed to me that with the flutter of his eyelids he mastered the moist mist that precedes tears.

"It is not necessary for you to know more, for the moment," he said, appearing to reflect profoundly. "A man kills and is killed in his turn. He forges for himself a chain of evil that has no end, but all of whose knots it will be necessary for him to undo—and with what difficulty! It is vain to enlighten too soon the man who ought not to see yet. Follow your path, which is the longest and hardest, and be content to make an effort to forgive others, and yourself."

He looked at me with an immense pity, and I could not help find that amusing, considering how paltry his form was and the wan pallor of his complexion. I quit him, very disappointed.

Winter was beginning to blow through the cypresses clinging to the slopes of the Château de Cabardez when Jordette Altaripa died in a strange fashion.

She was the daughter of a consul of Carcassonne and she loved Vicomte Roger Trencavel tenderly. After having dragged her away almost by force, Pierre de Cabaret had installed her in the finest room in the Château de Cabardez. She did not leave it, and every day she stood at the window watching the road to Carcassonne to see whether some peasant or merchant might be coming bearing news.

In the course of the autumn we had learned about the events that had unfurled among the crusaders. Comte Raymond had returned to Toulouse with his knights, and I knew his sentiments well enough to think that he must be filled with remorse. After the pillaging of Carcassonne and the acquisition of the houses by many thieving foreign hands, the papal legate and the Christian barons had proclaimed Simon de Montfort seigneur of all the lands conquered by the crusaders. The true master of those lands, Roger Trencavel, was locked in the prison of his own château.

Was he bemoaning bitterly his excessive confidence? Did he desire death? Did he converse during his final hours with his beloved Jordette Altaripa, as she believed? No one will ever know.

As Christmas approached, Jordette Altaripa never ceased to moan softly and to hold out her arms toward an absent companion. Extending her arms like those of a cross on the crimson brocade of her bed, she gave the impression of a crucified dove in a pool of blood. She wanted the window no longer to let in any light, in order to suffer the compact darkness by which the man she loved was enveloped. Sometimes, she asked him a question, as if he were present, and she seemed to hear a response that was not formulated. Her questions often implied responses that could easily be imagined. She asked: *Will you love me forever? Will you not consent to have me by your side?* But it was sometimes a matter of more precise things, such as the place where he was imprisoned, the possibility of corrupting the guards and the treatment to which he was subjected. And the words devoid of resonance that she perceived cast her into an ever more profound desolation.

A moment came when she refused to take any nourishment; she even broke the goblet and the jug that were presented to her, saying that the man she loved no longer received anything to eat or drink in the dungeon to which no one any longer descended.

One evening, at sunset, the women keeping vigil over her in the dark heard her utter a faint cry. She was found dead, her arms making the gesture of hugging an invisible creature.

We learned the next day at Cabardez that Simon de Montfort had just let it be known in Carcassonne that Roger

Trencavel was dead, without further explanation. He had him buried in the Church of Saint Nazaire with a certain pomp. No one doubted that he had caused the legitimate possessor of the lands of Béziers and Carcassonne to die of starvation in his prison.[15]

---

[15] Author's note: "Pope Innocent III himself mentioned that murder in one of his letters and qualified it as a 'violent death.'"

VII

All the souls in the Château de Cabardez were troubled. Chagrin had a curious influence on Pierre de Cabaret. He dressed from head to foot in the Arab manner and acquired the habit, while supervising the measures of defense or exercises in arms, of uttering oaths in the Syrian language, which no one but him understood.

Brunissende, Nova and Stéphania did not allow any sadness to show. Death is a blessing, they said, since it permits us to attain a purified state, more fortunate than that of life. When those we love are deprived of their form, we ought to rejoice for them. And they affected a certain delight.

But I was not sure that it was an affectation. I was even tempted secretly to believe that the delight in question had a more human cause. I scarcely dared admit it to myself. Perhaps it was because of me that there was a nascent flame of amour in the eyes of the three young women. Invisible smiles when I encountered them, and scarcely perceptible movements of the head, were certain proofs of it. But what would come of it? They were three, and the greatest affection united them. Was I about to cause their division? In any case, how could I distinguish myself the one that I loved?

One morning, I heard the resonation of the enormous timpani and buccinas that Pierre de Cabaret had installed in the southern tower. They were bizarre instruments with joyful sounds, which he had brought back from the Orient. It was agreed that they would resound when an advance guard of crusaders appeared on the horizon. That music ought to symbolize, according to him, the pleasure that he would have in combating the Northern barbarians. I was in the large courtyard, and I was about to hasten to my post in the western tower, the Albigensian perfectus with whom I had had an incomprehensible conversation outside the chapel emerged from a

137

low room. He made me a sign with his hand and he said to me softly: "Dalmas Rochemaure, it is necessary to leave."

And he drew away.

Why did he say that to me? Why did I have to leave at the moment when the château needed all its defenders?

As I was asking myself that question, Pierre de Cabaret came out of the same low room. He had just been in conference there with the Seigneur de Peixiora and the Seigneur de Brani, who had arrived from their châteaux and whose horses were steaming in the courtyard. He was holding a sealed letter in his hand, and on seeing me he uttered an Arabic oath to express his satisfaction.

Without losing a moment, before the place was invested and the roads cut off, I had to go to Toulouse across the Black Mountain and the plains of Lauraguais. No one was better qualified than me to talk to Comte Raymond, to tell him what had happened and to demonstrate what an interest he had in helping his besieged vassals. But the helmets of the crusaders were glinting in almost all directions. A rapid horse and a valiant man were necessary.

Certainly, I was that. The drawbridge was lowered and, to the din of trumpets in the sky, I raced down the unique path that clung to the flanks of Cabardez. At the bottom of that path, where cypresses stood watch at intervals, there was a crossroads with other cypresses around it, and a rock in the form of a dog. It was there that I risked being captured or killed and having the blue waters of the Orbiel as a shroud. I thought that, out of regard for the messenger, they might have decided the message a little sooner.

But I traversed the crossroads without being attacked, either because there was no one behind the cypresses or because those who were there preferred to lie low on seeing with what enemy they had to deal.

Then I was suddenly illuminated by a certainty. I was loved by Brunissende, Nova and Stéphania. Each of them had confided in the Albigensian sage, and the latter, in his wisdom, having foresight of the troubles and rivalries that amour engenders, had said to me in a peremptory tone: "Dalmas Rochemaure, it is necessary to leave." Certainly, I might have thought that the Albigensian sage, having taken part in Pierre de Cabaret's deliberation with the Seigneur de Peixiora and the Seigneur de Bram, knew the order that would be given to me and was notifying me of it, but I rejected that hypothesis as the less plausible.

I turned round. Far away, on the highest tower, to the dying song of the trumpets, I saw, or thought I saw, three white forms. But I had no need to turn round to see them. I distinguished them more clearly before me, when I closed my mind, and all three of them had Esclarmonde's face.

Preceded by that unique image of ideal feminine beauty, I flew along the roads all day toward my new destiny, far from the Château de Cabardez, whose three marvelous chatelaines I was never to see again.[16]

---

[16] Author's note: "The Château de Cabardez was besieged by the crusaders several months after the capture of Carcassonne, but it resisted all assaults and Simon de Montfort was obliged to lift the siege. Subsequently, thanks to his cunning, Pierre de Cabaret was always able to avoid the vengeance of the leader of the crusade."

VIII

I have seen the man known as the Antichrist in the lands of Toulouse, Albi and Foix. I have seen Pope Innocent III. He was not born in the tribe of Dan as the prophecies had announced. He did not cure paralytics and he did not have demons as servants. His face was not hideously ugly, as I naively believed. I was even amazed to see that the man who knowingly unleashed the calamities of the war had intelligent eyes, the forehead of a sage and the handsome and noble features that are seen in certain Roman Emperors on old medals.

When I arrived in Toulouse my horse was steaming so forcefully that I found myself in the thick vapor, and the men at the gate of the Château Narbonnais could not distinguish at first who I was. I was immediately introduced to the presence of Comte Raymond. He was pacing back and forth and finishing dictating his testament to the notary Pierre Arnaud, who was sitting at a marble table with his nose over his parchment because of his myopia.

"A man who is going to Rome ought to make his testament," he was saying, sadly, at the moment when I entered.

He considered Pierre de Cabaret's message as if it were utterly devoid of importance. He even crumpled it casually, while he looked at me with satisfaction and a smile illuminated his thin face. My return was visibly an event of a joyous order for him.

"Everyone thought that you had died at Béziers."

Suddenly, a thought occurred to him. That thought appeared to be so agreeable that he wanted to rejoice immediately in having had it. He went to the door and shouted for someone to bring him Comminges wine, very dry.

"I know," he said, winking at me, "that you have a horror of sweet wine."

I had nothing of the sort, but he had got it into his head, and I thought it unnecessary to contradict him for such a trivial matter.

"You'll come with me to Rome!" he cried. "Dalmas Rochemaure is my squire. It's him that I choose to company me to the presence of Pope Innocent III. There's no fault to find in that."

And he repeated it joyfully, savoring the enormous irony that there was in taking Pierre de Castelnau's murderer with him to see the Pope. If he was going to Rome, it was as much to complain about Simon de Montfort and the crimes of the crusade as to exonerate himself of the accusation of having had Pierre de Castelnau killed. That accusation still weighed upon him. It was maintained by the clergy of the Midi and had been repeated throughout Christendom. It had not been possible to furnish any proof. Of all the men on earth, I was the best placed to know how false it was.

"And I'll have you blessed by the Pope," he said, putting his hand on my shoulder. After a moment, he added, in a tone that was not so light: "As long as I'm not poisoned beforehand, for it appears that there's a lot of poisoning out there."

In Rome, we stayed in the palace that Guillaume de Baux, Prince of Orange, possessed there, which he had put at my master's disposal. While awaiting the audience with the Pope, the question of poison played a considerable role. Under the pretext that I was a lover of wine, the Comte very often made me drink before him and watched out covertly thereafter for the preliminary signs of a rapid death. He always chose that moment to enumerate the enemies that he had in Rome and who had an interest in making him disappear. I uttered a great sigh of relief when the Comte, after a month of waiting, was summoned to the Basilica of Saint John.

Since his arrival he had not ceased drafting a manuscript of the grievances that he intended to expose to Innocent. He had resolved to learn it by heart and then to simulate an improvisation, but his memory was rebellious; he feared being emotional at the last minute. He decided to read his manu-

script. He was very anxious about the costume that it was necessary to don, the manner of salutation and matters of precedence. Bernard de Baux, the brother of the Prince of Orange,
who lived in the intimacy of the Pope, gave him advice and
promised to accompany him.

He had to present himself without an escort, to be mod-
estly dressed and to penetrate barefoot and bare-headed into
the Basilica of Saint John. In the same apparel, I was to carry
his cloak and the parchment of grievances, but I would take
care to remain at the back of the church, in the part occupied
by men of the people. Since Innocent's coronation, all official
receptions were public, but Bernard de Baux assured us that
there was no need to be alarmed by that; in such cases, there
were never more than five or six beggars at the door. As the
Comte was tremulous at the thought that he might fail to recognize the Pope and throw himself at the knees of a cardinal
or even some ecclesiastical servant, it was agreed that Bernard
de Baux would hold him by the arm and take him to Innocent
personally.

On the morning of the ceremony the Comte waited for
Bernard de Baux in vain. That absence threw him into an extraordinary distress. He thought of treason and told me that
perhaps he had only been summoned in order to be murdered.
Bernard de Baux was, in his opinion, a hypocritical individual
who, in addition, nourished a great admiration for Simon de
Montfort. He sent for wine, but when he invited me to drink I
did not have the heart to support that anguish and I dropped
the bottle. The Comte considered that a presage, and he renounced drinking. He thought of presenting himself at the
Basilica of Saint John with his sword and breastplate, and
even gave me an order to carry a crossbow on my shoulder.
Then he wanted to have the horses saddled and to quit that
accursed city precipitately. He only resigned himself at the last
minute and I climbed up behind him in a sort of dilapidated
carriage that belonged to the Baux palace.

An extraordinary crowd had gathered in Saint John's
Square and the environs of the Basilica. The Comte thought

that the coachman has mistaken the church and wanted him to turn back. It was a ragged, disrespectful, monstrous crowd. I had never seen its like. That crowd, moreover, makes the law in Rome, imposing its candidates for the Papacy and massacring the cardinals if they do not satisfy it with their votes. We traversed it, not without difficulty, amid Italian insults that, fortunately, we did not understand.

The bronze doors of the Basilica opened before us as if by enchantment at the moment that my master gave the coachman the order to turn back. Armed guards threw themselves in front of the people who attempted to rush forward. The Comte de Toulouse advanced with an uncertain stride over the cracked mosaics, in the midst of a thousand candles that were flamboyant between the twin shadows that are the lateral chapels, and I remained motionless, struck by astonishment.

Between two pillars, the door that opened to the Lateran Palace suddenly opened. I saw a file of silent individuals enter, with automatic movements and impassive faces, as if they were made of stone. Each of those individuals stopped in front of the main altar, bent a knee mechanically, and went to occupy a place fixed in advance, in a circular arc. They each wore a black chlamys over a violet mozzetta. The cranium was covered by a quadrangular biretta drawn down as far as the eyes. Their hose and their shoes were red, as if they had plunged into a bath of blood. They were the cardinals. I counted eleven cardinal bishops, eighteen cardinal priests and twenty-four cardinal deacons. And there were also the chamberlains, the officers of the apostolic chamber and other religious functionaries in white, black and violet robes, with scintillating rings, jeweled crosses on the breast ad impressive waxen hands under the fabric of robes, as unreal as those credited to phantoms.

A cardinal who was wearing an archbishop's pallium and was visibly striving to appear majestic came in last. I thought that he was the Pope. He seemed astonishingly young. I heard voices in the crowd designating him as the doyen of the cardinals and I thought that they were joking, but he was indeed the cardinal of Ostia, who consecrates Popes after their election and has the title of doyen whatever his age.

The Comte de Toulouse had fallen to his knees in front of the altar. He made a semblance of praying fervently. I could see his back and I divined the anguish that he must be experiencing. But providence protected him for, if he had turned his head and perceived the cardinal of Ostia, he would have mistaken him for the Pope and would doubtless have thrown himself at his knees

Suddenly, there was something akin to the passage of an occult breath in the Basilica that immobilized the audience and caused a wave of silence to radiate. A monk entered at a rapid pace through the door by which the cardinals had entered and, to my great amazement, he headed directly toward me. He was clad in a very simple white robe, the hood of which was thrown back behind the neck, with the consequence that he seemed to be moving against the force of an invisible wind.

Suddenly my blood froze. I had just seen that the monk was wearing a crown of peacock plumes on his head. I recalled having heard that the Pope, instead of a tiara ornamented with precious stones, wore in ceremonies that bizarre crown, which symbolized the fact that his gaze, like the eyes of the plumes, were aimed in all directions in order to look out for the birth of heresies. It was the Pope who was coming toward me.

So the Pope knew that I was there and he had no other objective than my person. I had time to wonder by what mystery he had been able to discern the murderer of his legate. I had time to be astonished by the intelligence of his gaze and the active nobility with which he was imprinted, while his clairvoyant eyes were fixed on mine. And he was also gazing at me with all the eyes of the peacock plumes of his crown. I had time to glimpse the spiral staircases that wound down toward the subterranean dungeons, the glint of the scalpels with which the torturers dissect. I had to commit myself to the hands of God.

But the Pope stopped. He made the sign of the cross, and with the thumb and the first two fingers of his raised hand, he blessed me.

I understood then that it was not Dalmas Rochemaure in particular that he was blessing but the malodorous, grimacing, sovereign crowd that was behind me, and which he was obliged to flatter and bless. Before I had recovered from my surprise, he had traversed the church at his rapid pace, lifted up the Comte de Toulouse, taking him by the shoulders, and had kissed him on both cheeks, calling him his dear son.

I held up lightly, in the direction of my master, the parchment of which he had such great need. But he did not summon me by any sign, as I expected. He spoke familiarly with the Pope; he seemed full of ease, he expressed himself abundantly and his voice became increasingly firm. I only heard certain words because of the distance and I only understood the meaning of a few phrases. One name, however, took on the lips of Innocent III an unexpected sonority and always reached my ears. It was the name of Pierre de Castelnau.

Thus, the evil man that I had struck because of the evil he had done was only dead in his physical representation. He still lived for the Pope, for the cardinals, for the great ecclesiastical sect of which he had been the redoubtable defender. He was now causing evils greater than when he was alive in the flesh. It was to his manes that the city of Béziers had been offered in holocaust. He was serving Simon de Montfort as a vengeful pretext for massacres and pillages in the Occitanian lands. It was his name that Innocent repeated in an irritated voice to the Comte de Toulouse, now kneeling on the flagstones in the pose of a penitent.

On the bank of the Rhône, in the morning twilight, I had only felled a simulacrum. I had not attained the veritable cause of the evil. I had even multiplied that evil with my arrogant desire to punish. The cause was not in the visible form but in the spirit, and the spirit had remained beyond my reach. Pierre de Castelnau would not cease to torment and to put to death and to disinter the dead who could not do anything about it, with the pretexts of heresy. I thought that at that moment, he was standing to Innocent's right.

The disorder of my soul was at its peak. I remember that the vapor of which the dead are made is dissolved by the tip of a steel blade, and if I had had a sword I would have run forward to attempt to pierce that shade.

Now, in a loud voice that had a simulated tremor, I heard the Comte de Toulouse confess. He said that he had made every effort to discover the murderer of Pierre de Castelnau and punish him, that he was a good Christian, that he loved the Church and defended it with all his power. Innocent's noble visage filled with a mendacious indulgence. Before the enemy's humiliation, the eyes of the cardinals shone like the pupils of cats when, in the gloom, they see a prey captive within their ferocious circle.

I was witness to a ceremony of lies. The Comte, my master, was lying. He detested the Roman Church for its insolent tyranny, its insatiable thirst for riches, and the misfortune with which it was threatening him. He cherished the heretics and he had made a perfectus swear to bring him the consolamentum at the moment of his death.[17] He enumerated insignificant sins, passing over in silence the pillages of abbeys, notably that of Saint Gilles, which was known to everyone, in any case.

Pope Innocent was also lying. He had extended his hand over the head of the Comte de Toulouse as if he were about to crush it, and he gave him absolution. But that was only a false pardon. Also false were the promises he now gave him. He promised to return to him the domains conquered by the crusade, and he had just given those domains irrevocably to Simon de Montfort. He had confirmed that donation the day before by the envoys of his legate. Now, in calling Comte Raymond his dear son, he was thinking about the city of Toulouse, the queen of the lands of the Midi, the hearth of heresy,

---

[17] Author's note: "The *consolamentum* was a Catharist extreme unction. Its rite, practiced by the Perfecti, permitted the person who received it to escape the chain of reincarnations."

and he was asking himself by what ruse he could dispossess the legitimate seigneur whose head he held beneath his palm.

In the empty space of the basilica I saw the splendid city that sheltered the men of my race, with the red girdle of its ramparts, the wings of its bells, the flames of its houses, and the radiation of its eternal soul. But that clairvoyant apparition only lasted for a second. Gray clouds enveloped it in every part. Nothing any longer emerged but a confused silhouette of Saint Sernin, in the midst of a fog woven of lies.

Then the beauty of the truth appeared to me. The truth was what was important in the world. The elect were those who lifted that living word above the shadows in which inferior souls struggled. I had killed Pierre de Castelnau, I ought to proclaim that action and submit to the human consequences, raising the hands that had shed his blood toward the sunlight. I felt an extreme buoyancy, such as one experiences on reaching the summit of a mountain and discovering a limitless horizon there. I took a step forward, filled my lungs with air and with all my might I shouted: "It was me who killed Pierre de Castelnau!"

But I did not hear the resonance of my voice beneath the fived arched naves of the Basilica of Saint John. A savage clamor had just resounded around me, and at the same time I was jostled and knocked down in the midst of a rain of gold coins.

I had vaguely perceived, through the dazzle of sincerity in which I was bathed, that a functionary clad in violet, adorned with a cross, had approached the Comte de Toulouse and murmured something in his ear. Once the pontifical ceremony was terminated, custom dictated that the person who had received it from the Holy Father, should throw a large offering to the sovereign populace. My master, digging into his pockets, had thrown their contents in front of him and, careless of the majesty of the place and the presence of the embalmed heads of the apostles Peter and Paul under the altar, all those Roman beggars had precipitated themselves on all fours, had drowned out my voice with their cries and had

147

caused me to fall from the luminous height where I was floating.

My forehead collided with the bronze foot of the green basalt basin in which the Emperor Constantine had bathed several centuries earlier. When I got up again, the people, doubtless deeming the largesse insufficient, were proffering insults against the Comte de Toulouse and Toulousans in general. On all sides I heard the word "heretic" pronounced in Italian.

The Pope descended from the main altar and with a familiar gesture he drew away his dear son, purified by repentance and absolution. All the kneeling cardinals got up simultaneously and it seemed to me that the pilasters were about to break and the vault shatter, by virtue of the secret force that emanated from their collective movement. They must have been accustomed to the cries of the crowd, for their faces expressed neither terror not disgust. Slowly, they deployed in a circular arc, elongating like a serpent of which each ring was a cardinal with feet the color of blood, and they disappeared through the lateral door in order to go and coil around the earth.

I made my way painfully through the populace in delirium. I was bruised, and I was sad. It seemed to me that I had just contemplated the inverse of a medal whose face would never be revealed. And all of life was seen thus, backwards. I lived in confrontation with the caricature of souls. I never saw any of them in its true aspect. I could not even distinguish my own.

That evening, the Comte de Toulouse, with a puerile joy, showed me a ring enriched with an antique cameo that the Pope had given him.[18]

"This ring is worth at least fifty silver marcs," he told me. "In any case, its value is of no importance."

_____

[18] Author's note: "In addition to that ring, the Pope made him a gift of a cloak and a horse."

He never ceased gazing at it, and even kissed it respect-fully. Suddenly, he uttered a cry. He had just thought about poison. He had a very old wine brought and he steeped the ring and its cameo therein for a long time. Then he asked God's pardon for that evil thought.

IX

If one could collect in the same receptacle all the blood that has flowed from my wounds in the course of my life, it would fill a vat large enough to contain the wine of a season, between Toulouse and Muret. Now my body is covered with scars, like those great resinous pines on the slopes of the Pyrenees that have been slashed in order to make the resin flow out. I have shed my blood on the ramparts of all the besieged cites, in all the fields where the southerners fought for the independence of their land.

It has flowed uselessly, since my land has been vanquished, since Toulouse is submissive to a Seneschal of the King of France and the Pope's inquisitors, but I have no regrets. There is a hidden virtue in futile courage that is not wasted. The suffering of the oppressed falls into a spiritual balance in which the cry of a little child weighs more than an army on the march, and sooner or later, an invisible hand reestablishes the equilibrium of justice.

I participated in the defense of the Château de Montréal and I was, I believe, the only man who was able to escape therefrom, for Simon de Montfort had the soldiers and inhabitants massacred to the last man. It was me who, disguised as a peasant, aided by a few good companions, came by night to set fire to the crusaders' war machines and tents under the ramparts of Carcassonne. At the right hand of Gérard de Pépieux, I defended Puyserguier and I mounted with him the assault on Montlaur.

Disguised as a monk after the capture of Bram, I saw the eyes of those who had fought put out and their noses cut off on Simon de Montfort's orders, as well as those of the people who had remained quietly in their houses. I mingled with other monks in order to save my life. They were covering the screams of the tortured by singing canticles. Fortunately, I remembered those canticles, which I had once learned in the

Abbey of Mercus. When it was the turn of a young woman whose eyes resembled Esclarmonde's it seemed to me that as she struggled she held out her arms to me. My song became a frightful scream, and all the monks inclined their heads in my direction.

A single man of Bram was protected by some lucky star. Only one of his eyes was put out, in order that, with the half-light of the other, he could lead the troop of the blind to Cabaret's fortress and show its defenders that there was only darkness for those who resisted de Montfort.

In Minerve, when the place was taken by assault, I was one of the twenty-four combatants, almost all nobles and knights, whom Simon de Montfort ordered to be hanged in order that they might suffer in death an ultimate humiliation. I stood among the brave men of Minerve, hands bound, before twenty-four hastily-erected scaffolds. Those to my rights and left, all being wounded more or less seriously, never ceased groaning or abusing the crusaders. For myself, I tried to resuscitate in my soul the features of Esclarmonde de Foix in order to die with that image.

Suddenly, I emitted a loud burst of laughter. Accompanied by a troop of German soldiers, Simon de Montfort's wife had recently joined her husband and was sharing his warrior life. She had just appeared facing us, on a little mound, in order to enjoy the hanging of the twenty-four vanquished of Minerve. She was frightfully yellow in the complexion, the color of the oil of the banks of the Rhône. Devotions had mummified her skin and lack of care had decomposed her teeth. She was so prudish that she punished her maidservants when their unknowingly lifted dresses allowed glimpses of their ankle-bones. Leaning on the arm of an infamous scribe named Pierre de Vaux-Cernay,[19] notorious throughout Christendom for his lies and the villainy of his writings, she di-

---

[19] Author's note: "Pierre de Vaux-Cernay accompanied Simon de Montfort and was the vilely partial historian of the crusade."

rected eyes filled with hatred toward those who were about to die.

And I, at the limit of joy, laughed so loudly that the good Seigneur de Mercoriole, who had just been seized in order to be the first to be hanged, thought that I had lost my reason. It was simply that I had heard many times that Simon de Montfort, although he delivered beautiful female prisoners to his knights, did not personally pose any risk to their honor because of the fidelity sworn to his wife and his respect for the sanctity of marriage. I thought then that he had beside him every evening in his tent that sort of withered vulture, that hateful face, which resembled an incarnation of hypocrisy. I pictured the pious embrace of the warrior and that larva desiccated by interior malignity, and I burst into loud laughter. I also praised God for his skill in punishing without appearing to do so and for rendering my death joyful by the knowledge of that punishment.

Now, the Seigneur de Mercoriole was very fat and his weight broke the gibbet that had been prepared for him. It was perceived that none of the gibbets was solid. Dusk was falling and word was sent to Simon de Montfort, whose wife was becoming impatient. Someone was already whispering that the execution would be postponed until the next day when Simon de Montfort sent the order to massacre immediately, by means of swords and spears, those who could not be hanged.

A certain confusion ensued. A seigneur with an honest face was in command of the execution, but he was doing so in a detached manner and I noticed that his gaze was attached to mine with an unexpected sympathy. Was it because I had laughed and gaiety reaches certain hearts? He made a sign to a soldier to untie me, and, not without having darted a glance at Montfort's horrible spouse, he shoved me toward the open country.

At Lavaur I witnessed the torture of Guiraude de Laurac. Wounded, I had gone to seek refuge with her and had been cured by the Arab physician Mohammed who was part of her court of scholars and poets. I fought by the side of the warrior chatelaine during the thirty-three days of the siege, and on the thirty-third day, as the crusaders were about to attack, the beautiful Guiraude, raising her crossbow toward the sky, said something ambiguous about her and me, the interpretation of which threw me into great disturbance, but I was never able to penetrate its meaning.

The city and the château were taken by assault and I only owed my salvation to the Arab physician, in whom I had inspired amity. In order to care for his wounded Montfort had none but ignorant northerners who, with their plasters and their balms, killed their patients with certainty. Mohammed's reputation must have gone before him, for he gave the order to save his life and put a guard around his person and his remedies. The excellent Mohammed, at the moment of the combatants' debacle, dressed me in an Arab robe and swore that I was his aide, as expert as him in the art of medicine.

We were dragged outside the city into a field to which the crusaders who had fallen during the assault were transported. From there, while I pretended to obey Mohammed, I saw the immense pyre built on to which three hundred perfecti were thrown and burned alive.[20]

I saw from a distance Simon de Montfort beside the young Alix, his wife. His enormous stature and the mass of his head deprived of eyes gave the impression of an extra-human force unleashed in order to destroy and cause suffering. I had just drawn water from a well in order to moisten a plaster of herbs when I saw the crusaders' leader make imperious signs toward the well.

Two men dragged the chatelaine of Lavaur, whose hair was loose and whose face was divided by a trickle of blood. She straightened up for some supplication, or perhaps male-

---

[20] Author's note: "Pierre de Vaux-Cernay reports in his chronicle that they were burned 'with great joy.' It is impossible to determine exactly from this phrase whether he meant the great joy of the crusaders or that shown by the Albigensians, on being rid of life."

diction, and her palpitating bosom showed outside her robe, ripped by a dagger. Alix de Monfort made a gesture of disgust in order not to see that flesh soiled by sin and not to hear a scandalous speech. Then the men holding the rope let the chatelaine of Lavaur down into the well. For a long time I heard them throwing stones and pebbles into it. No cry reached me, but only a dull sound mingled with splashing, and that eventually died away.[21]

I have seen other scenes as frightful, and witnessed other battles. I have often been courageous, sometimes cowardly and I am astonished by the immense love of life by which creatures are possessed.

I have traversed villages from which all the inhabitants had fled. I have passed over the drawbridges of silent châteaux where my footfalls made the empty rooms resonate and where the fear that had opened the doors still vibrated.

But one thing remained mysterious to me. Simon de Montfort was always victorious. That constant victory might be explicable by his personal courage, by luck, by the number of his soldiers and the terror he inspired, but I discerned another element. His victory seemed to me to have a hidden cause in the very root of destiny. It was inscribed in a book in ineluctable characters. At that time, on the excessively beautiful land divided by the Garonne and its cerulean waters, evil had to triumph. Evil was incarnate in that pitiless man. It was written that everywhere that his shadow extended in the region where the philosophical poplar and the poetic fig-tree grew, the taste for beautiful things, and the love of songs that come from the heart, youth and intelligence were extinguished. For ends that I do not understand, my homeland, perfumed by the amber of the Orient, had to be ravaged by hatred, and accursed.

---

[21] The narrative of this execution became one of the most oft-repeated and widely-commemorated; the alleged site of the well is still commemorated by a stele bearing the emblem of the Cathar dove.

Now, the mosaics of the beautiful fountains are broken, the marble statues no longer ornament the thresholds of dwellings, the part-Arabic and part-Roman cities have lost the turban of their turrets and the toga of their ramparts. But glory to the unknown force by which the proprieties of the soul are condensed, and which permits them to lie dormant in a silent crucible in order to awaken later! Thus, like stratified plants that commence to live again at the stroke of the wand of a geomantic magician, with their petals in flower and their stamens living, the Occitan soul will one day be resuscitated.

PART THREE

I

My sister Aude had become the most charming young woman in Toulouse. Her beauty was not obvious; it was necessary to look attentively to perceive it, just as, when one has before one's eyes a landscape in which there is a delicate measure of colors, it requires a mental effort to conceive its poetry.

It was a great joy for me to find her again when I returned to Toulouse after years of absence. Comte Raymond had spent that time in vain negotiations and petitions to legates. He had been humiliated and deceived. He had finally decided to break with the Church and with Simon de Montfort and I had come to resume my service with him.

I had the gift of making my sister Aude laugh. Many very ordinary things took on a comical reach for her in my mouth. But that hilarity was not mockery; it was a manner of manifesting her affection. Thus certain domesticated birds sing when one approaches them. There was, moreover, a rather mysterious relationship between my sister Aude and the inhabitants of the air. She walked so lightly that she often appeared to be flying. And sometimes, leaning on her windowsill, from which Saint Sernin was visible, she repeated the same sound indefinitely, giving it sweet or heart-rending modulations until she had fallen into a kind of ecstasy. I noticed that her eyes then took on a color that I have only ever seen once, in a lake lost in the Pyrenees, which is a blue approaching violet.

Aude had been instructed in the Albigensian religion and she was able to discourse on the philosophy of that religion. She sometimes tried to explain it to me and what she said was always very beautiful, but sometimes incomprehensible. She told me everything that happened to creatures after death, entering into the most minute detail, and I wondered how things that are completely unknown to the vulgar could have come to her knowledge. I learned from her that all the evil that one does to others returns to you, via a bizarre curve, and strikes you in exactly the same fashion. The curve is sometimes very long and when it cannot attain you in this life it attains you in a subsequent life. Aude assured me that I had lived before and that I would live again, in order to receive the good and evil that I had done.

I asked her whether a man who had traversed the breast of another with a thrust of a lance, after having meditated that action all night, would surely receive a thrust of a lance in the same place of his own breast. She laughed, as was her habit, not knowing that I was talking about myself. Then she said that the man in question would assuredly die a violent death if he were devoid of intelligence and love, but that there were means and practices to avoid renaissances with their harsh regulations of account. It was not given to everyone to understand such practices, however, and they required a perfect purity of heart of which very few were capable.

At first I was proud of the love that Aude had for me, but I perceived that she loved with an extraordinary love not only her father and her mother, but her friends, her dog, the austere Albigensians with whom she conversed, the people that she encountered, those who passed by in the street, and those she did not know. When someone said to her "It's cold," she began to weep, because of all the animals that were going to die in the fields. When the sun was hot, red patches were visible on her face because of the mosquitoes she refused to swat. She did not admit it for fear of being mocked, but when we went for a walk I saw that she made it a scruple not to trample any blade of grass on the path.

Aude was often sad and I asked her the reason.

"I would like to accomplish a truly good deed," she told me, "and I can't succeed in that."

I made the remark that she gave all her savings to the poor and devoted herself to them. The day before, the executioner Tancrède, the most evil man in the city, had been attacked in a side street near our house. All the doors were immediately closed, everyone hoping for his death. Only Aude had run to bandage his wound. She had moreover, received nothing but imprecations by way of thanks.

"All good deeds give joy when one accomplishes them," she replied, "and because of that, they are not so desirable. It is only in suffering that one becomes purer. I would like to accomplish a good dead that only procures me pain."

With a vine branch in hand, the runner was announcing the arrival of fresh wine in a tavern near the Basacle Gate when I encountered the monk Petrus. We immediately went to sit down together under an arbor.

"You've become a filthy heretic dog," he told me, amicably.

Such words, which can be pronounced by companions that one sees every day, irritated me on the part of a friend that I had quit such a long time ago. I no longer know what reply I made to him, which was insulting with regard to Bishop Foulque, whose fanatical servant he had become. Under his orders, he organized bands that were known as the Whites because their members recognized one another by means of white jackets, and who pillaged the houses of heretics. I had projected since my arrival organizing a rival troop that would be called the Blacks and would rally to my black leather surcoat.

I saw hatred emerge from his person and it seemed to me for an instant that a furious black dog was circling around us. He lowered his voice and he said to me, like a confidence that he could only make to a friend: "Toulouse is accursed. But its destruction is now decided. It can no longer escape."

I asked him, with the mildness that Aude incessantly incited me to observe, who had decided that destruction.

He wanted to intimidate me and he pointed to a place next to me on the bench on the bench on which I was sitting.

"Look at that peasant," he said.

There was no one beside me.

"Well?" I said.

"It's Jesus Christ," he murmured, with a false respect. "He appears to me now almost every day. It's him who has informed me of the destruction of Toulouse."

I drew my sword with the calm proscribed by Aude, and, with the blade, I traced a sign of the cross on the spot where the peasant ought to be. Then, with a shrug of the shoulders I made Petrus understand that I was not his dupe. He clenched his teeth. His fists were closed.

He said to me: "It's Bishop Foulque who has decided thus. The Whites I command have divided up the city by quarters. When the moment comes, they'll set fire to it."

I invoked God internally in order to be able to control myself, and I succeeded. I promised myself to recount that victory over my natural violence to Aude. My smile brought Petrus' exasperation to a peak. In his rage he sniggered.

"Your house will be burned too," he said. "You'll be spared because you're my friend, but as for your sister Aude, we've promised her to ourselves for a long time. We've drawn lots, and it's me who won her..."

The universe was tinted red around me and as the last syllable of that speech was still resonating, I struck Petrus in the face with my dagger over the table. I wonder how he did not die from such a blow. Doubtless a movement that he made saved his life. He got up, crying out. Blood was running from his left eye, which I had punctured. I heard him call for any Whites that were in the vicinity. I felt that I was ready to take on an army. I had tipped the table over to make a barricade. But no one came. Thus, friendships end in the times in which we live.

That evening, without any other explanation, I asked Aude whether someone who punctures his friend's eye in a moment of violence during an argument had his own eye put out in a future life. She was content to reply: "Wouldn't that be justice?"

I replied that it would indeed be justice. I thought then about the arrows I had launched after having taken careful aim, the blows that I had delivered in battle, and it seemed to me that the surface of a man's body would be insufficient to bear wounds as numerous as those I had inflicted. And I felt pity for the creature who would be me, whose martyrdom I was preparing.

II

The battle of Muret had been lost.[22] The King of Aragon was dead and his army dispersed. Simon de Montfort might force the gates of Toulouse at any moment. A breath of catastrophe blew over the city, all the more intense because the annual plague was making greater ravages in the poor quarters because of a recent heat wave.

I exhorted my parents to leave and go to a little estate that one of my uncles had near Rabastens. My father refused. In any case, Aude was incapable of attempting the shortest journey. Since there had been fighting around Toulouse she had become extremely weak. Her body was incessantly agitated by tremors, as if she experienced all the blows that were delivered. She never ceased praying.

Comte Raymond made the decision to quit the city before Montfort's troops occupied the roads to the north. A large number of cavaliers were to accompany him.

The baggage and the horses were already waiting at the Matabiau Gate. The moon rose over the brick roofs and the Saracen turrets. I joined the Comte in the garden of his house. As I advanced along the principal pathway I was enveloped by a whirlwind of wings. All the aviaries were open, but the

---

[22] Author's note: "The King of Aragon had come to the aid of the Comte de Toulouse with a considerable army. They attacked Simon de Montfort near Muret. It was there that the fate of the Midi was decided." The battle of Muret, in which Simon de Montfort's forces defeated the Toulousan militia, allied with forces sent by Peter II of Aragon—Raymond's brother-in-law—was fought on 12 September 1213. The inexperienced Aragonese cavalry was crushed by Simon's seasoned troops and Peter was killed, whereupon the rest of his forces fled; the Toulousans also attempted to retreat but were overtaken and slaughtered.

birds, instead of taking advantage of their liberty, were perching on the low branches of the trees and appeared to be waiting. The Comte was immobile alongside his favorite stork and from a distance, in the moonlight, with his stout belly and the wings of his cloak, he gave the impression of being the bizarre and desperate seigneur of an avian people.

He did not know what to do. The stork that he loved did not want to be separated from him. Doubtless it had understood the gravity of events, for it refused to allow itself to be seized, but attached itself to his footsteps. He dreaded abandoning it, but he could not travel at the head of an army with a stork in his arms. He added that he would rather know that it was dead than abandon it, and gave me the order to kill it as rapidly as I could.

But I did not have to carry out that disagreeable order. Scarcely had I taken a step toward the stork than, by virtue of a singular coincidence or a mysterious comprehension, it flew up above the garden and over the houses, God knows where. The Comte made me a sign to follow him.

We traversed streets through which silent cavaliers were passing, heading for the Matabiau Gate. We crossed the bridge over the Garonne and reached the Saint Cyprien quarter, the one most tested by the plague. Many house seemed abandoned and the two or three glimmers we perceived in windows were those of candles keeping vigil over the dead. In a street bordered by walls we stopped in front of the door of a convent. I knew that it was a convent of women.

There were two litters outside the door. I recognized by the golden cross on the black key that the first litter belonged to the Comte de Toulouse. Four of his guards were sitting a little further away. The Comte considered the second litter with surprise and his expression darkened.

He knocked on the door of the convent. It took a long time for anyone to open it. A toothless old woman holding a tallow candle in her hand uttered a cry and nearly fell over when she saw us. She explained things that were difficult to understand because of the faults of articulation caused by the absence of teeth. I thought I grasped that the plague had claimed several victims in the convent and that all the nuns had abandoned it. Someone had to remain, however, for the old woman made us a sign to follow her and started walking along a gallery with stone walls. The Comte followed her without hesitation, as if the route were familiar to him.

We stopped before a door that stood ajar, within which a faint light was shining. The woman pushed the batten with her outstretched hand and immediately stood aside. Four candles illuminated the room, indicating by their geometry that the creature around whom they were flickering was dead.

I saw a meager silhouette and a face that had conserved an atrocious laugh beneath tangled white hair. Dementia, more powerful than death, still marked he tormented features. A man was on his knees in a corner of the room. Without getting up he looked in our direction and his gaze met that of the Comte, who knelt down beside him. I recognized Arnaud Bernard.

I was witness to the final scene of the drama that had agitated Toulouse thirty years before. Alix Bernard had loved Comte Raymond, she had gone mad, and she had been kept since then in this convent in Saint Cyprien. Now, the two men who had shared her love unequally were kneeling beside her form, all of whose beauty had fled. They had come in the danger that Toulouse was running to attempt to save the still-living symbol of their youth. The two faithful old men were side by side, united in the same prayer. But Arnaud Bernard would have his belated revenge. It was to him that the responsibility for the sepulcher belonged, the final adieu next to the coffin. The Comte doubtless understood that. He got up, suddenly timid, and went out backwards, his head bowed.

When we were in the street, he asked me whether I knew what became of the souls of the insane after death, and whether they recovered their reason. I replied that I did not know, but that I would not fail to interrogate my sister on that subject.

III

Men-at-arms, bearers of a square head with features of a frightful ugliness had assembled around the capitulary house. I occasionally lifted up the monk's hood that I had allowed to fall over my face in order not to be recognized, and it seemed to me that I was living a nightmare. The people of Toulouse were assembled and waiting.

Facing me, in the middle of the crowd, I saw Petrus surrounded by a troop of armed Whites. His unique eye was shining like a terrible lamp.

There was suddenly a great rumor, followed by an abrupt and crushing silence. A magnificently dressed individual appeared on the threshold of the capitulary house. He was holding a large parchment from with rutilant seals hung, and he darted an anxious eye over the windows opposite. I recognized him as a cowardly cleric. He unrolled the parchment with a trembling hand and he began to read in a toneless voice, uniquely preoccupied with the reckoning arrow that might spring from a window. What he read, in a stony silence, began thus:

"Philippe, by the grace of God, King of France, to all his friends and vassals, to which these present belong, greetings and dilection. Know that we have received for our liege-man, our dear and loyal Simon de Montfort, the Duché de Narbonne, the Comté de Toulouse..."[23]

That was all I heard. The rest was only a sequence of those official and incomprehensible formulae by means of which the great have the habit of expressing themselves in

---

[23] Author's note: "This is the commencement of the charter of investiture that Philippe-Auguste signed in June 1216 in Melun. Simon de Montfort was recognized thereby as Duc de Narbonne, Comté de Toulouse and Vicomte de Béziers and Carcassonne."

parchments. My master Raymond VI had been despoiled of his city and his Estates. When the cleric had concluded, the spoliator emerged from the capitulary house and stopped momentarily in the steps. The block of his cranium sketched a sign of respect before Bishop Foulque, who came out behind him. Foulque seemed prodigiously fat and I thought that it was because of his coats of mail, which he had tripled beneath his sacerdotal vestments. He raised his hands to his face, making a semblance of hiding his tears. I knew from Sézelia that they were produced by the pepper introduced into his fingernails. Behind him came Guy de Montfort, Simon's brother, the horrible Alix, in a robe streaming with stolen jewels, other spoliators and other bishops.

The Capitouls appeared last. They seemed to have difficulty breathing, doubtless because of the burn they must have on their tongue for the oath of obedience given to their new seigneur. And I thought I distinguished that their right hand was hurting because of the signature that had confirmed their oath. Bernard de Colomiès was no longer wearing jewelry. Étienne Carabordes, the fruit and vegetable merchant, had become thin. Pons Barbadal, the wine merchant, had lost his colored complexion. And while the accursed troop marched in the midst of soldiers I recalled what Petrus had said to me and what Sézelia had told me before. The destruction of Toulouse was imminent. The man barded in iron and the man bearing the miter were the incarnations of evil announced by Marie the illuminate. It was because of the prophetic words of that seer that the third person of that infernal trinity had had the dust of her body thrown to the wind. And the prophecy had been realized.

On the evening of that day I barricaded the door of my house and disposed a ready-primed crossbow at every window. Several times, as I looked out into the Rue du Taur, I seemed to see Petrus' eye shining.

I had made Aude party to my fears and she had said that the greatest evils can sometimes be deflected by prayer, like a storm by the crown of a tree, if the person praying consents to attract the evil to themselves. And that night, through the partition that separated our rooms, I heard her repeating:

"Let all the suffering of Toulouse come into my body and my soul."

I did not believe that such an attraction was possible, but I thought it imprudent to attempt it. I often begged my sister to stop, but it was always in vain.

The destruction of Toulouse had commenced. Many palaces in the city's interior were fortified. Simon de Montfort prescribed that their towers, which might serve as refuges in case of riot, must be dismantled. The chains of the streets were suppressed in order that his German cavaliers could sweep them without obstacle. Finally, hundreds of workmen were attacking the ramparts. But those ramparts, constructed in part thanks to Arnaud Bernard's science of stones, were a prodigious, cyclopean monument. It was necessary to be content to make breaches in them.

I perceived with horror that Aude's continual prayer had a commencement of efficacy. A mysterious link was established between her and the Toulousan city. When the tower of the Palais de Commenges was attacked, a sort of wound appeared on her shoulder. And when the crown of rose granite was removed from the queen of towers whose stump still dominates the Sardane Gate, a bloody crown formed around her forehead.

Sometimes, at daybreak, she called to me. She had been informed by a pain in her body that a new destruction was beginning somewhere. All that was done to the tower of Mascaron had an echo in her throat. The fall of the doors of the fortress of Basacle was inscribed in the palms of her hands. She felt in her heart the fall of the tower of Saint Rhemesy. I ended up having the certainty that the life of my sister Aude was linked to that of Toulouse. And when I begged her to interrupt the prayer that she was continuing internally, she replied: "The sacrifice I'm making isn't a true sacrifice, since I'm glad to make it."

I shall not recount the terrible years that followed. My mother died. My father was one of the eighty hostages that Simon de Montfort demanded of the Toulousans after their first revolt, and whom he had massacred under a false pretext. With Arnaud Bernard and a few valiant men I went begging from door to door to obtain the thirty thousand silver marcs that Simon de Montfort demanded after the second revolt, which saved the city from pillage.

I was favored by luck on the night when Petrus, with two of his companions, leapt into my garden with the aim of taking possession of Aude. I killed all three of them before they had time to cry out and I buried them at the foot of a laurel. I do not know whether they rest in peace. The laurel has continued to grow.

Fate was against me when, lying prone on a roof, I fired an arrow at Simon de Montfort as he emerged from Saint Étienne, when he was standing under the porch. Scarcely fifty meters separated me from him; I was sure of my shot. A hidden force deflected the arrow, for the time had not yet come.

When it was necessary for every inhabitant, on pain of death, to deposit outside his door all the weapons he possessed, I organized workshops in cellars where new swords were forged and wood was shaped into lances. At the time of the third riot, I was with the men who drove Simon de Montfort and his men back into the Château Narbonnais. I was one of the seven delegates who went to humiliate themselves before him.

We were on our knees and we heard Bishop Foulque beg Montfort to put us to death. His face was not clad in any hypocritical mask and his fingernails must not have contained any lachrymatory pepper. He let his sincere hatred show. The seven men on their knees were, however, a very little thing for him. What he wanted was the death of the heretic city. He demonstrated the necessity of it with eloquence. He swore that God wanted that sacrifice and inspired it.[24]

And while he spoke I heard a slight vibration in the air, a sound that did not seem to be produced by anything, and which was the mysterious note modulated on certain evenings by Aude when she fell into ecstasy. Was it her prayer that, by a magical secret, penetrated into the souls of the evil and influenced them without them knowing it? The troops massed in the squares and at the intersections of the streets, awaiting the order to precipitate themselves into the houses, were abruptly sent back outside the city. The seven Toulousan ambassadors emerged from the Château Narbonnais, amazed to be alive.

There were nights on which Aude had no more breath and when I believed that she was about to expire. Then I looked out of the window to see whether the light of the conflagration that the Whites were charged with consummating was visible. Once I stabbed a man who had piled bundles of dry wood again the door of the Roaix house and approached a lighted taper to it. On another occasion, in the cemetery of the Place Saint-Sernin, I heard noises coming from underground, and was never able to determine whether it was the dead who were walking or miners sent by Foulque to undermine the church.

However, Aude recovered her health and Toulouse survived. Simon de Montfort left the city with his cavaliers to make war on the banks of the Rhône. The monuments sunk their foundations into the ground with more solidity. It seemed that the dismantled towers put down roots. I was able to remark that what remained of the ramparts swelled and enlarged naturally. The bell-tower of La Dalbade gained a good few meters in height.

---

[24] Author's note: "Simon de Montfort had ceded to Foulque's insistence and was about to destroy Toulouse, which then had more inhabitants than it does today. It was his brother Guy and some of his barons who dissuaded him."

And one sunny day in September, for the first time in a very long time, my sister Aude went down into the garden and made a bouquet. Immediately afterwards, there was a prodigy of sorts. A thick fog, such as never happened in that season, fell upon the city in order to hide what was about to happen to Montfort's soldiers and the traitors.

That fog extended a denser veil over the part of the Garonne that flows at the extremity of Toulouse, especially over the Basacle ford. It was via that ford that, at five o'clock in the evening, Comte Raymond VI, still Seigneur of Toulouse in the heart of Toulousans, crossed the Garonne, with Roger Bernard de Foix to his right and Bernard de Comminges to his left, and valiant and invincible men behind him.

It was me who, going into the water up to my knees, first grasped the bridle of his horse and said the necessary words, while Étienne Carabordes and Pons Barbadal wept with emotion and Pierre de Roaix uttered inarticulate cries, for his tongue had been cut out at the Château Narbonnais because he had spoken ill of God. It was me who, when the Basacle Gate was taken, as if in play, seized the annunciatory trumpet and made it resound with a formidable blast. At its resonance, the two hundred thousand inhabitants of Toulouse appeared at their windows in the same second, while the foundations of their houses trembled beneath them, rediscovering the immortality of their stones.

At its resonance, Alix de Montfort took refuge precipitately in the Château Narbonnais with the few soldiers who escaped the Toulousan fury and had the four drawbridges raised, her teeth chattering with terror.[25]

And that evening, when I walked through the city, I heard that there was no topic of conversation on the thresholds and among the hilarious groups at the street corners but Alix de Montfort's nose. It was long and unsightly. Everyone

---

[25] Author's note: "The Château Narbonnais was not situated within the city itself but outside the ramparts.

claimed to have seen it at a window in the Eagle Tower, enormously elongated.

IV

Delga du Lauragais was at the Baziège Gate. He claimed that he fought better because he could see, on clear days, the village where he was born. The brave Palauqui de Foix had chosen his post at Saint Cyprien because it was the part of Toulouse closest to the Pyrenees, from which, he said, the breath of their forests reached him. The Seigneur de Montaut was in command at Bazacle, the Seigneur de Pailhas at the Sardane Gate. Arnaud Bernard was at the Villeneuve Gate because that was where the largest breach in the ramparts was, and it was the most dangerous post.

The scholar Émeric de Rocanaga was at the Gaillarde Gate. A servant followed him incessantly, charged with his books of philosophy. He had very poor eyesight and it was necessary that someone read to him even when he was on the rampart in the midst of a rain of arrows. He claimed that reading Plato was like a marvelous shield. The lector cleric did not share that opinion, for his voice sometimes failed. One manuscript was pierced clean through. The Seigneur de Rocanaga took great satisfaction from that, because it proved him right, Aristotle having replaced Plato that day.

At the barbican of the Old Bridge the astrologer Sicard de Puylaurens was in command. He knew by virtue of his studies of the stars the date of everyone's death, but he refrained from revealing it, saying that such knowledge is dangerous. He was extremely prudent, in spite of the fact that he knew by means of astrology that his life would be prolonged for another forty years. Doubtless he had committed some error of calculation because he drowned in the Garonne after wanting to bathe there in the moonlight.

Dor de Barsac the Child-like and Guillaume de Balafar the Experienced rendered the Barbican of Pertus impregnable by their presence. Bertrand de Pestillac the Magnificent was at the Montolieu Gate. He wore a cassock embroidered with pearls over his armor, and was so covered in jewelry, plumes and ornaments that he resembled one of those Spanish saints that buckle on their pedestals under the wealth of ex-votos.

I was at the Matabiau Gate with Frédéric de Frezols the Pious. His prayer was so profound that no bell or alarm trumpet could extract him from it; he said that God was on watch then. He had enjoined me to take command every time he knelt down, because God might keep a poor watch, favoring the party of the bishops.

At all the gates, at every hour, there were admirable man careless of their lives. But it was near Saint Sernin, in the Rue du Taur, that the heart of Toulouse beat with the heart of my sister Aude.

For nine months Simon de Montfort attacked the city from all sides at once. He had received immense reinforcements from France. He had had an immense war machine constructed that we called "the Gate"[26] and he dominated all our towers with that mobile monster. The terror that he inspired was augmented by the prospect of the repressions that would not fail to be carried out if he became master of the city again. At that same time as that terror, the desire grew to be delivered of it, and that desire took body in the person of Comte Raymond.

Throughout his life the Comte had given proof of a certain timidity in battle and his lack of heroism was well known. Without any reason, the people considered him on his return to be the most valiant warrior in Christendom. That faith had spread spontaneously and had gained the heart of the Comte himself. It was now necessary to beg him not to expose himself. He wanted to challenge Simon de Montfort to a single combat to take place between the two camps, and he did not doubt the outcome of that insane combat. That conception of his valor, which everyone shared, had rejuvenated him. He held himself straighter. He charged me with buying him cos-

_____

[26] This word appears thus in the text, presumably intending the English meaning.

metics for his moustache. For many years people had been calling him Raymond the Old. He confided to me that it was his enemies who had given him that ridiculous nickname. He felt younger than his son. He had noticed that his strength was increasing every day. He was thinking of remarrying for the sixth time. He nearly wept with joy when an old woman, on seeing him pass in the street, cried: "There goes the Archangel Michael!"

A renewal of youth circulated in reality in Toulouse, as if the liberty of the city were causing the blood of men to flow more freely. Pierre Carabordes, in spite of his obesity, practiced running in order to be able to pursue the enemy when he participated in a sortie. He was seen passing along the round-path of the ramparts, naked to the waist, streaming with sweat, waving his black Capitoul's wand. Pons Barbadal claimed that song has a considerable effect on courage, and in front of the Church of Saint Étienne he taught choirs of the militiamen that he commanded.

The quadrilateral of Arnaud Bernard's face rounded out because of the joy he experienced in considering the re-edified towers and ramparts. He had put a strange coquetry into leaving open the Villeneuve Gate, of which he was in charge. His soldiers were arranged in six rows of helmeted and armored men, the foremost of which were on their knees firing cross-bows and the last of which dominated the others by virtue of their taller stature. That phalanx was as broad as the Ville-neuve Gate and the length of the spears was proportionate to the position of the combatants. It advanced or retreated at a signal, but never surpassed the city boundary. It was like a living gate, bristling with iron, against which hundreds of horses and soldiers came to die, but which remained more inexorably closed than bronze or stone.

However, when the tenth month of the siege arrived, it appeared to the most judicious minds that the situation was desperate. The circle of the city was so vast that the combatants could not be transported rapidly enough to the sides under attack. Simon de Montfort was now multiplying surprise attacks and throwing all his war machines and cavaliers at the same point. The food supplies that the Comte de Foix and the Comte de Comminges sent by boat along the Garonne had been cut off by chains extended across the river. The Bordelais archers that Arcis de Montesquieu had introduced were beginning to get discouraged.

I remember that there was such a delicate tint of orange in the sky that morning, which Aude pointed out to me with the tip of her little finger, making the remark that it was the same shade as her robe.

As I went out to go to the Saint Sernin Gate, my sister followed me. She had an air of resolution and she told me that she had reflected and that she too wanted to participate by action in the defense of the city.

Almost all of the women of Toulouse, under the direction of the Dame de Roaix, spent all day on the ramparts, repairing weapons, bringing arrows and stones and caring for the wounded. The Dame de Roaix wore a breastplate and a sword and participated in the sorties.

I tried to dissuade Aude from accompanying me. She had been known to lose consciousness after touching the blade of a sword. She was too frail even to hand someone a crossbow. She could not render any service.

But Aude shook her head and I saw her marching by my side with a firm step, in her dress the color of the sky. She went more rapidly than me, and I remarked that there was something strange about her.

Perhaps, I thought, she had had a presentment of my death the night before. I remembered having had a dream that could be interpreted in that sense.

That was it! She wanted to be present in my last moments.

I was touched by the effort she was making, but I felt pity for myself. Around Saint Sernin, armed men were passing at a run. They were shouting that the Montolieu Gate was under attack. I recognized Ratier de Caussade the Rapid, who was in charge of grouping the available soldiers and taking them to the point attacked.

I had been instructed not to quit the Saint Sernin Gate whatever happened. I was satisfied. The place where my sister was would be exempt from attack since the fighting that day was at the Montolieu Gate. I guided her up an improvised stairway to the roof of the former Saint Sernin cloister. It was partly demolished, but the section of the roof that remained was higher than the ramparts and all kinds of catapults had been installed there, several of which, invented by Bernard Paraire, could hurl large blocks of stone. There were usually women whom Aude knew there. I laughed as I went up the stairway, and said to myself: *Dreams and presentiments are vain fictions*.

From the roof of the cloister one overlooked the devastated countryside. Frédéric de Frezols, who was in command of the Saint Sernin Gate, was on watch there all night, and went to sleep when I arrived, but that morning, he had not waited for me. He was on his knees, his hands joined, and the fervor of his prayer had thrown him into a profound trance.

As I looked into the distance I saw that the horizon was abnormally barred by a hill of dust. The air around me was motionless. What was that abrupt wind, which was not making itself felt in Toulouse? I heard the dull sound of an enormous number of hoofbeats. Almost at the same instant a trumpet burst forth beneath me. Voices cried: "There they are!" The Seigneur de Frezols woke up and started running, giving incoherent orders. Then I suddenly remembered that I had put on, without thinking about it, a helmet devoid on a metal visor. It was too late to go and change it. Death would strike me in the face, doubtless by the intermediary of an arrow.

The entire countryside was now covered with cavaliers. They had slowed their march, but their horses could be heard whinnying and their arms could be seen glinting. And their number was immense. The attack on Montolieu was a feint. The entire army was about to mount a mass attack the foot of Saint Sernin.

I shouted that it was necessary to maneuver all the catapults and attempt to stop the enemy under an avalanche of stones. By my count, there were no more than fifty archers on that section of the ramparts.

The cries stopped momentarily. All eyes turned toward the enemy. Simon de Montfort had just detached himself from the line of his cavaliers. He knew the effect of terror that the sight of him produced and he always strove to appear theatrically. The solar light made his helmet, shield and even his spurs radiant, so that he gave the impression of being molded in light from head to foot. His raised sword was like a supernatural ray that communicated with the sun.

As if in a dream, I saw men jostling one another in order to obey my voice. Two men came to set themselves at the tourniquet of the largest of the catapults. A dwarf, shouting in order to manifest his zeal, was hauling a basket overflowing with stones. I recognized that the stones were fragments of broken statues. The previous year, Bishop Foulque had had all the pagan statues that were in the houses smashed. He had exorcized the fragments solemnly in the Place Saint-Sernin, and those fragments had remained heaped up in a corner of the cemetery. We had been making use of them for days to load the catapults. I recognized in the basket a head of Minerva that seemed to be looking at me. That face resembled, in a marvelous fashion, Esclarmonde de Foix. Esclarmonde de Foix, decapitated, reposed in the dwarf's basket.

A symbol of the times! I thought.

All of that only lasted a few seconds. The dwarf took the head of Minerva and placed it in the leather pocket of the nearest of his catapults. The cord was taut, but even though the catapult was very small it was very resistant. The dwarf made a futile effort to trigger it, and as the thoughts precipitated in my mind with the same ardor as the Toulousans during the assault on a tower, I thought of Ulysses and his divine bow. But the dwarf uttered a howl. An arrow had just traversed his ear and entered his neck at an angle. He fell, and remained sitting down in a stream of blood.

Then my sister Aude, who had remained motionless, took a step forward, seized the cord of the catapult, triggered it with a single easy movement of her arm, and sent the head of Minerva, the head of Esclarmonde, soaring through sunlit space.

I did not see the curve of that predestined stone. An immense clamor told me toward whom a sage and inexorable destiny had carried it. In the midst of the splash of radiance, the luminous knight, the conductor of the evil, the chief, his body henceforth headless, remained upright on his horse for one more second. Then he collapsed at a stroke on the Toulousan soil that he hated, and in which he had sown so much suffering.[27]

"Simon de Montfort is dead!" clamored a voice that seemed to emerge from the Basilica of Saint Sernin.

"He is dead!" cried the ramparts.

"He is dead!" cried the city.

Through several gates, the Toulousans emerged and surged forward. An enchantment was terminated, a diabolical magic had just come to an end by the play of a stone launched by an innocent hand. It appears that the force of evil, when it is struck at its source, collapses suddenly, seems to dissolve, as if it were made of nothingness. The immense army that enveloped Toulouse was obliged to flee precipitately. In the direction of the gallows, the monks and the priests were heard for a long time singing funerary hymns around the body of the headless warrior.

In the evening, exhausted by a day of combat but satisfied that no arrow had struck me in the face, I returned to the Saint Sernin Gate and I climbed up to the roof of the abbey.

---

[27] Simon de Montfort's skull was smashed by a stone hurled by a catapult during the siege of Toulouse on 25 July 1218. It was reported that the stone had been launched by one of the women assisting the warriors in the city's defense, and the assertion became a matter of legend.

Tents were still burning in the distance, casting an uncertain glow.

To my right, the skeleton of "the Gate" was smoking and falling apart. The dead formed small tranquil hillocks. A crazed horse was spinning round and sometimes rearing up on its front feet. A breastplate glistened like a forgotten sun. In a charred wheat-field, a tall thin man was running. His hands were tied behind his back and he had a sword embedded in his chest. Doubtless one of Montfort's soldiers had struck that prisoner before fleeing. He was running with what remained of his strength to die among his brothers, a symbol of the martyrized city, eternally alive in spite of the wound in the heart of its stones.

V

Aude died. At least, she died according to the conception that humans have of death. One day, the movement of the blood stopped, the breath ceased to exhale. There was an increasing deterioration of the flesh beneath the apparent immobility of the physical form. Next to her, I understood for the first time that such a phenomenon is wrongly called death.

Aude had been unable to console herself for having launched the liberating stone.

"I've finally accomplished a good deed that is making me suffer," she said, with a sad smile.

She became silent, attentive to voices and signs that she alone could comprehend. She grew weak. When she had the certainty that life was about to withdraw from her body she displayed an altogether unhabitual joy. Her final days were passed in expectation of the light realm to which she was about to go. It made me think of the period of my childhood when I was waiting to be taken to the country to the home of my uncle de Rabastens. I was the only one to hear her final words, for Aude did not want to be assisted by anyone.

"May he pardon me for having taken his life, as all those he has caused to die will one day pardon him."

An improbable wish, I thought, through my tears.

I was tempted to follow my sister into that world, the desirability of which she had praised to me, and which drew its beauty from the absence of any sensible form. But life was solidly attached to my body by carnal roots. I resolved to study the Albigensian religion and to strive to become pure, as she prescribed. I went to find Frédéric de Roaix, the Capitoul's brother, who had once taken me to a heretical gathering where I had heard mention of the Holy Spirit. I said to him that I wanted a higher knowledge than that possessed by ordinary men, and I added that I believed that I had become more intelligent than I had been in the past.

At first he did not seem to believe me; then he told me that I was a worthy man full of courage and that it was necessary for me not to worry about anything. I persisted, and he decided to give me the instruction that I requested of him.

Like all persons who deal with subtle things, he did so in a deliberately complicated language and with which he strove to mingle words little used in ordinary parlance. I asked him several times whether he could not explain himself more clearly. He smiled benevolently then and I understood that he was making an effort not to send away the imbecile that I was. I remain convinced, however, that it ought to be possible to say everything in clear language.

I understood that there had been a primitive teaching reported by Bartholomew, one of the twelve apostles of Jesus Christ who had been sent to evangelize Persia and India. In distant India Bartholomew had been instructed instead than instructing. He had returned to Hieropolis in Phrygia, and there, while continuing to preach the gospel, he had given orally an instruction that was different in many points from that of Jesus.[28]

His disciples, struck by the radiant force of the truth, had collected his words and had transmitted them in a secret manner, for they enclosed a substance contrary to all human society.

Life is evil in its essence and it is necessary to destroy the desire that everyone bears within him, and which is the cause of all evil. The force of that desire precipitates us after death into a new terrestrial incarnation and that course through human forms is endless if we do not discover the secret by means of which one attains the bliss of perfect intelligence. That secret is revealed to the person who attains the Holy Spir-

---

[28] Author's note: "The origins of the Albigensian religion are obscure. One of the less well-known hypotheses is one that attributes it the first foundations of the heresy to the apostle Bartholomew."

it, the divine wisdom. Then, the course is terminated, and the human being reenters via love into the serenity of God.

I was touched by the verity of those things, but I could not forbid myself a great sadness because of that condemnation of life. The splendor of the sun, feminine forms and the stones of Toulouse continued to enchant me. Sitting in my garden, meditating on the Sophia of the Perfecti, I watched a bee settle on a fruit, a branch agitate, or the shadow of a bird pass over a flower-bed, and I felt remorse in finding the charm of perishable beauty in those images. I was only able to understand much later that the bee, the shadow of the bird, and the moving branch, are all the more beautiful when one has arrived by detachment in the plenitude of love.

One evening, at about five o'clock, a messenger summoned me on behalf of the Comte. He had made me a knight and now treated me as an equal. Almost every evening I went to converse with him in the home of a certain Hugues Jean, whom he liked because of his great simplicity and who lived in a house in the outlying district behind Saint Sernin. I put a certain malice into not hurrying.

The Comte must have been waiting for me with a certain impatience, for I perceived him making signs at me from a first floor window. Now, it happened that while I was climbing the staircase, the Comte suffered one of those internal shocks that are sometimes produced in old men. As he opened the door, he let himself fall into an armchair.

"You've taken your time," Hugues Jean said to me. "The Comte de Toulouse has been waiting for you to make us both a communication of great importance."

I understood, in looking at the Comte, that he was about to die. He did, in fact, have something to say, but he had just been struck by a paralytic immobility that only permitted him to emit inarticulate sounds. Only his feet were stirring. Eventually, they stopped. His gaze expressed a formidable desire. Hugues Jean and I were of the same opinion. That desire concerned religious assistance. But which? Doubtless he wanted to confess. But to whom?

For years the Comte de Toulouse had been accompanied everywhere by the Albigensian perfectus Bertrand Martin. He had often said to his intimates that he adhered fundamentally to the new religion. When he felt ill he said: "Quickly, go fetch Bertrand Martin." On the other hand, he had recently confessed to Catholic priests, and he had secretly taken communion at the Church of La Daurade. Numerous excommunications weighed upon him, but the priests had turned a blind eye.

A few months before, Bishop Foulque had returned to Toulouse and the Comte had been obliged to treat him kindly. The Bishop had hastened to remind the clergy that the major excommunication that weighed upon the Comte could only be lifted by the Pope. He had promised to write in his favor, but time had passed and the Comte had summoned Bertrand Martin again. Who was he asking for now with his twisted and silent lips?

"It doesn't matter; it's the same God," Hugues Jean said to me in a low voice, a man of good sense, but a trifle vulgar.

I laid my master down on a bed that was at the back of the room. The imploring and terrified expression of his gaze overwhelmed me with pity. I regretted not being a priest in order to give him the absolution and peace for which he was asking. I even deliberated as to whether I ought not swear to him by Jesus Christ that I had become a perfectus without telling him and make a simulacrum of a consolamentum.

I did not have time. There was a racket in the house. The door opened noisily. I saw the Abbot of Saint Sernin appear. He was followed by several of his canons, whose file I saw filling the staircase. The Abbot, recently returned to Toulouse with Foulque, was a hard-hearted man with an ill-omened visage. Doubtless some servant had informed him prematurely of the Comte's death. I assume that the latter's immobility confirmed that death for him, although he scarcely darted a glance at him. He said in a severe voice: "The body of the Comte de Toulouse belongs to the Abbey of Saint Sernin.

I leaned toward him swiftly and said in a low voice: "But, thank God, our Seigneur the Comte is not dead. He is only paralyzed."

From the corner of my eye I could see that on his bed, my master was making an enormous effort to recover the power of speech.

Instead of verifying what I said, the Abbot of Saint Sernin recoiled in disgust and said, turning to his canons: "Throw this disgusting heretic out. His presence is a pollution next to the body of our Seigneur Raymond."

I had neither the time, nor the desire, to express the comicality of inviting the canons to throw me out.

"The Comte is alive," I said, turning toward those faces of stone.

Then the stairway filled with tumult and, jostling the canons, who were trying to prevent them from passing, several Knights Hospitaller of Saint John of Jerusalem irrupted into the room.

"The Comte's body belongs to the Abbey," proclaimed the Abbot de Saint Sernin in a peremptory tone.

"It belongs to the Hospitallers," replied the prior of the Hospitallers, in a thunderous voice.

Comte Raymond was narrowly linked to the Knights Hospitaller. He gave them alms. He had confided his testament to them. He had probably asked them to bury him. That privilege involved precious prerogatives. The community to which it belonged received offerings of all kinds for three days.

"The Comte isn't dead!" I shouted with all my might.

But the tumult drowned out my voice. The prior of the Hospitallers, depriving himself abruptly of his white cloak ornamented with a golden cross, threw it over the bed as a sign of possession. The Abbot de Saint Sernin tried to tear him away. The prior struck him on the shoulder with the palm of his open hand. The Abbot uttered a strident cry and attempted

183

to claw the prior. Coming to grips, the Hospitallers and the canons tried to throw one another out of the room.

I precipitated myself toward my master and succeeded in casting the cloak aside. But now the Comte was gasping. The horror of the scene unfolding around him or the terror of not receiving absolution had hastened the advent of the power that takes human souls elsewhere. His eyes were no longer soliciting any pardon. When Hugues Jean and I leaned over their extinct flame, they no longer reflected anything but a void.

VI

The Comte de Toulouse was not yet buried.[29] The Hospitallers carried him away by force and placed him in an open coffin before which the Toulousans came to weep. But Bishop Foulque gave them an order not to deposit the excommunicate in holy ground. To the lamentations of the people, he replied that it was necessary to await the decision of the Pope. It never came. The coffin was closed and it passed from the Hospitallers' reception room to a corner of their chapel, and then to a more obscure corner of a small lumber room, in which gardening tools were stored.

In that epoch, I meditated a great deal on the manner in which events are connected and the destiny that had presided over all my actions. As Marie the draper had once prophesied, evil, in order to make my homeland suffer, had incarnated itself in three men, the one clad in red, the one barded in iron and the one who wore a miter. I had pierced the heart of the first with my own hand. My sister Aude had killed the second by throwing a stone. It was up to me to cause the death of the third, who was the most evil.

Bishop Foulque feared the anger of the Toulousans and only came to the city for religious ceremonies. He lived in the Château de Verfeil, which Simon de Montfort had given to him. Isarn Nébulat, the seigneur dispossessed of that town had

---

[29] Author's note: "He never would be. The chronicler Aymeri de Peyrat claimed, in the fourteenth century, that the Comte's cadaver was eaten by rats. The coffin was still in the same place in the sixteenth century. Bertrandi, the author of *Gestis Tolosanorum*, saw the bones then and reported that a fleur-de-lys was designed on the posterior part of the skull. He judged it to be a natural mark and a presage that the Comte de Toulouse ought to be united with the French crown."

taken refuge in Toulouse and was secretly recruiting partisans in order to take back his château and domains by armed might.

I went to find him. He was a grim and wily old wolf. With simplicity, I made him party to my resolution. He sniggered and said: "It all depends on the sum you're asking."

I replied that my name was Dalmas Rochemaure.

He asked me again to name a figure.

I renounced chastising such a stupid man and decided to act on my own.

I went to install myself in Verfeil under a false name. After a few days I knew the Bishop's habits. He never went out without several men-at-arms. On a slope of his château there was a garden in the Arab mode, uniquely planted with very old and very dense box-trees. Now, Foulque had a passion: he liked snails. He slept very little and got up before sunrise. The box-trees contained snails by the thousand. Equipped with a basket, at daybreak, when the snails were enjoying the humidity of the dew, he went through the narrow pathways. When he had filled his basket he came back to the terrace of the château, spread the snails over the stones and played a mysterious game with them. Doubtless he ate them afterwards for breakfast.

My plan was rapidly settled. I had rented a room from a blacksmith from which I could get out without being seen. When the stars paled, having put on a green doublet and equipped with a pointed dagger, I climbed over the wall of the Episcopal garden. The box-trees were higher than a man and they were hick and leafy. I plunged between their branches toward the central pathway. It had rained a few hours before. Thousand of snails were moving around me.

The perfume of box is melancholy and penetrating. Perhaps it contains a magic. After half an hour, I was soaked to the skin, and singular images were presented to my eyes.

I never thought about Pierre de Castelnau, not even to rejoice in having expelled him from the earth. From one end of Christendom to the other, priests had put around the rumor that in expiring on the gilded beach of the Rhône he had only pronounced words to forgive his murderer. I had never believed it. I had contemplated him on the sand and I had had the sentiment that he had died in silence. Now, in the midst of those wet box-trees, with snails climbing over my shoes, I saw Pierre de Castelnau again, in the same morning freshness, lying with his chest opened. Someone had leaned over him immediately. A vague memory came to me of his arm lifting to seize his companion by the neck. Perhaps he had whispered, hastily, words of pardon.

A rosy radiance began to bathe the pathway while, involuntarily, I posed myself all the elements of that bizarre problem. So what? What if it were true? Perhaps the evil were not so inexorably separated from the good. They followed different paths but forgiveness remained the supreme ideal in which all took refuge at the moment of dying.

A small sound was audible, doubtless the crack of a snail-shell underfoot. In the light air, in the increasingly roseate light, I distinguished he silhouette of Bishop Foulque. He was advancing slowly, examining the ground attentively. I drew my dagger while reflecting on forgiveness and I put my finger on the tip in order to assure myself that it was not blunt.

Forgiveness was impossible for me. It was an abdication of the human, a cowardly consent to evil. But what if Pierre de Castelnau really had pardoned?

Very close to me, Bishop Foulque bent down, with great difficulty. He had shrunk. How old he was! His face was a jaundiced mask in which bile flowed just beneath the skin. However, the love of snails gave his gaze an unexpected flame. That face became brighter, for he had just perceived a snail larger than the rest, whose minuscule horns were extended toward the sky and which was situated on a branch at the height of my face. He reached out to grasp it, and he perceived me.

He saw through the foliage a man ready to pounce, but whose face reflected perplexity. The naked dagger left no doubt as to his intention.

187

We were close enough to touch one another. My mind was singularly active. I noticed how hideous the Bishop's face was. His sterile cranium was bare. His nose was swollen. His cheeks were slack. He had the inhuman, extraterrestrial expression that the absolute love of money gives.[30] I read as in a book the thoughts that were agitating him: what he had dreaded so much had arrived. An assassin had reached him. Crying out would be futile. Ought he to flee or to deposit in the basket the snail that he was holding and pretend not to have seen anything?

Had Pierre de Castelnau really forgiven? That problem was above all the others. I sensed that it was insoluble. I formed the unrealizable project of finding in Rome the man who was supposed to have heard that pardon whispered. Oh, why had I not jumped from my horse after having delivered the thrust of the lance and leaned over the stricken legate, close enough for him to bite me and for me to carry away the certainty of his hatred in the mark of his teeth?

Bishop Foulque, quivering with terror, had taken a few steps along the path, simulating calm. Then he threw down his basket and started to run. And I, a prisoner of the funerary enchantment that came from the box-trees and memory, watched him draw away. I had not a minute of pity for that old man whose lifted robe allowed the sight of his legs, ridiculous and deformed, as if his executioner Tancrède had exercised his instruments on them. Not for one minute did I think of forgiving him for the torture of my city and that of my race. And yet I remained immobile, because the man that had been his other self, his brother in evil, might perhaps have forgiven me before dying.

The first cry for help that he uttered woke me up. I launched myself along the narrow pathways, under the shadow on the box-trees. When I reached the breach in the wall

---

[30] Author's note: "Bishop Foulque had become so rich that when the King of France came to lay siege to Toulouse he was able to receive him and his entire army at Verfeil."

through which I had entered, no head had yet appeared at any window in the château.

Thoughts change like the images of life. My mind, while I fled, was entirely occupied by the representation of the instrument of torture of which Tancrède flattered himself with being the inventor. That instrument, in order to hasten the confessions of the patient, broke the arms and legs at the same time. It gave me wings through the forest of Verfeil; it enabled me to traverse the Tarn like a fish when its waters barred my way.

While I swam against the current, I saw a white bird above my head. It was flying in the same direction as me. But I did not know to which species it belonged. I thought of the dove of the Holy Spirit. When I arrived at the opposite bank, I observed sadly that my dagger had slipped from its sheath and had fallen into the water.[31]

[31] Author's note: "Bishop Foulque died peacefully in his bed, in 1232. His final days were devoted to writing poems to the Virgin."

VII

Now, enveloped in a shepherd's cloak and mounted on a mule, I am quitting Toulouse definitively. It is dark. The autumn wind is blowing over the banks of the Garonne. A man has just lit the two lanterns of the drawbridge. I hear him singing in the language of my ancestors. Thank God! He is a Toulousan; I have nothing to fear from him. The guard at the Narbonnais Gate is a little further away. I distinguish the stature of men of the North carved on a template of ridiculous size. I see their frightful blond beards, their bellies swollen by beer, their strange halberds. In their midst a Dominican friar is sitting, a subaltern of the Inquisition, watching those who are entering and leaving.[32] He gazes at me with the eyes of a pious cat. He does not recognize me. He is deceived by the empty jars that are hanging from the flanks of my mule. He thinks: *It's a poor man going back to his village.* He is only partly mistaken; it is a poor man, who is quitting the beloved city of his birth forever.

I plunge into the tenebrous route, where the nascent moonlight outlines the silhouettes of poplars. How fortunate those trees are to be solidly attached to this earth by roots and to be able to respire with their leaves the air that has passed

---

[32] Author's note: "The tribunal of the Inquisition commenced functioning in Toulouse in 1233. The first autodafé provoked a popular uprising. A little later, the Council of Narbonne was obliged to ask the Inquisitors to reduce condemnations because material were lacking in all the cities in the Midi for the construction of prisons." Although Magre does not cite Étienne de Lamothe-Langon's 1829 history in his bibliography, he does cite H. C. Lea' *History of the Inquisition*, which drew its accounts of events in Toulouse from Lamothe-Langon's partly-invented history, and he probably obtained these data from that tainted source..

over Toulouse! I hear the waters of the Garonne along the slopes of Pech David. I draw further away. And suddenly, I turn round. I see La Daurade, I see La Dalbade, I see Saint Sernin.

O Toulouse, what has been done to you? There are your houses, your lamps, and your towers, but you are no longer the same. Your soul has been changed.

A Seneschal of the King of France now has more authority than your Capitouls. Raymond VII has been deprived of the city of his ancestors.[33] It is the terrible sect of Dominicans that renders justice.

There are so many people accused of heresy that the house of the Inquisition is overflowing and the neighboring streets are filled with captives awaiting their turn to be judged. The judges are exhausted by dint of condemnations, but they condemn untiringly. Night and day, groans rise up from the subterrains of the Château Narbonnais. Dark Auvergnats who resemble tree-trumps, and fat Normans with cunning faces, are installed in the palaces of literate and delicate Toulousans. Young men dare not sing free songs in the evening under the fig-tree in the Place des Carmes. Young women attenuate the Saracen colors of their robes and adopt French fashions. The Baths have been closed because it is a sin to care for one's body. The manuscripts in the Bibliothèque du Taur have been burned because they contain mysterious characters that might express an impious wisdom. Where now are the philosophers from Granada with their beards and turbans, who once chatted among the tombstones under the cypresses of Saint Sernin? Where are the Moorish musicians who made the sand of Asiatic deserts vibrate in their darbukas? Not a single Roman

---

[33] Author's note: "In 1229 the Treaty of Paris consecrated the fall of Raymond VII. He submitted to the Pope and the King of France. He beat himself with rods at Notre Dame as his father had done at Saint Gilles. He received absolution. His Estates reverted to the crown on his death."

statue remains on its pedestal. No one dares recite a page of Plato aloud.

O Toulouse, I bid you adieu! I shall no longer hear the crier announcing that the fresh wine has arrived. I shall no longer laugh with the children as the Matrons of Expertise go past.[34] I shall no longer see the bread being weighed in front of the capitular house. I sense, at the moment of losing them, how great those petty pleasures were.

I resume my route. The foothills of the Pyrenees are nearer. I have reached Ariège. I can no longer distinguish in the distance the contours of your eternal mass. The poplars already have another language. If I picked a fig, it would have a different taste. How could the air is when one draws away from Toulouse!

I am the guest of Montségur. From all the persecuted towns, the heretics who do not want to renounce their faith have come to take refuge in Montségur. On a mountain in the region of Foix, encircled by the gorges of the Ers and the Lectorier, deafened by rocky precipices, Esclarmonde, Vicomtesse de Gimoez, has had an impregnable fortress constructed. I find there all the faithful of the religion of the Holy Spirit. The Canastbrus are there with their fathers, their grandfathers, their sons and their grandsons, who are all animated by an excessive liking for generation. The Malhorgas, who are hairy and have blue eyes. The Nolascos are there, who are musicians and make the tower they inhabit vibrate with the perpetual sound of instruments. The western barbican is full of orphan children. The soldiers camp in the courtyard, under tents. The perfecti are in the eastern tower, and when they march at its summit, meditating in the starlight, the radiation of their thought is so powerful that the tower gives the impression of being surrounded by a blue-tinted aureole. There is a

---

[34] Author's note: "Women charged, at the moment of marriages, with determining whether the fiancés were well-constituted."

field of daisies planted by the beautiful Alix d'Escaronia, and the beautiful Pélégrina de Bruniquel can be seen with a watering-can in her hand, lavishing her cares upon a rose-bush with white flowers.

But the life of Montségur is extended underground in the forty-eight floors that are hollowed out in the mountain. Along stone galleries, subterranean rooms are superimposed that overlook the gorges of the Ers through narrow loopholes. Down below are the baths, the reserves of salt and wheat, the jars of oil, everything that Esclarmonde's foresight has accumulated in view of a siege. There are the libraries of all the châteaux of the Midi, which, menaced with burning, have been transported one by one. There are stables, workshops for the armorers and grottos for those who, making progress toward perfection, attain it by mans of immobility and prayer. There are cells for deaconesses and rooms where they gather in order to form the mystical chain.

The deaconesses are all women who have taken a vow of chastity. When they emerge in the evening in white robes and make a tour of the château I recognize among them prostitutes from Toulouse alongside chatelaines with illustrious names. Somewhere—but no one knows where—the one whom no one must know, the invisible Pope, elected by the Synod of the Perfecti, is meditating. On the highest tower, the one turned toward the Orient, it is said, Esclarmonde de Foix is lodged. When the nights are clear, her silhouette can be seen outlined against the sky. An astrologer and a geomancer are incessantly by her side; both are seeking, in the study of the stars and the analysis of the earth, the enigma of life and death.

For a long time I have believed that I am not growing old. My strength has scarcely diminished. I have neither the time nor the possibility to count my hairs, but I am sure that they are as numerous as of old. Only their whitening betrays the presence of the years. There are the mountains where I wandered when I fled Mercus, there are the torrents where I drank, and there are the trees under which I went to sleep.

Then, I came to ring the tocsin without knowing that that prophetic bell was announcing the thousand tocsins that would ring in the bewildered towns from the Rhône to Toulouse. I was young and joyful then. Now, I am aging and full of experience.

On the narrow road that I am on, there are almond branches that I move aside with my hand. It is hot; it is midday. I look between the trees and I see a stream flowing. I am going along the banks of the Ers. I remember that I once went along that river under an analogous sun. Was it the same place? No, undoubtedly, but the vegetation is the same. At the noise I make, frogs jump to the right and left, and I take care not to crush them, for parcels of the divine soul are enclosed beneath the envelope of those creatures. It was on the bank of the Ers that extended over a little beach of gilded sand that I saw the miraculous form of Esclarmonde de Foix for the first time, asleep.

What is the aspect of that form now? As the spirit of Esclarmonde has become more perfect, the flesh that was the expression of it must have withered and lost its beauty. No one can see her at Montségur. She never descends from the tower where she resides. Perhaps old age has exerted ravages on her more terrible that on other women. Perhaps she no longer has any but astrological preoccupations. How sad the law is that dictates that beauty bears the principle of its death hidden in its substance! But might she not be an exception?

Branches obstruct the path in front of me. I move them aside and am about to advance when I have difficulty retaining a cry. On a strip of sand bathed by the Ers, a woman's form is extended beneath a veil that is partly unwound. It is evident, by the evaporation of water on her flesh, that she has just been bathing. She has three tresses, like the other. I see her face and I recognize her. It is Esclarmonde de Foix! But how is that possible? She seems younger than before.

Doubtless the sound of the shifted branches wakes her up momentarily. I distinguish beneath her eyes the metallic flash that struck my eyes when I carried her in my arms and I had, for the first time, the revelation of the mystery of the spirit. Am I not the victim of a magic spell? No, magic spells do not exist. In that case, Esclarmonde possesses the unique secret, the secret of eternal youth.

A gust of wind, come from I know not where, passes over me. And suddenly, I take a step backwards and recoil through time. I become a hirsute young man again, clad in rags, the soles of whose feet are horny by dint of having walked. I feel a desire to laugh, to run, to sound the tocsin without reason, as before. I sense that if I were thirsty I would lap instead of taking water in my hand.

Obscure larvae have taken possession of my flesh and they are stirring there in darkness. I feel a desire to pounce and seize in my arms the woman who, throughout my life, has symbolized spiritual perfection. To hold the tabernacle and profane it! An odor of oleander, an odor of sap, rises around me. The earth encourages me.

I am about to launch myself forward. I chance to look at the sky and I see a white bird flying above my head. Is it a miracle? Is it the dove of the Holy Spirit? The bird descends to the height of the treetops and then draws away. But I have received its message. I turn round on the path. In a matter of seconds I traverse the years of my life. My hair, which had blackened, becomes white; my feet are no longer horny; if I wanted to lap up water, I could not.

I return at a slow pace toward Montségur, toward its knights, toward its deaconesses, toward its subterranean city, wondering whether I have contemplated a reality or a dream, and meditating on the eternal youth of Esclarmonde.

Men posted on the heights signal with flames by night and the sound of trumpets by day. Cavaliers are incessantly running along the road to Lavelanet. The people arriving from Foix and Toulouse bring bad news. Pierre des Arcis, the Seneschal of the King of France in Carcassonne, and the Bishop of Albi, have gathered an army that is now within the walls of Toulouse. They have resolved to destroy Montségur, the hearth of heretics who, from the height of her rock, defy the Pope and France. As was done thirty years ago, they have promised indulgences and they have put crosses on the breasts of knights to stimulate their ardor.

From all the Pyrenean châteaux where there are Albigensians, voluntary defenders come running. They are seen on the narrow path that snakes in zigzags and climbs to the gate of the château turned toward Lavelanet. There are peasants carrying their entire fortune, sacks of flour, or vegetables on their back, and knights that only come with their sword and lance. Old Raymond de Pérelha, who is the titular Seigneur de Montségur, stands on the threshold to welcome them. I have been there for a long time like an idler, and I marvel that such a great quantity of men, mules and horses can find places in the subterranean galleries of Montségur.

Here is the taciturn Roger de Mirepoix, who is charged with commanding the combatants. Dispossessed of his château, where Simon de Montfort put his companion Guy de Lévis, he set forth with a few cavaliers on a moonless night to attempt to take it by force. He has renounced it now and his face is as redoubtably closed as the gate of his lost fortress. Here are Palauqui de Foix, Delga du Lauragais and Louis du Gers, by whose side I fought in Toulouse. They are valiant. Were they the same age as me before? They are now much older. The problem of time is a mystery.

Here are Loup de Foix the Intrepid, and Jean Cambitor, the warrior magician whose buckler has two sides; the face protects from swords, the reverse is a mirror in which, with the point of his dagger, he makes phantoms appear. Here is Roger de Massabrac, who has the evil eye. He turns away as he speaks to his friends and widens his eyes in the presence of his enemies, because, he says, he can fell them with his stare. Here is Amaury Nebulat, the crank; every day, at noon, he throws his helmet on the ground and tears off his clothes; he swears that he will live naked henceforth, in order to rediscover the veritable purity that can only be obtained in the state of simplicity of the first man.

Suddenly, my eyes widen and I start trembling. A woman on horseback, whom one might take for an adolescent, advances toward the gate of Montségur. She wears a sword, she has a silver helmet and is armored like a knight. I recognize the oval of her face and the profundity of her eyes. It is Esclarmonde de Foix, in whom the ideal of my youth is incarnate. I was not dreaming when I saw her on the water's edge. The pure spirit has been obliged to take up the sword and don iron because of the harshness of the times. But here it is, alive, climbing toward Montségur.

The young woman leaps down from her horse slightly. She addresses a few words to Raymond de Pérelha and immediately seems to be looking for someone. I had noted with surprise that men of some importance who were entering did not fail to salute respectfully a little, insignificant old woman who was sitting under a fig-tree on the threshold of the interior courtyard. I had scarcely glanced at her. There are two men clad in black by her sides. She is extraordinarily wrinkled and her dress is so simple that one might take her for a servant. It is her for whom the young woman is searching. Scarcely has she seen her than she runs forward, falls to her knees and kisses hr hands.

Before whom can Esclarmonde the eternal be prostrating herself thus? I lean toward one of the innumerable Canastbru sons, who is standing beside me, and I interrogate him about the wrinkled old lady. He considers me with a dolorous amazement, as one might consider someone insensate or sacrilegious. He asks whether I am joking about that which is sacred. Then, seeing my innocence, he says: "But that's Esclarmonde de Foix, Vicomtesse de Gimoez, who has come down for the first time today in order to greet her niece, Esclarmonde d'Alion."

And he moves aside swiftly, for all the Canastbrus pride themselves on intelligence, and that one must blush to be near a man as ignorant as me.

But I stand aside even more swiftly. I have just felt the pain of a lacerating wound. I need to walk, to run, to exteriorize my disappointment. Woe betide the man who believes in a miracle, even a miracle of the spirit. Nature is atrociously deprived of them. The laws of the flesh are inexorable. No divine force can install itself in a form that does not perish, in order to make beauty radiate.

Old age is stronger than the spirit. My ideal chimera has faded since the time when I created it.

O Lord, if nothing endures, no living forms, nor monuments, nor the images of gods, no expression of perfection, it is because life, as my brothers the Albigensians say, is only an evil illusion, a succession of dolors that it is necessary to reject as quickly as possible, in order to attain the realm of the true life in which everything is stable perfection and immutable amour!

VIII

In the leaden circle of mountains, between the ferrugi-
nous streams and the mute firs, Montségur with the hermetic
towers gives the impression of a tomb looming up against the
autumn sky. Pierre des Arcis' army slowly envelops the plat-
eau bordered with precipices at the summit of which the château stands.

On the stone esplanade that overlooks the Ers, we gaze at
the floating banners and hovering crosses, and we count the
machines of war. We laugh at their pettiness. Night falls. The
stars light up. The valleys fill with fires. I am now almost
alone in front of the château. There is a twisted oak that de-
ploys its branches over the abyss. A stone bench has been built
beside it, on which I am sitting. But this place, at the same
hour, ought to be occupied by a person of importance, for I
have scarcely sat down when someone runs forward and
touches me on the shoulder with a hand. I barely have time to
stand up and move aside in the shadow, and I see Esclarmonde
de Foix advancing.

The rumor has been running round the château for several days that she is going to die. For me, that is a statement that
has no meaning. The Esclarmonde who lived in me died when
I saw her again and wept. But she has resuscitated slowly, a
little more every day, and I am beginning to understand that
the only ideal creatures are those that are deprived of faces and
bodies and are above death.

I watch the chatelaine of Montségur walk slowly under
the oak. I had thought her small. She appears to me to be tall. I
cannot distinguish her wrinkles. She gives the impression of
being carved in transparent ivory. The old Seigneur de Pérelha
has approached her and he tries to console her for some dolor
of which I am ignorant. Both of them lean forward, and scruti-
nize the darkness. I hear a term that returns to their lips: the
Holy Spirit, the spirit...

And suddenly I hear Esclarmonde say, wringing her hands and raising her head, as if to take the stars as her witness: "My God! With an entire life of efforts, I have not been able to do anything for the truth, I have not served the spirit."

Close at hand, a trumpet sounds. Six horsemen appear on the sheer road that leads to the château. They must be expected because the watchmen utter joyful appeals, waving torches. The gate opens. I see, under the helmets, six male adolescent faces. They are the six children that Esclarmonde de Foix has had by the Vicomte de Gimoez.

The Seigneur de Pérelha murmurs, while she goes toward them: "Look, life has taken charge of responding to you."

The siege of Montségur had endured for a month and I could not contrive to understand the mysterious intoxication that reigned in the château. I thought at first that it was the joy that war causes, but the joy in question was very different from the one that I had been able to see in the course of my life among combatants. It was a joy without exterior manifestation, a pure joy of the soul. It began to spread on the third day of the siege, when the rumor ran around that Esclarmonde de Foix was dead. That news was whispered from one to another, without comment. It caused no apparent affliction. There was no collective prayer. No one knew where on the mountain her remains had been deposited. Even in Montségur, the Cathar rite of secret burial was practiced, which had been in usage for a long time because of the folly that the bishops had of violating the tombs of heretics in order to rob them of the repose of death.

From that moment on, however, everyone had more feverish gestures and a bizarre glimmer of delight in the gaze. I could not understand that astonishing joy at all. It is true that the fortress seemed impregnable. The triangular mountain of Montségur was so vast, so bristling with precipices, that the royal troops would never be numerous enough to encircle it completely. But those considerations did not appear to me to be sufficient to explain the reigning state of mind.

It was the joyful Arnaud Boubila who enlightened me. He was a simple man who had a slight paunch and who slept in the cell next to mine. He was so cheerful that I often heard him laughing on his own behind the partition that separated me from him. He had been a shepherd in his youth and, in memory of the past, he nourished a goat-kid of which he was very fond and allowed to sleep in his arms. He glorified himself for having been with d'Alfaro at the Avignonnet affair. Several Inquisitors had been massacred there.[35] He showed me proudly the staff with which, on the celebrated night, he had broken the skull of Raymond de Costiran, nicknamed the Writer because he drew up lists of heretics for burning so long that no parchment could contain them. Arnaud Boubila's great anxiety was not being able to take that staff with him when he died, in order to present it to the Holy Spirit. Taking pity on such a simple man, I assured him that the phantom of the staff would not fail to accompany him, with its murderous virtue.

One night, I heard Arnaud Boubila singing for longer than usual. When his kid bleated plaintively and fell silent. I was woken up by something moist on my hands. By the light of a candle I saw that blood had flowed under the planks of my cell. I got up and went into the next cell. Arnaud Boubila had killed his kid, and then had opened his veins. His staff was placed against his heart.

"He's given himself Endura," said the man in the next cell along, simply when I woke him up and showed me Boubila's body. "He's happy now, with his kid and his staff."

---

[35] The massacre of the Inquisitors in Avignonnet took place on 28 May 1242. It was followed by a brief insurrection, which son petered out, and the massacre was the pretext for sending Pierre d'Arcis' army in 1243 to destroy Montségur, to which those responsible had fled.

And I understood by the attention with which he studied the cut wrists that he envied his fate and was thinking about the most practical way to imitate him.

What the Albigensians called Endura was the natural consequence of their philosophy. Life being evil, death is the fortunate deliverance therefrom.[36] When the soul is deprived of remorse, disengaged from the passions, it is permissible to anticipate the play of nature and deliver oneself from the chain of the body. That permission, in verity, was only granted to perfecti, but many simple believers, either to escape great dolors or to enjoy more rapidly the bliss of the formless world, deliberately gave themselves death.

The disappearance of Esclarmonde had given a mysterious signal. Several Albigensians put an end to their lives in the same fashion as my neighbor Boubila. It had been hoped in the first days of the siege that the crusaders would grow weary and depart. The rumor had gone around that the Albigensians of Toulouse and Albi would send an army of rescue. Then discouragement had come. Death, the marvelous death that opens the door of the world of light, appeared imminent and inevitable. Everyone extended his arms toward it, and summoned it with an ardent wish.

Holding hands one evening, at sunset, Jean de Cassanel and his two sisters threw themselves into the precipice of the Ers. The sage Bernard Ortolanus put on a white robe and sat down in the midst of his children, in order, he said, to give them a noble and useful example, and pierced his heart with his dagger.

"He was wrong," said the sage Philippe Pellipar. "It is necessary not to offer oneself as a spectacle. One lends reality to death by making it visible. The man who wants to die ought to disappear."

And that same evening, he disappeared.

---

[36] Strictly speaking, an Endura was a kind of penitential fast undertaken by Cathars, which often led to death, rather than an active suicide.

Others believed that it was necessary to respect destiny, that everyone had his marked hour. But it was not forbidden to hasten that hour by magical practices, by burning herbs and intoning chants. In the subterranean galleries, on the towers and even when sorties were made, the Albigensians waited for death with delight. One did not know in the evening whether someone was leaving in order to go to sleep or to open his veins during the night.

An immense appeal emerged from the cells, galleries and towers. The watchmen on the elevated towers were those who gave themselves Endura most easily because the purer air and the clouds that brushed them brought them, with the suavity of the mist, a foretaste of what they imagined the afterlife to be. Montségur was the château of death.

IX

Pierre Roger de Mirepoix hated me, with an incomprehensible hatred, and he had made Jordan d'Elcongost, who was second-in-command of the besieged, share it.

I had always thought that it was because I showed a valor at least equal to theirs when we descended the slopes from the château and attacked the crusaders unexpectedly. Certainly, I did not desire death, but I fought with a tranquil indifference, a valorous serenity that had to inspire envy in those agitated and violent men. I was always sent to the most dangerous posts, charged with missions that comported the sacrifice of life. A quotidian miracle preserved me. My companions felt sorry for me, and said that I truly had no luck in escaping beneficent death so frequently. I did not share their opinion. I had not extirpated within me the root that is the appetite for living, and every day I rejoiced secretly in seeing the light of the sun.

All the war machines that the crusaders had brought with them were too short. We saw woodcutters on the slopes of Serrelongue felling fir trees in order to construct taller ones. Slowly, an enormous wooden tower rose up facing us. When its giant scaffolding was completely erected, the tower commenced the ascent of the sheer slopes to the château. It was hooked on to stones, wedged against folds in the terrain, and rose up for five months until the moment when its platforms, laden with stones and catapults, were level with our towers. With the winter snows a rain of arrows and an avalanche of rocks fell upon us incessantly. The crenellations were splintered. The breached barbicans trembled on their foundations. Gaping holes opened up in the walls. The dead—the fortunate dead—became more numerous.

Help came to us from several châteaux.

When the nights were dark, a resolute troop conducted by a reliable guide sometimes managed to pierce the crusaders' line and reach Montségur. Once, it was the architect Bertrand de la Baccalaria, with Toulousan volunteers. He had the chimerical optimism of my compatriots. He walked in the midst of punctured towers and crumbled walls and rubbed his hands, saying that all that was nothing and could be easily reconstituted. We had faith in his genius as a builder. We set to work. But the château must have been possessed, like its defenders, by the love of death. There must have been a desire or ruination in the stones. We only succeeded in rebuilding the appearance of walls, towers that fell down again of their own accord. Without anyone being able to explain why, the wood that was to serve to build machines proved to be rotten.

Another time, it was Esclarmonde d'Alion, with a few Aragonese mercenaries. They had left eighty strong and only a dozen came back. Esclarmonde d'Alion came to embrace her lover, Jordan d'Elcongost. In the Château de Montségur all unions were mystical, there were only ideal embraces. That amour was an exception to the rule. While the battens of the great door were slamming shut again, by the light of a torch. I saw Jordan's lips met those of Esclarmonde, and in the pure air of Montségur, that kiss caught fire and cast a more vivid light than that of the torch.

The assaults became increasingly frequent and no one slept any longer. The women and children ran to the most exposed places in the hope of being struck by a liberating stone or arrow. The perfecti remained close to the combatants in order to give the consolamentum to those who were dying with a gesture of the hand and the light of the gaze. Thus they were delivered from the chain of reincarnations. But the majority had no need of the magic practiced by a perfectus. They had already broken the final thread that retained them to the earth and they died with the certainty of being liberated.

It was at the moment when the situation was at its most desperate that Bertrand de La Baccalaria's optimism gained the majority of minds. A flame appeared one night at the summit of the Bidorte. Everyone thought immediately that it was a signal from the King of Aragon who had sent a rescuing army. As the sun rose on one spring morning, a watcher at the height of the northern tower came down shouting that he had just seen an immense army advancing from the direction of Toulouse. He had recognized the banner of Raymond VII. At the same moment Raymond VII was prostrating himself at the feet of the Pope, as his father had once done in my company. He had no army. The watchman had been the victim of an illusion.

Many people were tormented by apparitions. They saw the companions they had lost, those that had been carried away by the waves of the Ers, and those who reposed in subterranean tombs. They lived with those shades in a strange familiarity. Nora de Marcilhac incessantly questioned an invisible creature, her sister India, who had died at the beginning of the siege. They had jumped into a precipice together but Nora had been retained by her robe; she had seen that as a sign from destiny that obliged her to live. Since then, her sister's phantom was always by her side, and her sole dread was that of distinguishing, on the part of the phantom, a slight impatience because she was lingering in life.

The Albigensian who had taken the place of Arnaud Boubila only occupied half the cell. He claimed that Arnaud Boubila was still in the other half. At night he heard the bleating of the kid and the tap of the staff that had broken the skull of the Inquisitor of Avignonnet.

The dead were not plaintive or dolorous. They did not ask to be avenged. They urged their brethren to rid themselves of substance in order to enjoy with them the estate of amour, of fraternity without separation. I could not succeed, in spite of the keenness of my hearing, in hearing their whispers. In spite of the excellence of my eyesight, I could not distinguish their contours. But the others saw and heard and I was sure that they were not deceiving me. There were dead men sitting under all the porches, wandering in all the corridors. The field of daisies was full of them. A large number were under Pelegrina de Bruniquel's rose bushes. The physicians obtained secrets from them for the fabrication of their medicines. Children made them play their games.

There was one point in the gorge of the Ers guarded by soldiers from Mirepoix who had remained devoted to their former seigneur. A perfectus entered into communication with them and it was agreed that they would let a few men and horses pass one night.

It was necessary to save the treasure of Montségur. It was immense. It had been accumulated in several rooms. There were the riches, in solid gold and precious objects, of many of the Albigensian châteaux whose seigneurs had fled before Simon de Montfort. There were ancient manuscripts brought from the Orient, notably a book written in the Zend language that was in the hand of Mani himself. There were the teachings of Nicetas and all the writings to which the perfecti had consigned the methods permitting humans to obtain perfection rapidly.

All of that was loaded on to mules whose feet were surrounded with felt. Loup de Foix and Esclarmonde d'Alion commanded the handful of men who were to fight and try to save the treasure in case of surprise.

From the height of the balcony of rock that overlooked the Ers, with the group of leaders, I watched the silent cortege plunge into the darkness. Esclarmonde d'Alion was the last, and as she turned round to make a sign to Jordan d'Elcongost she stumbled, made a noise and almost fell.

Jordan d'Elcongost watched her silhouette decrease. The perfecti followed the hope of Catharism with their eyes. Pierre Roger de Mirepoix, who was beside me, was thinking about the gold that was drawing away from him. Had he not been fighting for its possession? His face expressed despair. Never had the enigma of the man appeared greater to me. There was no Albigensian faith in him, and he was even scornful of the believers for their religious scruples, and their horror of bloodshed. He did not believe in anything except his own hatred. If Montségur held out for so long it was because of the determination of that inexorable leader. He never confided in anyone. The only words he spoke were military orders. But I sensed

207

that he was linked to the presence of gold in the château, and when the gold had gone, he found himself in the midst of empty stones. He fought with the same tenacity until the final hour, but perhaps without knowing why.

Very late, just as daylight as about to appear, a flame on the mountains of Serrelongue told us that the treasure had been saved.

Roger de Massabrac had inspired so much confidence in us in the power of his evil eye. To the west of the fortified part of the mountain he commanded a little redoubt above a sheer path. That path, known only to shepherds, was almost vertical. Its stones were hostile and vertigo troubled the mind there. It was thought to be impossible to climb by night, especially with Roger de Massabrac's evil eye above it. Doubtless a shepherd betrayed it. Doubtless there were particularly skillful mountain-climbers among the crusaders who possessed a talisman against the evil eye. It was by that path that defeat slid toward us.

From all sides at once an attack had taken place during the day. We were exhausted. In the evening, Bertrand de La Baccalaria made a tour of the broken walls in order to say that all was well. His joyful voice could be heard resonating through the ruins. We had scarcely fallen sleep in the subterranean ant-hill when the alarm trumpet resounded, followed by clamors. I threw myself on my weapons and launched forth half-dressed, scarcely taking time to wake my neighbor, the companion of the dead Boubila.

The stairway that I climbed ended in the great courtyard, where a torch was perpetually alight. By its light I perceived Roger de Massabrac, tottering and supporting himself with his hand against a wall. I thought he was drunk and I was about to reproach him sharply when a man appeared through a low door that I did not recognize. He looked to the right and left, seemingly frightened. I saw that he had a red cross on his coat of mail and that everything he was wearing was singularly bright and new by comparison with the rags in which the château's defenders were now clad. In my folly, I thought of some incomprehensible disguise.

But he suddenly turned round and shouted in the French language: "Come on, there are two of them here!"

Pouncing like a cat, he thrust with the point of his sword at Roger de Massabrac, and tried to lay me out with another. Roger de Massabrac fell face down. I think that he was already dying when he received that final thrust. I had time to see that his back bore several wounds. He must have received them while he was trying to get back to the château to warn us. The man was still bounding as if he belonged to the feline species rather than the human.

Albigensians emerged from all sides. A few pikes, behind which there were gleaming eyes, had appeared at the little door. We rushed in that direction. A small group of crusaders, driven back against the wall of a tower, were exterminated in the gloom. But there were others almost everywhere. Pierre Roger de Mirepoix had gathered the men of the guard who were sleeping, fully armed, in the main hall of the central keep. His stature had suddenly increased. His voice had taken on a metallic tone. A warrior spirit animated him. He was holding a short pike in his right hand and a dagger in his left. He had thrown away his helmet as if he were certain that he would not be hit. Thanks to his presence of mind and his divination of the danger that menaced us, we were able to repel the enemy from the circle of the four central towers.

But the enormous stone-throwing machines, grating and groaning, were set in motion in spite of the darkness. There was a rain of cyclopean blocks, as if the somber sky were against us and dropping fragments of stars. A procession of old men and children who had gathered and who emerged singing to ask death to come more rapidly had their wish granted immediately. The men posted at the ballistas must have been the first killed, or could not reach the towers in the disorder.

We perceived above us the skeletons of our own machines, dislocated by stones and motionless. It was impossible to tell what was burning, or how the fire had been ignited, but spirals of suffocating smoke blinded the eyes and blackened faces. The perfecti ran around, lavishing the consolamentum upon the dying. Jordan du Mas San-Andréo, whose chest was crushed, bid me adieu smiling and gave me a rendezvous in the other world, into which he was preceding me, at a precise hour on the following day. I saw Pelegrina de Bruniquel, who had received an arrow in the heart, raise the petals of a rose hastily to her lips. All those who were dying said: "Finally!"

Late in the night there were a few minutes of calm. I was surprised to see Bertrand Martin coming toward me. He took me by the hand and drew me through the wounded and along the interior staircase to a little bare cell. Bertrand Martin was reputed to be the most saintly of the perfecti. My master Raymond VI had held him in veneration. It was claimed that he was the Pope of the secret Church.

"I have chosen you," he said. "You must live."

I made a gesture to express the impossibility of realizing that wish, but he stopped me.

"It's necessary that a courageous man save the most precious part of the treasure of the Albigensians. You can still take advantage of the darkness, go down the mountain and slip through the crusaders' lines. Don't regret death. It will not be definitive for you. It will be necessary for you to be reincarnated very often in human forms.

He assured me thus of an imperfection of which I as well aware but that no one likes to hear specified. It was not a time for polite reticence and Bertrand Martin's purity obliged him to an absolute sincerity.

He took from his garments an oval object of which I could only perceive part beneath the hide that enveloped it. It was a glaucous stone, perhaps an enormous emerald, which as hollow and which contained some sort of red-tinted liquid.

He hesitated for a second, wondering whether he ought to explain the nature of the treasure to me. He simply said: "Give this to the perfecti who have taken refuge in the grotto of Ornolac. I have confidence in you. Adieu."

And he embraced me.

The grotto of Ornolac was the place near Castelverdun to which the treasure of Montségur had been transported.

I went back upstairs, reflecting on the means of getting out of the château.

Almost all of the defenders of Montségur were assembled in the great courtyard. Jordan d'Elcongost was holding a torch above a seated cleric who was writing. Beside him, Pierre Roger de Mirepoix was shouting names at regular intervals, and his voice resonated strangely. It seemed to me that there was no longer any sound from the direction of the besiegers and that silence seemed lugubrious to me. First light was beginning to appear. I interrogated Delga in a low voice as to the significance of the scene.

There was no more fighting. A negotiator had come. The whole mountain was full of crusaders. There were thousands of them and resistance was impossible. Pierre Roger de Mirepoix had made a treaty with the Seneschal of Carcassonne. He was surrendering what remained of the château but he had obtained a guarantee of life for him and his soldiers. He had just drawn up a list of combatants who, with their weapons, were about to leave the château with him.

There were scarcely more than sixty defenders still alive. Pierre Roger de Mirepoix ordered the cleric to read the list of names that he had just dictated. As no one could hear him, he took it and read it himself, pausing to curse because of the poor handwriting, which he had trouble deciphering. When he had finished, the cleric, who had stood up, sat down, livid, He was not on the list. Nor had Pierre Roger de Mirepoix read my name. But as he concluded, our eyes met. He hesitated, and articulated, regretfully: "Dalmas Rochemaure."

The silence that followed tore my heart. We were about to leave behind three or four hundred Albigensians, women and old men for the most part. They had appealed for death with such ardor that death was now there, under the arch of the gate, with crosses and pikes.

Pierre Roger de Mirepoix instructed us to pick up our weapons and hold ourselves ready in order to be able to defend ourselves if there was treason. A few minutes were wasted searching for a trumpet. All those who knew how to play one were dead. The man who took the instrument drew discordant sounds from it.

We went down the mountain to the bizarre sounds of that trumpet. The sun rose. An unusual number of crows filled the sky. A group of cavaliers with dazzling armor preceded us. Another followed us. We whispered to one another that they were going to surround us and massacre us. The fatigue was so great that, in spite of that prospect, several of my companions fell asleep as they marched. Jordan d'Elcongost stayed beside Pierre Roger de Mirepoix and listed, bitterly, the names of combatants who had been forgotten.

"No, they're dead," replied the other, indifferently.

At the foot of the mountain, near the Ers, at the entrance to a wood, there was a mass of cavaliers arranged in good order. Through the trees, tents could be glimpsed and a blazing fire with a soup tureen suspended above the flames, and soldiers at repose chatting and laughing.

"They're going to throw themselves upon us," said my neighbor, indicating the cavaliers.

And another murmured: "The bridge must have been sawn through, and it will collapse when we pass over it."

I saw Roger de Mirepoix's hand clench on his dagger.

Only Bertrand de La Baccalaria was completely reassured, and claimed that the crusaders must be preparing a meal for us.

We passed over the bridge. No one attacked us. The seneschal Pierre des Arcis prided himself on his chivalry. He was on horseback at the head of a further group of cavaliers. He looked at us with curiosity, his head tilted slightly forward. He did not salute. He remained motionless, but there was a hint of emotion on his face and I am sure that he would gladly have shaken our hands.

Beside him was a fat man with the expansive face of a sensualist. That was Pierre Amiel, the Archbishop of Narbonne, denounced the previous year by his own canons as incapable, debauched and scandalous. He winked at us benevolently.

We filed past without looking round, with all the dignity of which we were capable in our ridiculous accoutrements. But we were sad to find such a sympathetic attitude in those we had cursed throughout a year of siege.

The road to Lavelanet was cluttered with carts and mules. We took a small path that plunged into the mountains.

After walking for several hours I stopped on a platform of rocks at a place where the path, after having climbed the slopes of Serrelongue, descended again through a forest of firs.

In the distance, the water of the Ers was as blue and metallic as the reflection of a word. I saw a spiral of smoke that rose up swirling in the depths of the valley.

On the platform known as the Spaniards' Aerie, an enormous pyre had been built, whose framework I could make out. It had just been ignited in several places at once, and the flames were beginning to rise into the calm air. To the right, a mass of gold and miters had to be formed by the bishops with their crosses and their clergy. A circular forest of pikes and helmets surrounded the Spaniards' aerie. The neighboring woods were full of human silhouettes and flashes of armor.

And in front, the few hundred wretches that had been captures in Montségur were huddled together, giving the impression of a palpitating heap of human rags.

No sound reached as far as me. A mysterious silence reigned, with the result that what I saw seemed more like an image, an arbitrary tableau, than a living reality.

Suddenly, at an invisible signal, all the pikes lowered simultaneously, pushing the Albigensians toward the flames. I saw a man tear off his clothing, gesticulating. It was midday. It was the crank Nebulat. He had finally rediscovered the innocence of the first days. A few women ran back and forth. I saw others seize children and cover their heads with the flaps of their robes. Those who had so desired death seemed hesitant before it. The flame, now immense, was almost invisible under the light of the sun, as if purified by the blue of another universe.

Finally, I heard. An immense, grave, religious chorus rose up. It was the *Veni Creator*. Commenced by the bishops, it was intoned by the cavaliers on their horses, by the pike-bearers and by the entire army spread throughout the valley. Perhaps there was in that song a mysterious appeal of death heard by my heretic friends. As if the pyre was no longer anything but the gate of fire by which one enters the divine country, they all launched themselves into it simultaneously. The *Veni Creator* swelled, made the firs vibrate, and resonated in the mountains.

I perceived that Pierre Roger de Mirepoix was beside me, watching those who had been his companions for long months burn. He was impassive. Was he dreaming of vengeance? Did he regret not having died in combat in the ruins of Montségur? I attempted to speak to him but he did not reply.

As I was no longer under his command I thought about reproaching him in vehement terms for the hardness of his heart. Doubtless he would have thrown himself upon me to kill me. I reflected that there are closed and mute souls that it is necessary to leave in their darkness. We were both exhausted and we went to sleep side by side.[37]

---

[37] Author's note: "Not all the prisoners of Montségur were burned. A small number, including Raymond de Pérelha, were sent to the prisons of Carcassonne, where the denunciation of other Albigensians was extracted from them by torture." The burning of the captured Albigensians took place on 16 March 1244.

X

At the place where the Ariège receives the springs of Ussat, on the flank of the stony mountain, the grotto of Ornolac opens.[38] It extends over great depths; it has descending tunnels, others that rise in staircases, vaults higher than cathedrals and a lake with silent waters extends at the heart of its shadows. It was in that grotto that the last Albigensians, hunted throughout the Comté de Foix, took refuge one by one.

I had lived with shepherds for a long time. Then I had received hospitality in the Château d'Alion. But the Château d'Alion was burned. All the châteaux of the heretic seigneurs were destroyed by the seneschal of Carcassonne. In order not to die, a large number of Albigensians renounced their faith. Others formed bands and resisted in the mountains. I was one of them. But we became too few to fight in the open. I went to ground in the grotto of Ornolac.

Those who had been living there for a long time had lost the habit of seeing the light of the sun and consumed themselves in perpetual prayer. Pierre Pagès had succeeded Bertrand Martin and it was into his hands that I had put the emerald confided to me at Montségur. In the darkness of the grotto, where there were no birds or vegetation, by tremulous candlelight, I recognized faces encountered in the past that I had forgotten. I saw a workman from Carcassonne who had been under my orders at the siege of that city. I saw a nephew of Pierre de Roaix of Toulouse, and the peasant Ferrocas, who did not understand anything but was filled with love.

The circle formed by the seneschal's soldiers tightened around the entrance to the grotto. We learned that all the roads in the region of Castelverdun were guarded. Boats filled with armed men were traveling back and forth on the Ariège. The

---

[38] Author's note: "This grotto is now called the grotto of Lombrive, near Ussat in Ariège."

grottoes of Lherm and Badaillac had been occupied and their inhabitants massacred. The last fugitives that ran to us told us that the seneschal had decided to take the refuges of Ornolac by assault.

The men who were with me were worn out and discouraged by the miseries of their errant life. Their energy was exhausted. They expected nothing of this world and only had aspirations for the joys of the afterlife.

I succeeded, however, in uniting the most audacious. I grouped them at the junction of two narrow tunnels that bifurcated shortly after the entrance of the grotto. The disposition of the rocks and the inclination of the terrain rendered its defense facile. The first soldiers that appeared were transpierced by arrows springing from the shadows. The seneschal rapidly took his men backwards. Undoubtedly he had to know the length of the tunnels hollowed out under the mountains and understood the difficulty of pursuing us there. He used another, surer means.

All the Albigensians had gathered in a large space as high as a church. The treasure and the stores of provisions were there. The same little oil lamps had to serve everyone. Light was the rarest wealth in Ornolac, for oil and tallow were what had been transported there most parsimoniously. The perfecti charged with their distribution only surrendered it groaning, with exhortations to economy. A few families and hermits had plunged into corridors leading no one knew where in order to meditate and die alone. No one ever knew what became of hem. All the others had assembled, seeking in union the strength of soul necessary to struggle against the anguish of the darkness. In order not to reveal our presence, it had been recommended only to pray in low voices. The whisper of prayers alongside the palpitation of little lamps under the vaults rendered our assembly more lugubrious.

We perceived in the silence the sound of blocks of stone being shifted. The walls vibrated around us. Those who were charged with watching the entrance of the grotto came running and told us that the entrance was being walled up, in order to cut off the portal that led to the light.

Everyone got up and ran to see the sun one last time. Then everyone remained motionless. Everyone evoked internally the prisons of Foix with the torture chambers where their companions had perished in slow agony. The Albigensians sat down in the shadow, formulating a mute adieu to the sun.

But light is the radiant beauty of the world that no one can resign himself to forget. When after hours, the blocks could no longer be heard accumulating and the work of the masons ceased, despair raised the breasts of the immured. Cries resounded. Men who had been placid and resigned until then became furious. A few, deprived of reason, ran hither and yon, bumping their heads into walls. Others, whom rage rendered more insensate, tipped over the precious lamp-oil.

Pierre Pagès and the sagest made their way as best they could from group to group, trying to attenuate the dolor with their words without being able to remedy the darkness. They spoke about the spiritual sun that everyone bears within the soul, the marvelous sun of the Holy Spirit. Everyone tried to create internally the source of light forever lost. But in the damp air, the mysterious circle of the cupola extended so heavily above us that hope could not create daylight, and there was nothing but crepuscular phantoms of the sun that dissipated as soon as they were born.

"I want to see! Take me to the place where we can see!" repeated a little child to his mother with an unsuspected force of breath. That cry, which formulated the common desire, multiplied the anguish so much that some people proposed expelling the mother and child to a distant corridor in order that the voice would not reach us.

I thought I remarked that Pierre Pagès breast was emitting a confused light as he walked. I asked him for an explanation. He was carrying on him the emerald wrapped in animal hide in the middle of which I had seen a few red droplets trembling.

"It's the blood of Jesus Christ," he told me, "which was conserved in Caesarea and transported to Genoa. Faithful Albigensians received it as evidence of the truth of which they are the depositaries. When you sense your strength decreasing and death coming, fix your eyes on this stone, and your soul will be lightened."

I cannot evaluate the time that elapsed, or how life diminished in us. I know that many died quickly solely by virtue of the deprivation of the sun. In the beginning, we carried their bodies far away, into the depths of a tunnel, and we left a small lamp beside them. It burned for a while and then went out. But our strength must have diminished. We did not take the dead as far, and they were left without light.

A few perfecti were charged with the distribution of nourishment. At first they did it with economy and sagacity. Then a lassitude took possession of them and they ceased to supervise a just division. There were some who thought of hastening death and did not eat, others who wanted to obtain the same result by eating too much. There were some who grabbed everything they could and placed it in reserve in places that they were unable to find again.

We went to fetch water from the lake and brought it back in ewers. It was icy and had a calcareous taste. That water, drunk in abundance, was perhaps the cause of a poisoning of which some people died. The shores of the lake were impressive. It must have reposed on translucent rocks, because it gave off a vague green-tinted light, as if a subterranean planet were bathing it with its dead reverberation. People were afraid of being in proximity to those waters and only went down there in numbers, talking loudly.

A courageous hermit clinging to the asperities of the walls had succeeded in reaching the opposite shore of the lake. He was seen in the attitude of prayer that he had adopted in order to await death. He signaled to us with his hand from a distance, but he ceased making those signals. He was a man slightly above average height. His distant silhouette took on something grotesque and menacing. Some of my companions claimed that it was longer every time they saw it. That im-probable elongation of the dead hermit increased the terror that the lake inspired.

A languor took possession of those buried alive at Ornolac. Two or three young men who had departed through the dark tunnels came back and assured us that if one walked for a long time in a northerly direction one found a narrow corridor whose distant extremity was illuminated by daylight. They had taken reference points and offered to guide those who wanted to follow them. No one got up. Life had become impossible on earth for those who wanted to keep their faith. In addition, the lassitude was too great. It was better to die in the absence of effort. Everyone had abdicated the hope of see-ing the sun again.

It was also necessary to renounce the modest light of the oil. The little lamps went out, one after another. As the light of the last grew fainter I considered the faces of the creatures leaning over the heart of clay where the protective wick was expiring.

Among those faces I recognized that of Esclarmonde d'Alion. It had deteriorated, and was slightly puffy. The suf-ferings of an unhappy life had hardened the gaze and de-formed the oval of the features. The former suavity of the ex-pression still floated there, but as a mist floats that will soon vanish. The form in which I had thought I saw the incarnation of perfection had lost its purity; and that was the last image that it was given to me to contemplate before being enveloped by darkness.

There was a dull moan when the last glimmer of the lamp rose up toward the stalactites of the ceiling and illumi-nated the vastness of our tomb. I sat there, prey to a greater distress than the apprehension of death.

Later, someone called to me through the darkness. I groped my way, stumbling over recumbent bodies, touching stiff limbs and marble faces. The small number of us who were still alive had resolved to form a circle around Pierre Pagès and to die holding hands. I took my place in that chain and heard, as a kind of chant, the prayers that my companions were transmitting to one another. I did not understand their meaning, and they died upon my closed heart.

Later—perhaps an hour later, perhaps a day—in the semi-slumber in which I was plunged, images began to appear and to file before me. At first there were pleasant scenes that had made me smile in my childhood; then people that I had known, and must be somewhere, in Toulouse or elsewhere, and others who probably belonged to the realm of the dead that I was about to enter. But I could have pronounced the names of all of them, as if they bore them written on their foreheads. They were moving in a circle and their hub was the confused gleam that emerged from the clotted blood of Jesus Christ on Pierre Pagès' breast.

That light fascinated me. It became an increasingly phosphorescent green; it was miraculous, ineffable. And I marveled that a man as ordinary as I had been in my life, with passions so vulgar, had been chosen to save that divine blood and to carry it underground, into the midst of the elect of its faithful. I had always shown a very mediocre intelligence. I had never understood the elevated conversations that the wise men had in my presence, and now a belated regret came to me for having been so little developed in the spiritual order.

But at the same time as that regret, like a sort of recompense for having experienced it, it seemed to me that my comprehension increased and that an opaque veil placed over my intelligence had just torn. Words heard previously and not understood were suddenly revealed to me charged with meaning. Certain obscure theories unfurled with clarity. I was filled with gratitude for certain individuals because I understood their role. And at the moment when I thought of them, I saw them again. I saw the philosophers who had sought the meaning of the world. I saw Basilides, I saw Valentine, and all the gnostics with their luminous abstractions. The Alexandrians exposed the philosophy of divine emanations. I understood why Bartholomew had kept his teaching secret, why Mani had been flayed, why Hypatia had been stoned. I understood the meaning of the voyages of Nicetas and why he had thought that Toulouse ought to be the point on earth from which the truth would radiate. I loved Nicetas for that legitimate choice. I understood what I had never understood before: the Holy Spirit, the union of human being with the infinite intelligence.

I was plunged in an incomparable delight in having become intelligent after a long life of stupidity when an individual in a white robe appeared who dissipated all the other images. I recognized Pope Innocent, dead for a long time. He was marching at a rapid pace, his eyes fixed upon me, such as I had once seen him in the Church of Saint John. I experienced the same surprise mingled with terror. Suddenly, he bent down, and with an extraordinarily easy gesture, he stole Pierre Pagès' emerald.

"All relics belong to the Church," he said to me.

His visage was resplendent with intelligence and something that was above the cunning and skill of taking advantage of events. He agitated his tiara of symbolic peacock plumes and shoed me those plumes with his finger, saying: "I can see with all these eyes. I see all the heretics that appear on earth and I stifle them immediately."

As if to illustrate those words, to the right and the left of him, I saw once again Basilides, Valentine, Mani and Nicetas. They carried little lights in their hand. But Innocent blew on them and they all went out. Around me, the dead Albigensians got up, effortfully, and held out clay lamps in which the parsimoniously distributed oil, reanimated, spread a droplet of clarity. Protecting it with their hand, they tried to raise that flame. But Innocent shook his robe and that wind caused the lamps to die.

And I heard his severe voice addressed to me.

"Do you finally understand, Dalmas Rochemaure? I extinguish all spiritual enlightenment that does not come from the Church. No one has the right to think about God by himself. I even forbid the reading of the scriptures, because people can debate them while reading them. My power is one of fixation, of coagulation, of turning to stone. And woe betide those who rebel! I am always victorious, and I bury them alive in my subterranean cathedral."

Yes, I understood. Everything was clear. I was, indeed, in the monstrous cathedral of darkness. It was haunted by the phantoms of heretics, those who had disputed the dogma and attempted to light the lamp of their own truth. And, careless of those vague shades and of me, Pope Innocent now celebrated an inconceivable mass. The basilica was as vast as the planet. The altar, the extinct candles, and the symbols of the religion, were all carved in a species of obscure porphyry. Marmoreal cardinals with eyes of mica emerged from all the corridors. I saw the solid back of the pontiff, from which emanated his love for that which is hard, unchangeable and inert. He elevated in the darkness a mineral host.

But I was suddenly gripped by an appetite for aerial, subtle things devoid of weight. I had a desire to bathe in clouds, to flat in imponderable ethers. To my right and my left, the dead were holding my hand. I broke that funereal chain. I stood up silently, with a thousand precautions, in order not to interrupt the inanimate mass. My desire to escape the terrestrial condensation was so great that I launched myself forward to take light. I fell, to get up immediately.

Around me, I had the sensation that the walls of the grotto had solidified in elements denser than those the earth knew. The pillars of the stalactites shrank. I perceived petrifactions of rock in the cupola that were descending to crush me. Everything was in motion. Liquids were stirring in mud. The mud hardened. I felt currents of inferior attraction. Nature was going backwards. And in the accumulation of that cathedral of matter, Innocent III, arms open, was fused with the substance, having become a pope of stone.

But I fled, lightly. The spirit breathed within me and it lent me a power stranger than death. I recalled that the young men had mentioned a tunnel open to the solar air. It was in a northerly direction. I had no difficult heading in that direction. I had the habit of noting every evening, no matter where I was, the direction of Toulouse, That city of favorable attraction lay to the north in relation to the grotto of Ornolac, and it was toward her that I had turned my face when I had lain down to die.

I leapt over recumbent bodies and my first bounds took me as far as the lake. I went along the waters, remarking that the hermit had collapsed. That did not appear to me to be important. I was uplifted by a force that had its source in the utmost depths of my being. Everything that I had accomplished in my life had only been a game, a series of insignificant actions. I had devoted myself to my race, and had done nothing for it. It was now that my mission was about to commence.

I had just received a mysterious investment. A gift of speech possessed me, so great that I had a desire to orate while running. An unexpected intelligence had descended upon me, as if those who had disappeared had bequeathed me parcels of their thought. I was proud of that heritage, but it was necessary to make it fructify. I had to recount to people the story of my brothers, the story of the truth buried and resuscitated, and that message was as precious as the blood of Jesus Christ recovered in Caesarea.

I did not have the sentiment of walking for very long. At an intersection where the corridors became narrower a snake, slithering underfoot, indicated the right path to me. I glimpsed in the far distance the inimitable clarity that daylight produces.

But the corridor was obstructed by rubble. It was a fissure where the clay resisted, where there was a reflux of matter endowed with a sort of activity. It was necessary to lie face down. I crept like the snake; I hung on to stones; I struggled against the living molecules of the primordial substance, which conspired against me in order to stifle me.

Finally, I felt plants on my hands and bats fluttered around me. I had escaped the embrace of matter.

The Ariège was flowing at my feet. The sun was radiant in the infinite azure. I fell to my knees and extended my arms toward it. It seemed to me that I was the symbol of my race. The wicked had tried to bury it alive, but it would hold out its arms eternally toward the sun of the spirit.

Glory to the winged speech that resuscitates the dead and gives youth to the living in evoking the visages of their forefathers! Glory to the magical speech that, in launching the deeds of men through memories, causes them to fall into balances more impeccable than those of three judges seated in the Hell of the ancients! Glory to the archangelic speech that tears the shadows of forgetfulness!

Silence is the most powerful weapon of evil. Evil has passed over my homeland and has left behind silence, with its companion, fear. Half a century has sufficed for the men of the Midi who suffered in their flesh and in their belief to have almost forgotten the history of their dolor.

Leaning on a staff, with my cranium on which my hair is dead and my beard immeasurably elongated, I go from village to village. It is believed that I beg, but in reality, it is me who gives. I give memory.

By virtue of a singular curve I have rediscovered the folly of my youth. It is thanks to that that I can live. The priors of the abbeys have changed. There are new magistrates everywhere and seneschals arrived from France. No important man knows me. Who would think of imprisoning as a heretic an old man who dances without reason when he encounters a small child and prostrates himself in a grotesque fashion when an Inquisitor goes past? Every time I see a pot of milk outside a door beside a sleeping man, I empty the pot over the man. When I go past a bell I launch myself upon the rope in order to pull it and make it resonate.

I search in every village for the man who is susceptible of hearing me out. I do not address myself to those who have children. The state of father of a family renders a man hostile to anyone opposed to the social order and the established religion. Nor do I address myself to the most learned. I choose for preference a stupid man with wonderstruck eyes, for the stupid have more faith than the intelligent. I tell him how beautiful and flourishing the soil of the Midi was when the men of France had not yet come, how the literate were honored, how thought was reflected in matter, becoming beauty naturally. I recount the death of Béziers, that of Carcassonne and that of Toulouse; I show him by what mystery a city can perish and nevertheless retain its palaces and bell-towers. I explain to him that an injustice remains alive and gives birth incessantly to the effects of injustice, until it is, not repaired, material reparation being unimportant, but understood by those who have committed it and pardoned by those who have suffered it.

It is the pardon that is the most difficult to understand. The beauty of vengeance is so easily accessible! It seems to have a sort of courageous nobility. Vengeance is the first thought that occurs to the stupid man full of faith who listens to me. He immediately talks about killing. I have a great deal of difficulty explaining to him that one death is linked to another death with more force than a sin to his father, and that all deaths form a chain that will never end unless it is broken by some action as surprising as forgiveness. While speaking, I rebel myself, not understanding very well the forgiveness that Albigensian wisdom prescribes to me. But what does it matter if I understand the message poorly? It is sufficient that the message be transmitted.

I shall transmit it eternally. As Bertrand Martin announced to me, my imperfection will oblige me to return often to the earth to inhabit new human forms. In every one I shall recall the terrible forgotten history. All the books have been burned, all the texts of prayer, all the evidence of Albigensian thought. The calcined towers have been reconstructed, new columns added to the monuments, sculpted with caricatures of saints instead of Greek goddesses. But I shall not weary of tearing the silence of evil. I shall evoke the defunct towers, the old house of the Toulousan chapter, with its Capitouls with ivory wands, the cemetery of Saint Sernin where the dynasty of Raymond Saint-Gilles reposes. I shall make the dead live again, for as long as they are not in peace.

In order for them to rest in peace, forgetful of past evils, and for their animating force to be emitted with serenity by their bones, I shall resume my Toulousan body with every wave of incarnation. And my effort will be constant, my sincerity will be luminous and my love for my brethren ever-increasing.

May my future form become increasingly clairvoyant and sage, being molded of a more purified matter, like the wine of the hills of Pech David, which divest themselves with the years! May the sword of the word launch a brighter flash every time! May my words, animated by life, fall more perfect and more veridical! In order that I might gaze once, my heart liberated from all evil, upon Toulouse, without distinguishing the blood of the Albigensians in the red color of its bricks! In order that injustice might be effaced from the hearts of the unjust! In order that forgiveness might be understood by those who give it!

THE UNKNOWN MASTER OF THE ALBIGENSIANS

The Unknown Master

Was there an unknown master whose word gave birth to the Cathar verity?[39] Did an instructor bring the eternal verities from the Orient to the Albigensians and Toulousans? Was he the man that a peasant from Rouergue encountered on the side of the road one evening when he was returning to his farm: the man who had, according to what the peasant reported to the tribunal of the Inquisition, in addition to a strange persuasive power, a Moorish visage and a blue-tinted aura around his hair? Was he the Pierre, a disciple of Abelard, who began to teach in the twelfth century? Was he one of those anonymous preachers who stopped at the crossroads of towns in order to tell simple men that the poverty that constituted their misfortune was the pledge of an immense bliss after death?

Was the veritable initiate, the great propagator of Catharism, Nicetas, the Bulgar mystic who traversed the south of France several times, laid at Saint Felix de Caraman the foundations of a new church and confided to certain men he

---

[39] Author's note: "The origin of the word Cathar is obscure. Derived from the Greek, *cathari* would signify those who tend toward perfection and to be the name that the members of the sect originally gave themselves. Pronounce Cazari it might designate the inhabitants of Cazères, a small town near Toulouse that was a center of the heresy and, in the same fashion as the word Albigensians, was subsequently extended to all the heretics of the Midi."

recognized as pure in spirit the book in which the spiritual doctrine was summarized? Nothing is known about him except the great impression that his passage left and the extension of the Cathar movement that followed his departure for Sicily.[40]

The greatest masters remain hidden and one cannot discover with certainty at the origin of the Albigensians any sublime individual playing the role of initiator. Perhaps. by virtue of the expansive force of verity, heretical doctrines from the Orient traversed Europe to invade France and extended as far as Germany likes the pollen of a tree transported by the wind, which geminates everywhere that the soil is propitious.

In Greece the monk Niphon, a man full of wisdom and virtue, is condemned to lose his beard by the patriarch Oxites, which is a very mild and slightly singular torture. He is also imprisoned, but he is freed by another patriarch. His beard grows back and his ardent preaching stimulates disciples who set out to spread his doctrines through the world.

Near Turin, an exalted Contessa who lives in the Castello Monteforte forms a community with a mystic named Girard whose members try to live a perfect life. All men are equal

---

[40] Author's note: "It is worth noting that after Nicetas' sojourn in Sicily a group formed of the Faithful of Amour, whose doctrines had much in common with Catharism. Frederick II, a protector of heretics, was said to be an initiate. One of the masters of that group was Guido Cavalcanti, a friend and initiator of Dante." Magre's account of Nicetas is based on Napoléon Peyrat, who appears to have invented it, but Nicetas became sufficiently renowned in the wake of Peyrat's championship that he now has a highly fanciful Wikipedia entry that identifies him as the Bogomil Bishop of Constantinople. The second reference is to the Holy Roman Emperor and King of Sicily Frederick II (1194-1250), who was frequently at war with the papacy and was excommunicated four times, named as the Antichrist by Gregory IX.

there and property is held in common.[41] No use is made of meat, for it is not appropriate to take the life of animals. Wine is not drunk, because its vapors obscure presence of mind. Life is a kind of penitence and of one does not want to reenter new bodies eternally it is necessary to arrive at the detachment from all things that alone permits reintegration with God. One ought, but only when one has attained a certain degree of perfection, refrain from marriage and the act by which life is perpetuated.

The Archbishop of Milan directed an expedition against the Castello Monteforte. He captured the heretics and had them all burned. The historian of those facts notes that he would have preferred to let them live, without explaining why he did not.

And then, the words that Girard spoke before dying are true:

"It is not only me that the Holy Spirit visits. I have a great family on earth, which includes a great many men that it enlightens, on certain days and at certain hours, and to whom it gives illumination."

One sees that illumination manifest everywhere.

An unknown woman arrives in Orléans, and after listening to her, all the canons of the collegial Church of the Holy Cross become heretics. Two clerics, Etienne and Lisoi, are the theologians of a new church in which it is taught that Jehovah, the God of the Bible, was a bad God who, after having had the imprudence to create, only occupied himself with punishment, a church in which baptism is rejected and remission from sins is only obtained by the perfection of life.

On the orders of King Robert, those heretics are seized in a house in Orléans where they had gathered. They are taken to a church where Guarin, Bishop of Beauvais, interrogates them

---

[41] This assertion is derived from Carl Schmidt's *Histoire et doctrine de la secte des Cathares ou Albigeois* (1849) which is one of the sources listed in the bibliography of *Le Sang de Toulouse.*

while a pyre is being built for them outside the city. Queen Constance waits at the portal of the church for the condemned to emerge and uses the end of her cane to put out one of Etienne's eyes because he had been her confessor and had made her run the risk of hearing a false doctrine. The historian notes that one nun preferred to abjure her errors rather than perish on the pyre, without indicating the number of those who preferred to die rather than abjure.[42]

The spirit blew at hazard, touching the extravagant as well as the reasonable. One day, when the Breton Eon de Loudéac was listening to mass in a church he fell asleep. The priest who was officiating had a resounding voice and that voice woke Eon by pronouncing the line of the liturgy: *Per eum qui venturus est judicare vivos et mortuos*.[43] Eon thought that he had heard his name pronounced in the syllables *Per eum*. It was God who was inviting him to judge the living and the dead and to recognize the pure and the impure. He left the church precipitately and his mission commenced.

---

[42] The notorious trial of several clerics, including two named Stephen and Lisois, of which this is a garbled account, occurred in 1022, and seems to have been a politically-motivated stitch-up. Magre seems to have based his version on an account included in Gabriel Daniel's history of the church, published in 1755. Daniel expressed the opinion there that it was the residue of the "cult" in question that gave birth to the Albigensian heresy.

[43] "By him to whom it belongs to judge the living and the dead." Éon de l'Étoile, as he became known, castigated the wealth of the church but was accused by his enemies of accumulating a fortune by pillaging churches and abbeys between 1140 and 1148—accusations that had also been leveled at the next charismatic preacher he mentions, Tanchelm of Antwerp, a.k.a. Tanquelin, who flourished a generation earlier, before being murdered by a priest in 1115. After being captured and tortured, Eon died in captivity in 1150; most of his followers were burned.

He started to preach. He attached the wealth of prelates and the harshness of the powerful. All those who possessed anything were the dead. He, Eon, conferred life by the imposition of hands. He judged, as God had prescribed for him, by addressing himself to him directly. He exposed the Cathar doctrines that had reached him mysteriously and his sincerity, allied with a kind of folly full of delight, rendered him popular wherever he went. Disciples grouped around him and their number increased. Having traveled through Brittany Eon headed southwards. He camped with his troop on heaths and in forests. He organized a Church of priests in accord with God, who possessed nothing, and went almost naked, followed by an immense cohort of devotees.

The Archbishop of Reims succeeded in dispersing the menacing flood of those pure men. Pope Eugene III came to preside in person over the council that judged Eon, but to all interrogations Eon responded that he was the one who ought to judge the living and the dead, because of an order from God.

In Flanders it is Tanquelin who speaks to sinners like Jesus. He enthuses the populations of the North by proclaiming that the sacraments are unnecessary and that women ought to be held in common because of the vanity of the pleasure they procure. But success causes him to lose his reason. He allows himself to feast with his disciples. He recovers the taste for wealth that he began by proscribing. The former apostle of simplicity dress in the costume of a prince, surrounds his hair with gold bands, and is betrothed one day to the Virgin Mary before a statue.

But it is in the regions of Albi, Carcassonne and Toulouse that the mystical revolution takes place. There is Pons in the Périgord, Henri in Toulouse, Guillabert in Castres, but they are literate men and philosophers who explain the wisdom of Catharism in writing. The Roman dogma had closed its iron door and elevated the forever-immutable walls of its principles. With the Cathar philosophy, many minds welcomed the possibility of seeing the spiritual meaning of the

Scriptures opened by free research and the metaphysical questions that had always haunted the minds of the intelligent resolved. The others, those who did not read books but who saw and were indignant at the sumptuousness and immorality, listened to ascetics at crossroads because they had souls similar to those of the first Christians and they found in their words the pure doctrine of the master Jesus.

What the Church called "the abominable epidemic leprosy of the Midi" was manifest as an epidemic of disinterest, a communication of goodness, a chain of sacrifice.

A rich bourgeois of Carcassonne wakes up in the night because he can no longer abide the idea of his wealth, when there are so many poor people who have nothing. An interior voice tells him that it is necessary not to lose a minute and that he must obey it scrupulously. He loads his precious furniture on to his shoulders and transports it into the street so that anyone who is passing can take what he wishes. As the night is dark the lights two candles outside his door to facilitate the choice of the passers-by, and as the street is deserted he picks up a trumpet and blows it in order that people will know that his property is no longer his, that they will hasten to deprive him of it and that the rising sun will illuminate his redemptive poverty.

In Lavaur, a stammerer strives to speak and becomes eloquent by virtue of the desire to tell his brethren that there is not only a single life of dolor but that it is necessary to be reincarnated endlessly in new human bodies if one cannot escape that inexorable wheel by becoming perfect in one life.

In Montauban a man of Quérigut scandalizes the town by abandoning a wife whom he loves tenderly and leaving her to another man by whom she is loved. He retires to a hill in the vicinity haunted by wolves, nourishes himself on fruits and roots, sleeps joyfully on the bare ground, because, he says, one is educated by the companionship of wolves, and he more the body suffers, the more the soul is elevated, the more one triumphs over human amour and the more one gains divine amour.

Buddhist renunciation becomes a moral law, which spreads with astonishing rapidity. From Bordeaux to the limits of Provence, in bitter Languedoc, under the chestnut trees of the Albigensian region and the heaths of Lauragais, the roads are full of ascetics who travel barefoot and are avid to inform their brethren of what the spirit has revealed to them. And it is always the humble who are inspired. The spirit is driven away by the magnetism emitted by the gold of churches. On the other hand, it enters willingly into a hut isolated on a hill, the little house of an artisan backed up against the ramparts of a city or a placid monastery on the banks of the Ariège or the Garonne. In the path lined by poplars and the stone cloister where a hundred men with shaven heads circulate, it sometimes blows with a force so communicative that it causes the door to be closed, the garden and the chapel abandoned, and changes the copyists of manuscripts and illuminators of missals into the errant prophets of the new heresy.

At the end of the twelfth century the word of the Pelagians—Christ had nothing that I have not; I can divinize myself by virtue—appears essential to the majority of the people of the Midi. Increasingly estranged from the God of the churches—the God who has excessively gilded images on excessively magnificent pedestals; the God of rich prelates and pitiless lords—they honor the interior God whose light is all the more visible because it leads to a purer life more filled with love for their fellows.

The crime of disinterest and love! There cannot be any greater in the eyes of egotistical men. The hatred that moral superiority provokes is always pitiless. The Christian Church, with its priestly hierarchy, its fraternities of richly endowed monks, its powerful abbeys, cannot forgive the Cathars for setting an example of an asceticism greater than its own. There is no tragedy in history crueler that that of the almost complete annihilation of the southern race by the King of France and the Pope, by the Barons of the North and the Church of Jesus.[44]

---

[44] Author's note: "All the histories of France are histories of the unity of France and not the impartial history of that land. The idea of unity is used to oppose the most elementary justice. The war against the Albigensians seems to have served the future unity of France, so it only provokes an incomplete indignation among those who relate it. Everywhere, it is summarized hastily; people want to forget it; it is inconvenient. Even Michelet, the apostle of right, cannot prevent himself from letting show through the scorn that has always been inspired in the men of the North by 'the eaters of garlic, oil and figs.'"

The Crusade

In those days, the land that extended from the sea of Provence and the towers of Fréjus to the maritime pines of Guyenne was, after the savant Spain of the Arabs, the most civilized on earth. The light of Athens and Alexandria still illuminated it with a radiance that did not want to be extinguished. The thermes and the Imperial triumphal arches had not fallen into ruins in its cities and there was no hill on which the whiteness of a Roman statue did not stand between the vines and the olive groves. Aristotle and Plato, who had been translated into Latin in Granada, were the nourishment of the literate. The cities had municipal liberties unknown in the cities of the north. In Toulouse, the power of the Capitouls elected by the people tempered that of the Comtes. The immense literature of the troubadours flourished even in remote villages in the Pyrenees. And the Saracen invaders had left behind when they departed theorbos that came from Damascus and on which the music of the Orient still resonated.[45]

But the men of the south then seemed to the men of the north what they still seem today: a loquacious, vain and idle race. Their joyful levity was a lack of seriousness and their mysticism could only be heretical. Memories of paganism were more alive there than elsewhere, and liberty of thought was greater, translated in the satirical verses of poets, the proclamations of monastic preachers and in popular movements so audacious and disrespectful that Saint Bernard, after a triumphant tour of France, was jeered by the Toulousan crowd. The crusaders who came back from Constantinople and Palestine,

---

[45] The kind of lute known as a theorbo was a product of the sixteenth century; in the novel Magre substituted the much older darbuka, a kind of drum, as the symbolic transmitter of Oriental culture; the ancient Oriental stringed instrument ancestral to the European lute was the oud.

and who disembarked at Fréjus and Marseille in order to go home, could not help perceiving a strange resemblance between the bronzed and thin southerners with excessively prominent bones and overly long faces and the infidels that they had fought with such pious ardor and such a great thirst for pillage.

It is true that the seigneurs of Provence and Gascony had been their companions. But in traveling up the Rhône in order to reach the forests of Armorica or the heaths of Flanders, they saw excessively bright cities whose architecture differed from their own, cities that distantly resembled those they had just besieged and before which so many knights avoid for riches had fallen for an insufficient booty. They saw the detestable residues of the Saracen invasion. Not far from Saint-Tropez was the mass of the Château Fraxinet, from which the infidels had commanded the Mediterranean coast for such a long time, the fortifications of Narbonne with dentellate towers and the Abbey of Saint Donat near Grenoble and its octagonal towers on the heights, guardians of the passages and crossroads, which testified to the sojourn of the Moors arrived from Spain. The robes of the women were too colorful and had something Oriental and immodest about them. The language had a barbaric resonance. The cities contained a large number of Jews, and not only did they practice their religion freely but they maintained a prosperous commerce, professed letters and medicine, and were honored by an insouciant nobility.

So, when, under the orders of Pope Innocent III, the monks of Cîteaux spread out throughout France to preach the war of extermination against Raymond VI, Comte de Toulouse and against the entire Midi, they found the ground prepared. The operation was a thousand times more profitable than the one they had attempted by going overseas under the pretext of liberating the tomb of Christ. The same spiritual advantages were assured by the Church—the redemption of sins, and even eternal life—and the material advantages were immediate and known: the wealth of the châteaux, the beauty of the women and the abundance of the wine. It was to be a work blessed by God to invade that land as ocher as a land-scape of Palestine, to put to death the turbulent and rebellious men of Oc, and to possess their perverse spouses, like daughters of Satan, amid Moorish fabrics.

Three terrible figures dominated the great Albigensian massacre. For that massacre to be possible, it required simultaneously the extraordinary genius of violence, organization and hypocrisy incarnate in three men equally devoid of pity and perhaps equally sincere in their hatred of heresy and their love of the Church.

It was Pope Innocent III who wanted and decided the crusade with an obstinate determination. The assassination of the legate Pierre de Castelnau was only a pretext. All historians are unanimous in glorifying the genius of that Pope. The great men of history are those who do something, who exert a powerful will toward a goal. No one is preoccupied subsequently with whether the goal was sublime or vile, and success provides the measure of genius.

Scarcely has he been elected Pope than Innocent III begins to talk in all his speeches about "exterminating the impious." That is the dominating idea of his life and he has realized it fully. He thinks with a powerful conviction that any man who tries to formulate a personal opinion about God discordant with the dogma of the Church ought to be pitilessly burned.

He goes even further. He deems that the cadavers of heretics, whose heresy was undiscovered while they were alive, ought to be disinterred, in order to deprive them of a peace to which they have no right. "In 1206 he excommunicates an abbé of Faenza who refused to allow the remains of a heretic laid to rest in the Abbatial cemetery."[46] "It is necessary that the skillful investigation of Catholics," he says, reveals the

---

[46] Author's reference: "Luchaire, *Innocent III*." The reference is to a six-volume biography by Achille Luchaire (1846-1908), published in 1904-08, which is still in print. The second volume is devoted to the Albigensian crusade.

crime of those who pretend to lead a Christian life in order to lead opinion astray."

In a decree addressed to the bourgeois of Viterbe he asserts that "the divine sentence punishes the sons as well as the fathers, and canonical laws sanction that disposition."

He is very well informed about the purity of the mores of the Albigensians and Cathars, and yet he calls them "lascivious sects that, seething with libertine ardor, are nothing but slaves to the sensualities of the flesh." He exhorts his envoys unscrupulously to deceive the Comte de Toulouse by promises that are not kept because, for a cause as just as the destruction of a people, all means appear good to him.

He finds in Simon de Montfort the iron instrument that is to serve his apostolic fury.

Simon de Montfort is a noble and poor warrior. He is a sexagenarian when the crusade begins and deprived of the desire for women that might incite a leader to indulgence when he sees the massacre of a city's inhabitants.[47] His mores are austere. He cannot read and does not think of learning. Perhaps, in fact he could not; he is astonishingly myopic. When he fights he cannot see the enemy he strikes. His sword-thrusts are haphazard and he laughs noisily afterwards with his knights at having been able to kill blindly. His eyelids are perpetually closed and he is known as the eyeless knight. Perhaps a part of his cruelty comes from the fact that he never sees the expressions of despair on the faces of his victims.

He obeys the Pope's orders blindly. He is animated by an inconceivable cupidity, but he is prodigal with the clergy. He can see to further than his nose but he has the gift of seeing riches through walls and when he has traversed a city he knows which inhabitants he ought to accuse of heresy in order

---

[47] This estimate of Simon's age is highly dubious, although estimates by other historians that Simon was born circa 1175, and was therefore in his twenties when the crusade was launched, also seem a trifle dubious, given that his marriage to Alix de Montmorency took place in 1190.

to confiscate his wealth for himself. He ignores the chivalric honor of his era. It is as if he is possessed by a destructive fury, a cold passion for razing châteaux, slaughtering prisoners and spreading devastation. For the ten years that the war lasts no one can report a hint of pity on his part. He is devoured by hatred of the lands he conquers and of which he is named suzerain. He does not even like his own allies. When he lifts the siege of Toulouse he abandons the wounded that he could have taken with him.

He is pitiless toward the weak but prostrates himself before the powerful. He is the valet of bishops, the slave of the Pope. The lion is his heraldic emblem. Nothing expresses evil better than the face of that monstrous and ferocious feline. Simon de Montfort resembles a lion. He has the courage that the certainty of being the stronger gives him. He is the symbol of evil incarnate in man and that evil is exercised in a fashion all the more redoubtable because it has put over its face the mask of the Archangel Michael.[48]

A great saint lifts a cross behind the head of Montfort in order to make him a sort of aureole and permits him to draw from an ideal spring that exceptional power for the destruction of cities and slaughtering men. That saint is the Spaniard Dominic de Guzman. He is for the spiritual domain what Montfort is for stone and flesh. But the enemy he attacks has more resistance than the walls of Carcassonne or those of the Château Narbonnais. It is the hydra of heresy that he glimpses in souls. It is the thoughts of purity that rise higher than towers, the divine dreams lighter than clouds.

---

[48] Author's note: "Michelet, desirous of finding some virtue in him, speaks 'of his courage, his severe mores and his invariable belief in God.' He also recounts with admiration a story reported by all the chroniclers. Simon de Montfort once helped several of his soldiers to cross a river, at the peril of his life. And Achille Luchaire calls him 'a diplomat full of resources and a skillful organizer of conquered lands,'"

In order to arrive at his objectives, he imitates the Albigensian ascetics; he goes barefoot, asking for his bread, along the southern roads, avid to speak and to convert. His faith is as absolute, as disinterested, and as perfect as that of his enemies. But he does not know how to beg. He does it with pride, and desires to strike with his staff anyone who has filled his wallet generously but remains mute when he talks about the Holy Church. Those he encounters on his travels have heads as hard as his Spanish head, and in his rage in being unable to convert them he forges the plan for a terrible Order, an Order that will convert, a little later, by force.

The sound of his voice is hoarse and he has not lost his Spanish accent. On this side of the Pyrenees the voice is musical and the man of the south recognizes his race by a gleam in the dark eyes that the monk from Osna does not possess. He is incapable of winning hearts. He only finds those like his own among the Barons of the orth. Simon de Montfort never does anything without seeking his advice. The mystic follows the warrior. There is never a word of clemency. He never intervenes in favor of the wives or children of heretics who are massacred before his eyes and he assists in all the slaughter.

In any case, he regards the crusade as the just punishment of sins that do not merit pardon. At Prouille he says to the crowd: "Where the blessing is unwarranted, the rod is warranted. We will excite princes and prelates against you. The towers will be destroyed, the walls felled, and you will be reduced to servitude."

He has no scruple about installing himself in the dwellings that Montfort gives him, which are stolen from the seigneurs of the Midi, in order to make them monasteries of his Order. A globe of fire falling by night in a miraculous fashion on the domain of Prouille indicates to him that God wants to see the school of converters erected that will bear his name, and he does not hesitate to dispossess Guilem de Prouille of his hereditary property. His subsequent disciples glorify the saint and are proud of the miracle, without finding it implausible that God would send a globe of fire to designate the place of a rapine.

The significance of his life is indicated by another miracle that occurs in Toulouse in 1234, the day of his canonization. Bishop Raymond has just celebrated that canonization with a mass in the Dominican convent. As he goes to the refectory to complete the religious feast with a meal, someone comes to tell him that a heretic woman of Toulouse is dying in the Rue de l'Olmet and is waiting for the Cathar bishop to receive the consolamentum. Immediately, he sets forth with his soldiers. The dying woman's relatives cry: "Here comes the Bishop!" The deceived woman thinks that he is the Cathar bishop and delightedly affirms her faith before Raymond; she replies to all his questions, giving him the names of the believers she knows.

The Bishop and the Dominicans have her condemned rapidly and there is time to see her burned in the nearby square without the meal having suffered an exaggerated delay. But such a fortunate error and a pyre so rapidly lit are signs of the favor of Saint Dominic. The monks return to the refectory singing canticles and celebrate with an unaccustomed appetite the miracle that marks the saint's canonization.

Everyone knows, or ought to know, the history of the Albigensian crusade. I shall summarize rapidly.

Catharism had spread with an extraordinary rapidity through the south of France. It was the radiant cult of the pure spirit that took possession of souls and caused the greatest danger to the materialistic Church of the Pope. Innocent III understood that and dispatched several apostolic legates to the south of France. These legates went to Toulouse, which was the capital of Catharism.

They were determined to strike a resounding blow that would make the Midi weep and terrify it.

There as then in Toulouse, in the Rue du Taur, a venerable old man named Pierre Maurand, who had been Nicetas' host and who held nocturnal meetings in his house in which he preached the new religion. He was compared to Saint John because of is illuminated eyes. He was a Capitoul and his fortune was one of the largest in Toulouse. The legates summoned him solemnly before the people, interrogated him, convicted him of heresy and condemned him to death. The strength of a martyr was not in him. He was afraid of death, harsher for a rich old man than another, and he promised to reenter the Roman Church; but a difficult return was imposed upon him.

He had to go barefoot to the prison of the Church of Saint Sernin between the Bishop of Toulouse and one of the legates, who whipped him forcefully with rods. There he begged pardon on his knees, abjured, and heard himself condemned to have his châteaux destroyed and his property confiscated. He had to depart for the Holy Land and devote himself for three years to assisting the poor of Jerusalem. In addition, before his departure, in order that no inhabitant of Toulouse should be unaware of his abjuration, he had to visit all the churches in Toulouse, flagellating himself, for forty days.

Pierre Maurand, who was then eighty years old, whipped himself and wandered naked in the streets for the prescribed forty days. He departed, crossed the sea and reached the Orient. In Arabia he went to discuss mystical subjects with the Persian sufi Farid Uddin, sojourned in Tripoli, became acquainted with the philosopher Maimonides, spent three years in Jerusalem and was able to return to Toulouse, where his friends had not expected to see him again.

His career was not over. It was almost beginning. A symbol of the tenacious race of the people of Toulouse, he recommenced preaching secretly and five times, every three years, he was elected consul of the city by his compatriots, desirous of honoring in him the national resistance to the foreign Pope. People were so accustomed to the idea that death could not strike him that he was reputed for a long time to have taken refuge in the forests of Comminges, and a century afterwards the people of the outlying districts claimed to have seen Pierre Maurand making a tour of the ramparts of Toulouse in order to examine their solidity, leaning on his staff and standing very straight, as of old.[49]

The Midi had been terrified by the condemnation of Pierre Maurand. The Pope who dared to touch an old man of such perfect virtue could only be a Pope of evil. Catharism grew; the churches were abandoned. A new spiritual church devoid of monuments, devoid of hierarchy and devoid of ceremonial costumes was created secretly. The voice of the Spaniard Dominic resounded impotently on the parvis of cathedrals.

The legate Pierre de Castelnau departed for Rome discouraged. He was a former abbé of Maguelonne. On the day when he was promoted to the title of papal legate he had been hit by an arrow; by a sort of folly of pride he had his guards dress in red and he traveled clad in a strange ecclesiastical uniform brocaded with gold. He had just excommunicated Raymond VI, Comte de Toulouse. He had gathered the Capitouls, the notable citizens and the people had repeated in addressing the Comte the terms of a letter from Innocent III:

"Pestilential man! Tremble, perverse individual! You are like the crows that live on cadavers. Impious, cruel and barbaric tyrant, are you not confused by protecting heretics?"

He had threatened Toulouse with destruction, and had asserted that by his personal care people would soon be tiling the land where its towers and ramparts stood.

---

[49] Author's note: "Not being able to believe in that astonishing longevity, some historians have wrongly claimed that the consuls who succeeded one another after his voyage to Palestine were his sons." The original details of Magre's version of the story of Pierre Maurand are ultimately derived from Lamothe-Langon, who gives as a reference the non-existent Annals on which many of the more colorful details of his history are supposedly based, although it was certainly his own invention. In the actual *Annales de la ville de Toulouse* published in 1772 and in the history of the city published by Jean Raynal in 1759, only the name appears.

243

A young man whose name has not been retained had keenly resented the insult addressed to his city. He resolved to punish the proud legate. He followed him as far as the Rhône, which must have been easy because of the brightness of his escort's costumes. Near Fourques, as night fell, as Pierre de Castelnau was preparing to cross the river, the Toulousan launched himself upon him and struck him with a lance, a blow of which he died. He was able to escape to Beaucaire and to return to Toulouse, where no one punished him for his action.

Pope Innocent III "sang the song of the crusade" on learning of the death of his legate "the affliction of which he had for a long time in his hand and his jaw, and invoking Saint Jacques de Compostelle." He was not to stop there. He sent messages to all the Christian kings. All the Roman pulpits fulminated with maledictions. The crusade against the Albigensian heretics was preached with the promise of the rich cities of Languedoc to pillage. The nobility of France, at the head of German mercenaries, got ready to descend southwards via the Rhône, the Velay and the Agenois.

The Midi could have stood up to the North. If Raymond VI, the most powerful lord in the Occident after the King of France, had united his armies and had reached an understanding with the heroic Trencavel, Vicomte de Béziers, victory might have remained with him. But he was more possessed by the love of women than that of his people. While still an adolescent he had excited the wrath of his father because he was obstinate in deceiving him with his mistresses. He had just married, for the fifth time, the beautiful Eleonore of Aragon, who was sixteen years old and whose father had been obliged to keep her captive in a tower because he could not see a man without swooning. He desired to savor the possession of such an ardent creature in peace. Albigensian at heart, he was beginning to get used to excommunications, but he feared an open struggle with the Church. Perhaps he had the taste for self-betrayal that one encounters in certain men worn away by the love of pleasure. In any case, one cannot expect anything great from a man who has gummed-up eyes and excessively flabby and soft hands that are always slightly damp. He submitted to the Pope. He was sufficiently wretched to guide the crusader army in the plains of the south and fight against those who were placed under his protection.

The crusaders arrived at Béziers, where the rural populations fleeing the invaders had taken refuge. With those who had accumulated there, the city contained more than sixty thousand people. A large number had not participated in the heresy and were excellent Christians. It was there, in the name of the religion of Jesus, by virtue of the fanaticism of one of its most venerated Popes, that one of the most savage massacres in history took place. In fact, history, so skillfully adapted for children by official historians, scarcely mentions in passing the taking of Béziers and seems to consider it as an event devoid of importance

The gates were forced on the first days by an advance guard of *ribauds*.[50] That was the name given to bands of brigands that accompanied armies in order to profit from pillages and robbing the dead. The crusaders launched forth behind them. The day before, a council of chiefs and legatees had decided on the extermination of the entire population.

"But how shall we distinguish the Catholics from the Cathars?" asked one ingenuous Baron.

---

[50] This word, the equivalent of the English ribald, normally signifies debauchery, and both here and in *Le Sang de Toulouse* Magre seems to have taken it literally, substituting *truand*—the equivalent of the English truant—in the novel and referring to *le roi des truands*, the title attributed to the leader of a legendary Medieval association of thieves and professional beggars, rather than *le roi des ribauds*, which was the title given in jest to the commander of a special guard of soldiers created by Philippe II, King of France from 1180-1223, which was actually responsible or forcing the gate of Béziers.

And the Abbot of Cîteaux had replied, doubtless suppressing the smile that such candor inspired in him: "Kill them all, God will recognize his own."[51]

As the streets were full of corpses and the doors of the houses had been broken down, the people sought salvation by taking refuge in the churches. The crusaders set fire to them. Twelve thousand people perished in the Cathedral of Saint Nazaire, whose roof and three sides collapsed simultaneously. The entire city was delivered to the flames, and the Pope's soldiers encircled that immense pyre, putting to death those who attempted to emerge from it.

"May God receive the souls of the dead in his paradise!" said one pious chronicler, after having narrated the taking of Béziers.

The Abbot of Cîteaux, in the letter he wrote to the Pope to inform his of the event showed a singular modesty, estimating the number of the dead at scarcely twenty thousand.[52]

The young Vicomte Trencavel, who was twenty-five years old, as courageous as Roland and as handsome as the hero of a chivalric romance, was enclosed in his impregnable city of Carcassonne. His skin was the color of milk and he was astonishingly beardless, with blue eyes full of credulity, which gave him a child-like appearance. But he had a square cranium that was reminiscent of the towers that the Templars built. He was confident to the point of absurdity, and extremely violent. In Béziers, once, he had cruelly avenged his father, murdered

---

[51] The Latin "original" of this notorious comment, which Magre refrains from including in the novel, was credited to the Cistercian abbot Arnaud Amalric by his fellow Cistercian, Caesarius of Heisterbach, one of the chroniclers of the crusade, as an item of hearsay.

[52] Although Amalric did report in a letter to the pope that the entire population of Béziers had been slaughtered, estimating the death toll at 20,000, some later historians have doubted the assertion—although, as Magre points out, they might have had reasons of their own for trying to minimize the incident.

by the notable citizens of the city. Not only had he put to death the notables but, as he had heard that their wives had played a role in the affair, he forced them to marry their husbands' murderers, men of low condition. His subjects had seen that as fine evidence of energy.

It was in vain that the crusade battered the stone towers and thick walls of Carcassonne with the joists of machines, rains of arrows and the work of sappers. The valor of the besieged repelled the attacks. A sort of legend was attached to Trencavel's courage. The northern Barons sensed that the young man full of faith was like the heart of Languedoc and that it was necessary to tear out that heart in order to obtain victory. In order to doom him they made use of his divine credulity. Under the safeguard of Christ, so authentically represented by the Roman legates, he was asked to come unarmed to the crusaders' camp in order to discuss the conditions of a possible peace.

The confident hero, incapable of suspecting an unprecedented treason, emerged from the city in spite of the anxiety of his companions in arms, who begged him to remain. Scarcely had he arrived at the tents where the elite of the French nobility were than he was seized and kept prisoner.

He was awaited all day on the ramparts. When night fell, the defenders of Carcassonne understood that they would never see their leader again. Then moans burst forth; they propagated from tower to tower, from street to street, and a funereal plaint rose into the night everywhere, the despair of the city deprived of the heroic leader who incarnated its life.

That was the fifteenth of August, the day of the festival of the Virgin, protectress of the Crusade. The night was extraordinarily bright. The besiegers thought they saw from afar the silhouettes of the archers keeping watch become lees numerous on the ramparts and then disappear. The nocturnal plaint diminished and died away, and an impressive silence descended upon desperate Carcassonne. The assault was to commence at daybreak. The fortress seemed dead, like an im-

mense stone tomb. Knights and soldiers advanced with pre-
caution behind their shields, believing it to be a trap.

They forced one of the silent gates and when it had fallen
they advanced at a slow pace, chilled with amazement, into a
deserted, mute city like a city of the *Thousand-and-One
Nights* struck by an enchantment. Through open windows they
could see the interiors of houses filled with abandoned riches.
At the crossroads, dogs were howling mortally. There were
empty suits of armor on the ground and horses were running
hither and yon. It was thought at first to be a miracle, and then
the truth was discovered.

The old baron Pierre de Cabaret, a friend of Trencavel,
had hollowed out a subterranean tunnel several years before,
going from the keep of Carcassonne to his Château de
Cabardez in the Black Mountains. The warriors, the consuls
and the entire population had fled during the night. The crusaders were only able to find, gone to ground in cellars, four
or five hundred forgotten Cathars for their gibbets and pyres,
and thought that very few.[53]

The Midi was virtually vanquished. The victors gave it
by election to Simon de Montfort, who stayed there to finish
extinguishing the heresy with his troops from the Low Countries and Germany.

The days after that election it was published that
Trencavel, Vicomte de Béziers, had died of disease in the
prison where he was locked. It was known throughout Christendom that Montfort had had the man he had despoiled murdered, but a murder was very little when it as a matter of heresy.

And the heresy was tenacious. It was necessary to take
the châteaux one by one, recommencing siege after siege. At

---

[53] The earliest easily-traceable reference to the improbable
story of this tunnel is in Jean Benoist's *Histoire des Albigeois
et des Vaudois* (1691), from which numerous subsequent accounts, including Napoléon Peyrat's—where Magre presumably found it—appear to have copied it.

Minerve, near Narbonne, at Limoux, not from the mountain of ruins and bones that was the unfortunate city of Béziers, at Pamiers and Mirepoix, Simon de Montfort raised scaffolds everywhere and burned heretics. The monks of the abbeys and the ecclesiastical functionaries, traitors to their homeland, summoned the man from the north, sent by the Pope, while the Albigensians retreated toward the forests of the Pyrenees. The tireless army of crusaders went along the Ariège and then the Garonne, drew back toward the Aude and recommenced a new massacre of the entire population of Lavaur, whose beautiful chatelaine, Dame Geralda, was thrown alive into a well in order that her death might be slow and worthy of the grandeur of her impiety.

"We exterminated them with an immense joy," said the pious Pierre de Vaux de Cernay, the chronicler of the crusade. Elsewhere he claimed that the Albigensians "precipitated themselves into the pyres, so perverse and obstinate in their malice were they."

One prey, however, and perhaps the most desirable, escaped Montfort's fury. That was the Château de Cabardez, with its three towers, situated in the foothills of the Black Mountains, where Pierre de Cabaret and the defenders of Carcassonne had taken refuge. Pierre de Cabaret was married to Brunissande, the most beautiful chatelaine of Languedoc, whose beauty had been rendered widely celebrated by the troubadours. He had a daughter of an earlier marriage, the blonde Nova, and a goddaughter, the brunette Stephania de Sardaigne, who were no less illustrious than Brunissande for the beauty of the body and the amorous sentimentality of the soul.

Montfort's knights dreamed of the three young women contained in the château with three towers. What a recompense for the victors! They were an aliment for heir lustful imaginations during the long evenings of the siege before their tents. There must have been quarrels, choices and divisions. Brunissande was reputed to have refused herself to her husband by virtue of the mystical chastity of a Cathar perfectus, and that was one attraction more. There was also an attraction in the virginal youth of Nova, and the savage warriors, habituated to rapes in the cities they had just captured, must have pictured their entry into the Château de Cabardez as the entry to a paradise of carnal pleasure.

But the paradise of stone that dominated the rocks and the trees remained closed behind its portcullises and drawbridges. The crusaders were obliged to lift the siege and return in long columns toward the fields of Carcassonne, without having glimpsed more than a white robe on a rampart, or a helmet of hair between helmets of steel, leaving behind them the three inviolate young women, like the symbol of the pure beauty of the spirit that, for the vulgar man, remains eternally inaccessible.

The Comte de Toulouse had implored the King of France, the King of England and the Emperor of Germany in vain, and had gone in vain to prostrate himself, weeping, at the feet of the Pope. He had acquired in the company of women an astonishing facility in weeping and falling to his knees. He finally understood that no baseness would save him. Heresy was only a pretext; it was his lands and his cities that they wanted. He finally decided to resist. It was too late. His Barons were decimated. He had delivered the best of his partisans to Montfort himself.

In Toulouse, Bishop Foulque had put to death ten thousand people accused of heresy. He was a former troubadour, an adventurer devoid of belief, who had found it sage on growing old to embrace the career in which one became rich most rapidly. He was so devoured by envy that it was said that he was even jealous of Christ when he saw an altar overloaded with gold. He left Toulouse, excommunicating for the tenth time in a few years the city, its Comte, its Capitouls and its people.

Toulouse was not taken by Simon de Montfort, thanks to the heroism of its inhabitants. Twice, the army of crusaders broke before its ramparts. "O Toulouse! O nest of heretics! O tabernacle of thieves!" cried Pierre de Vaux de Cernay, indignant at that resistance of a city that did not want to die. But the crusaders quit the impregnable city to go and ravage Albi, Quercy, Lauragais and the comté de Foix. Time passed. Reinforcements were still arriving from the north. Once, it was ten thousand armed pilgrims from Germany, another time it was the Comte de Bar and his battle-hardened troops. From Hautpout in the Black Mountains, to Lavelanet in the Ariège, Simon de Montfort, traveled untiringly, followed by a cortege of bishops and prelates, destroying amorously, patiently and methodically, as if they were obedient to a mysterious ideal of death.

A great battle takes place at Muret, where the King of Aragon has come with an immense army to defend the Comte de Toulouse. The Midi wakes up and hopes. The King of Aragon is a great captain and victory seems assured. But Montfort wins again. He is protected by the god of armies. He always wins the material conflict, for he is a man of the matter that, at this time and in this place, must vanquish the spirit.

Finally, under the walls of Toulouse, which he besieges again and where the old men, the women and even the children have been armed, the invincible falls. A stone launched by a catapult manipulated by a young woman shatters the skull of the soldier of iron, the man devoid of pity. A painting in a room in the Capitol of Toulouse represents her launching the liberating stone. Her face, whose anonymity destiny wanted to maintain, cannot be seen, but one can sense in the bracing of the arm and the neck, the sheaf of plaited hair and the movement of the upper body, the qualities of courage, mysticism and the independence of the southern race so unjustly crushed in the thirteenth century.

The body of Simon de Montfort was piously brought back by his son and brother through the region of Toulouse and Albi, the Black Mountains and Quercy. From abbey to abbey and church to church the funeral cortege traveled through silent villages on roads from which the peasants fled on recognizing the banner with the accursed arms. Sometimes, in a defile, a stone thrown from a height fell on the coffin like

251

the testimony of popular malediction. In the evening, in the monasteries where the dead man was welcomed, candles were lit and funeral hymns sung. But all around, in the houses, the lights were extinguished.

Finally, Simon de Montfort left the land of which he had been the scourge. The terrible paladin of the Pope was taken to Montfort d'Amaury, to the cloister of High Heather, and the symbolic lion, the beast that crawls and devours, was sculpted on his sepulcher, with the inscription: *Glorious Martyr of Jesus Christ*.

Six centuries later, the Revolution broke the sarcophagus and the sculpted lion in order that the wind could carry the dust away all the way to the Pyrenees.

The Two Esclarmondes

The movements of the spirit are almost always incarnate in the beauty of a woman, who becomes its living statue. The heroine of the Midi, the symbolic chatelaine of the Pyrenean mountain where the last refuge took refuge and died, was named Esclarmonde. And as the resistance was long and staged over half a century, as the death was slow, there were two Esclarmondes. There was Esclarmonde de Foix the chaste, she of the châteaux. who became a sort of female pope of Catharism, and there was Esclarmonde d'Alion the amorous bastard, she of the forests, of the mountain of Capsir, who wandered with the hunted Albigensians, fighting like a man, loved like a woman, and died with those she loved.[54]

Esclarmonde de Foix had made a gift of herself to Cathar purity as soon as she reached adolescence. She had worm to consecrate herself to the spirit. That was in her twelfth year. In the château of her father, Roger Bernard de Foix, she had seen the Bulgar Nicetas, who was wandering through the Midi bringing the teaching of the Orient. She had not had the possibility of hearing him. He had only darted one glance at her, and on perceiving her he had made a slight sign with his hand. Had he recognized in the silent child someone who was made to understand and defend the truth? Esclarmonde was to live with the flame of the gaze that Nicetas sent her.

But before being the apostle, the organizer and the soul of Catharism, a long martyrdom was reserved for her. Her father made use of his daughters as a commercial means of aggrandizing his seigneurial house. He gave Esclarmonde to Jordan, Vicomte de Gimoez, a brutal warrior who laughed at

---

[54] The idea that Esclarmonde de Foix was an Albigensian, and the entire substance of her legend as reported and further embellished here, appears to have been invented by Napoléon Peyrat.

the new mysticism and took possession of the platonic adolescent in order that she would be the obedient instrument of his pleasures after his hunting and horse races. Esclarmonde submitted to the quotidian rape that sanctifies for men the sacrament of marriage, and it was only on the death of her husband that she commenced an apostolate that was to last thirty years. She converted to Catharism in an ostentatious fashion, in order to set an example to her people. She allied all the seigneurs of the Pyrenees against the authority of Roman pontiffs and the local tyranny of abbeys. She spoke, she applied the religion of the Spirit and she became the learned Esclarmonde.

Legend took possession of her and people who did not know her created her with the richness of the soul, for it is necessary that a high ideal taken a physical form, and becomes alive and active among humans. The Albigensian martyrs of Avignonnet, Lavaur and Pamiers, when they mounted the pyre and felt the flames lick their feet, were glad to think that somewhere, in a distant fortress of the Pyrenees, on the tower of Montségur, in the midst of the clouds, there was a beautiful chatelaine clad in white, who was raising her arms toward the sun and who incarnated the perfect purity of their faith.

Glimpsing the future and the defeat of the Midi, the sage Esclarmonde had the impregnable château of Montségur built as a supreme refuge of the Cathars in flight, between Lavelanet and Quillan, above valleys of stone, silver torrents and mountains of firs. It was toward Montségur that all those who did not want to deny their faith, those who escaped the massacres of the pious soldiers of the Church, the denunciations of monks and the subterranean prisons of the Inquisition made their way by night by roundabout paths.

For the stone of justice that had broken the skull of Montfort had only rendered Toulouse to its Capitouls and it seigneur for a while. The day of the municipal liberty of the cities of the south was over. The Kings of France stole the Languedoc from the Comtes de Toulouse; the Pope's bishops returned on their caparisoned horses with their corteges of Roman prelates to their fortified bishoprics. The tribunal of the Inquisition, created expressly to discover hidden heresy and composed of pitiless Dominicans, began functioning in all the cities.

The history becomes incredible, so terrible is it, and the forgetfulness into which it has fallen is inexplicable. The fearful great seigneurs returned to Catholicism, to the religion that does not pardon the slightest parcel of difference with the intangible dogma, and delivered their subjects to the church themselves.

The Comte de Toulouse goes to flagellate himself at Note Dame to demonstrate his fidelity to the Church and the King. But that is not enough. Cardinal de Saint-Ange, the legate of Rome and the lover of Queen Blanche of Castille, drags him behind him to Toulouse in order that he can bow down at his feet in a ceremony of humiliation on the parvis of the Toulousan cathedral. At the same time he brings a legion of professors in order to reorganize the excessively independent university and inform the Toulousans of the theocratic law, the harsh Roman theology and the bitter Picard and Beauceron patois then spoken in Paris instead of the bright language of the troubadours.[55] It was not enough to take the fields of maize, the blue vines and the beautiful houses of Saracen architecture; it was necessary to modify the brains of those rebellious people, to conform their thoughts to the icy bronze of Roman thought.

In Toulouse, the profane symbols that ornamented the facades of dwellings were destroyed by hammer blows and on the site of the house where Saint Dominic had resided, facing the Château Narbonnais, the palace of the Inquisition was built. A miraculous fig-tree that the saint had planted redoubled the ardor of the Inquisitors by its presence. The portal of the palace still exists; on its fronton a bucolic sculptor, doubtless arrived from Italy in the wake of the legates traced in

---

[55] Author's reference: "Napoléon Peyrat, *Histoire des Albigeois*."

stone gracious bouquets of lilies and a dove carrying an olive branch.

For having eaten the fruit of the sanctified fig-tree the Inquisitors of Toulouse work marvels. The existing prisons are insufficient and it is necessary to undertake major works to construct new ones in haste in every quarter. On the Place du Peyrou and the Place d'Arnaud Bernard gibbets are set up every day, and as the executioners are ignorant and too few in number more are brought from Paris. Sometimes a citizen disappears and is never seen again; he has been immured. People are imprisoned on the slightest suspicion of heresy. All denunciations, even those that are baseless, are treated as veritable. The clergy make use of that means to confiscate the property of the richest citizens.

There is no longer any security in any city in the south. Denunciation lurks behind every door. It is the moment when torture is introduced into the procedure as a legal means to obtain confessions. That innovation causes a breath of fear to pass over the peaceful people of the Languedoc, but the result is extraordinary. Confessions multiply in proportions that surpass the hopes of the judges. Everyone is a heretic. It is sufficient to have listened once in the previous thirty years to a sermon by an Albigensian preacher to be arrested and obliged, if necessary by torture, to search the depths of your memory for the names of the people who listened to the sermon with you thirty years ago.

Human cowardice multiplies treasons and denunciations. An Albigensian perfectus is seen to denounce all those who have sheltered him during his flight between Toulouse and Marseille, and the stages have been numerous and the hosts have been welcoming and filled with love. Men traverse cities on their knees in order to beg forgiveness in front of the house of the Inquisition for a heresy to which they have never adhered, in order to put an end to the terror of being suspected. The dead can be suspected and judged. They are solemnly disinterred and the property of their children and grandchildren, even if they are good Catholics, is confiscated because they have no right to anything acquired by a heretic.

The time when the greatest number of pyres blaze and the greatest number of the immured disappear is when the marriage of Saint Louis, the model of kings, is celebrated in Paris. Terror puts an end to commercial transactions, marriages and relationships of amity. In Albi and Castelnaudary people are imprisoned because their faces are too pale and are suspected in consequence of practicing the Cathar asceticism that proscribes wine and meat. In order to avoid suspicion some no longer go out without make-up, and feign drunkenness.

And as the bourgeois of cities sent a complaint to the Pope in 1245, the bishops of the Languedoc, in order to counterbalance the effect of the complaint or by virtue of a ferocious humor, complained in their turn about the extreme indulgence of the Inquisitors, whose weakness, they said, was aggravating the heresy.

Despair took possession of souls. For those who had conserved the Albigensian faith in the depths of their hearts, there was nothing more to expect from humans. Henceforth, there was only hope in God. But God was about to betray the purest and most disinterested of those who turned to him.

Montségur

In the clouds of the mountains of the Ariège, like a celestial fortress, the Château de Montségur, built with care by the sage Esclarmonde de Foix, remained impregnable to the armies of the Pope and the King. The treasure of Catharism, its bishops and its perfecti, had taken refuge there. In the distance, in the mountains, seigneurs and peasants who had remained faithful to the pure doctrine had gathered in armed bands and lived nomadically with the complicity of the peasants. The villages had been rallied to Catholicism by fear, but every inhabitant knew in the secrecy of his heart that the truth was up above, with the last of its faithful, and in the depths of grottoes, along the emerald-colored torrents and on the slopes where the snows commenced.

Two generations had passed and Catharism still resisted. It clung on his habitations suspended above precipices, hid in profound forests, lit fires by night on the heights like fraternal lights responding to the fires of the towers of Montségur. There were epic battles in the mountains, unknown heroisms, martyrs whose names will never be known.

It is the time when the solitary Saurimonde, the inspired sibyl of the region of Mazamet, walks naked as in the days of the world's birth, because her soul is as bright as he sun she invokes. It is the time when, at Hautpoul, the highest peak, Guilhem d'Airens cures the wounds of Cathars merely by extending his hand over them, which has magical virtues.

It is the time when Guilhabert de Castres, the saint, transports himself with inexplicable velocity to give the consolamentum, the extreme unction of the Cathar religion. He appears everywhere when a devotee of the faith of the spirit is about to die. Sometimes dressed as a beggar, sometimes as a pilgrim, he looms up on the threshold of grottoes or his footsteps resonate in the streets of cities as the death-throes begin, in spite of the Inquisitorial guards and the watchmen at the gates of ramparts. When the pyres blaze it is sufficient for the burned individual to glimpse, lost in the crowd, a perfectus making the mysterious sign of salvation for him to die consoled and without suffering. For the love exchanged between the two saves the soul and projects it into its veritable abode. And the ungraspable Guilhabert de Castres is always before the pyres to make the sign and give the love.

He died very old and the greatest miracle was that he escaped the pyre himself. Death, which was for him only the road that leads to a better estate, attained him at Montségur and his bones were laid in crypts so profound that they could never be discovered, and the Inquisitors were unable to disinter them in order to throw the heretic ashes to the wind.

Next to him reposed Esclarmonde de Foix. She had become a legendary enchantress, a female pope with silver hair. Her face had as many wrinkles as Catharism had martyrs. Her body was so desiccated that it seemed incorruptible. She resembled the divine wisdom that only traverses the human envelope in order to purify itself and raise itself in the scale of divine wisdoms.

It is then that the second Esclarmonde, the niece of the first, Esclarmonde d'Alion the bastard, appears. She was the daughter of Roger Ramon. One evening, Roger Ramon, who was a bold hunter, became lost in the Ariégeois valleys pursuing a wolf. He reached the wolf, cut of its head, and as he was seeking shelter or the night he perceived the door of an abbey of nuns hidden in the fig-trees, myrtles and wild vines. He nailed the head of the wolf to the door, went in, supped, and as the abbess was young, noble and beautiful he spent the night with her. In the morning, he left The abbess gave birth to twins, Loup de Foix, thus named because of his father's exploit on the eve of his conception, and Esclarmonde, who was to become by her brother's side the heroine of the last Albigensians.

Around Montségur, at So, Tarascon and Lavelanet, the supreme effort of the resistance is groped. Esclarmonde is twenty years old. Before dying, her father married her to Bernard d'Alion, the seigneur of a petty Pyrenean principality. She makes her château a refuge of Cathars and orders the drawbridge to be raised when royal troops pass by. Her brother, Loup, commands the insurgents in the mountains; she goes to join him on horseback, clad in a man's armor. She fights in the defiles; she supplies food to besieged Montségur; she lights the nocturnal signals that enable the Albigensian groups to communicate with one another; with shepherds she pushes the rocks that crush the King's soldiers in the depths of gorges. More than one knight dreams, in the evening, of the face of that ardent young woman, her eyes the color of a torrent, and, as she is overflowing with passion, she gives herself to more than one in the shade of firs, in the midst of Pyrenean ferns, beside her horse, beside her sword.

Montségur supported on its squat escarpments, above its stages of granite, with its tunnels opening into precipices and its subterranean reserves, which hides within its walls the sepulchers of saints, whose towers are bristling with the spears of its defenders, is still holding out against the King, against the Pope, against the malediction of the Christian world.

Ramon de Perella is in command there. The Barons expelled from their feudal dwellings, the Lantars, the Belissens and the Caramans have come with their men-at-arms. Wheat has been accumulated there for years, alongside stables for the horses and cells where hermits pray. Corridors plunge into the earth and spiral stairways piece the immense fortified rock. As in Toulouse, women share in the defense, for Montségur is the last refuge of the perfecti.

A new crusade has been decided and an army under the Seneschal of Carcassonne and the Bishops of Albi and Narbonne circles all the defiles, blockading all the Ariègeois valleys. Machines of war of an astonishing force have been brought to batter the towers. Reinforcements arrive every day. Lavelanet has become a camp for carts and Tarascon shelters the spare ballistas. And the siege lasts for two years, with daily combats.

Help also comes to the besieged, for the Comte de Tou-louse and the Comte de Foix, terrorized by the Church, protect the Albigensians secretly. Once, it is the son of the poet Pierre Vidal, a poet himself, who succeeds in piercing the lines and throwing himself into Montségur to announce good news. On a road by night he has crossed the path of a phantom paladin on horseback with a crimson cloak and sapphire gloves, which is a certain presage of the victory of the believers. Scarcely has he brought the hope than he dies in combat. Another time, it is Esclarmonde who erupts into the place with a little troop of armed men. She soon leaves again, taking responsibility for taking away a few Cathars.

But the heroes fall one by one. There are no more than a few hundred left. From the depths of the gorge of the Ers or the vale of the Abès, the royal army can count their broken suits of armor, still glinting, on the high stone barbicans, min-gled with the white robes of perfecti. They have been told to wait. A great movement is in preparation. The south is about to rise. The Comte de Toulouse will cease to flagellate himself and kiss the Pope's feet. His armies are advancing toward Montségur. Another seven days, the messengers say. And they murmur on the towers: "White Doves, can you not see the host of Toulouse coming?"

The host of Toulouse never comes. Driven by a presen-timent, Ramon de Perella has sent away the Cathar treasure by night, with a few men to guide it and hide it in the grotto of Ornolhac. Shepherds betray Montségur and reveal the narrow path by which the treasure had escaped. The Seneschal of Car-cassonne's soldiers penetrate the tower of the Ers under cover of darkness and force the posterns. The general massacre is only halted by the promise of surrender, the following morn-ing. The heroic Albigensians have one night to bid one another adieu, and when the sun appears over the mountains of Belesta, they deliver themselves to the power of the Catholic bishops. Only Pierre Roger de Mirepoix, who commands the combatants, obtains permission to leave with his arms and his soldiers.

All the others are chained by the neck and led to a vast platform overlooking the Ers. A formidable pyre is constructed with oaks and beeches from the forest. The Bishop of Albi, out of the goodness of his soul, promises eternal prison to those who abjure. No one accepts. Priests and soldiers intone canticles and precipitate the three hundred perfecti of Montségur into the flames.

The flame rises so red into the sky, the smoke rises so high and to straight, that the people of the Toulousain, the Lauragais and the Albigeois who look in the direction of the Ariège with anxious hearts know by that flaming sign of death that their heroic brethren have perished and that the last hope of the Midi is extinct.

The Château de Montségur was destroyed. Apart from its calcined stones, there was nothing but the name of Esclarmonde, which survived in the popular soul and in legend Esclarmonde de Foix the chaste and Esclarmonde d'Alion the amorous were confounded in a single creature who was Esclarmonde de Montségur. For a long time the people of the villages claimed to see her wandering in the cloudy mists that rise in the evenings from the steep banks of the Ers.

After six centuries she still stands on the vestiges of the tower that faces north. She will always stand there. Her hand will be seen above the clouds. She makes a sign that she has come back and that no ecclesiastical tyranny and no dogmatic wrath can get rid of her. For where the spirit has breathed, it remains. Esclarmonde has come back to the heart of the Pyrenean mountains to affirm that humans ought to reach for spiritual perfection and that, in order to find the way that leads there, one can give one's life joyfully.

The Grotto of Ornolhac

In the region of Sabartez, in the place where the forests of Serralongue expire, there was a cavern famous for its depth and its labyrinthine tunnels. It opened half way up the mountain above escarpments overlooking the Ariège, at the spot where the springs of Ussat fall in the icy waters of that river. The druids had celebrated their mysteries there. The Saracens had stopped to sleep there. The Albigensians were to sleep there in their turn.

Those who still remained were hunted in the mountains like wild beasts. In the same way that there were later to be lieutenants of wolf-hunting, there were officers appointed to the pursuit of Cathars, who had packs of dogs at their disposal trained to track them down. The fugitives lived amid the brushwood of the plain or the stones of the heights. They lived in huts that it was necessary to quit in haste when the hunters were announced. They sometimes lived in the trees like monkeys.

A large number of these accursed wanderers retreated toward the grotto of Ornolhac, where it was known that the Cathar treasure was hidden. A new center was constituted there, a new Montségur, but it was as profoundly hidden underground as the other had been resplendent in the sky.[56]

The untiring Inquisition could not lave that refuge of the wretched in peace in its darkness. In accord with the Seigneur

---

[56] The legend of the grotto of Ornolhac as a "new Montségur" was invented by Napoléon Peyrat. Magre's comments are a paraphrase of his. Two years after the publication of *Magiciens et illuminés*, however, the cave was visited by the unorthodox German historian Otto Rahn, subsequently an officer in the SS, whose writings helped to repopularize the legend.

de Castelverdun, to whom the land belonged, it sent troops commanded by the Seneschal of Toulouse.

Legend relates that when those troops advanced, either out of heroism in order to share the fate of a young man she loved, Esclarmonde d'Alion raced along the Ariège on horseback and arrived at the sheer path leading to the grotto, abandoned hr mount, climbed the stone zigzags on foot and went to join those of her faith.

The grotto had two entrances, which were surrounded, but the Albigensians hoisted themselves up on ladders, which they withdrew to a deeper, more inaccessible grotto. It seemed to the Seneschal of Toulouse that it was impractical to attempt an assault. He thought it wiser and perhaps more humane to exchange for the Albigensians torture and the pyre for a silent death in the darkness. He had all the entrances to the cavern solidly walled up. He camped for some time on the banks of the Ariège. He waited. He listened to see whether any sound was reaching the surface from the interior of the granite, and then he quit the mountain, which had become a tomb.

The Albigensians must have lived for quite a long time in the darkness, for they had stored grain in the grotto. Several bishops and a large number of perfecti were among them. In the silence of the night the bishops must have pronounced the words announcing the grace obtained by imminent death and deliverance of the spirit. They must have extended their hands to make the invisible gesture of the consolamentum over prostrated heads. And perhaps, for the embracing Albigensians, for the groups that said adieu in the darkness, for Esclarmonde herself, clinging to her lover of flesh, a magnificent light made the vault resplendent with a thousand extinct crystals, the petrified sweat of the rock and the age-old stalactites. Perhaps, by the miracle of the love that united them so closely, they were projected together, as it is taught in their religion, toward the abode where matter no longer has weight, water fluidity and fire heat, and where one enjoys the bliss of endless love.

The Ariégois mountain has kept the secret of the mass without candles, the death without graves and shrouds. The book of Nicetas conserved in the treasure, the kisses of lovers, and the bishops' gestures of benediction, must have been mineralized, mummified by the absence of air. The last Albigensians, immobile, clad in stone, are still celebrating their supreme ceremony in the middle of frozen ferns and dead mica, in a basilica of darkness.

The Doctrine of the Spirit

What, then, was the spiritual poison, the mortal error of souls against which the indignant Occident rose up and caused so much blood to flow? The books in which the ancient verities were enunciated, where the tradition of the spirit had its written bases, were carefully destroyed, to the last page, and we can only recover Cathar thought in the bitter refutations, full of imprecations and threats, of the monks of the time.

The mysterious Nicetas, before departing again for the Orient, to disappear from the society to which he had brought the word, is reputed to have left a written monument of his doctrine. The manuscript must have been conserved with the Cathar treasure in the Château de Montségur and must now repose underground in the grotto of Ornolhac, between the bones of a faithful guardian.

A certain Ramon Fort of Carmanan had one of the sacred books of the Albigensians in his possession at the end of the thirteenth century. Sensing that his life was insecure because of the possession of that book, he confided it to the Seigneur de Cambiac. That seigneur's wife belonged to the Christian faith and animated by an appetite for treason. She ran to inform the Inquisitors, but when they came, the book had disappeared. Torture made it known that it was in the hands of a certain Guilhem Viguier. Men went to his house to arrest him. He was found dead, seemingly by suicide. What had become of the book? It escaped the fury of the Inquisition. None of those who had kept it amorously and preserved it from destruction were Albigensians. There were no more Albigensians then. The radiant power of the doctrine had disengaged from the parchment the vivacious force that permitted the book to subsist, engendering fidelity in the hearts of those who possessed it but were no longer able to comprehend it. It must have been conserved for a long time in the archives of a château blackened by the old sieges of the time of faith. But where is Ramon Fort's book now?[57]

Almost all the authors who have studied the doctrine of the Albigensians have affirmed with the powerful authority that Christian prejudice gives and the ignorance that renders it invulnerable, that the Albigensians were either Manicheans or Catholic heresiarchs, of which the religion of Christ engenders so many. They are mistaken.

The Roman Church, in burning and extirpating, was logical from its own point of view. History shows that it had vowed the destruction of everything that was not in accord with its intangible dogma. With the Albigensians it was in the presence of an Occidental branch of the Asiatic tree, the flower of the millenarian Vedas, the pure truth of the Orient. The Albigensian belief that, after having spread through the south of France, might have extended its tolerance and its purity throughout the Occident, but which was to expire under the Pyrenean trees, was born under the fig-tree of Kapilavastu where the Buddha preached his reform.

The Albigensians were Occidental Buddhists who impregnated the Oriental doctrine with a mixture of Gnostic Christianity. How the words of the Indian sage were able to fly across the continents and fall into the souls of the people of the Languedoc we do not now, and it is, in any case, of scant importance. Thought has such a great fluidity that we are not sure whether it can act, even without means of expression, simply by the fact of being thought, by virtue of a subtle quality that escapes us. Buddhism traversed the world and it stirred what Catharism was in the people of Oc, then more mystical then sensual. It is probable that after the great surge toward the spirit, persecution and misfortune changed the race, caused it

---

[57] This story is another Peyrat invention. The remainder of this highly speculative section is, however, save for one acknowledged citation, the syncretic product of Magre's own imagination.

267

to retrogress and brought it back to the materialism of the southerners of today.

For the Albigensians, the origin of God was unknowable, in the same way that, for the Hindus, Brahma, the cause of causes, is enveloped by a sextuple veil and remains closed to human conception. At a given moment in time, the souls of humans, by virtue of a force of desire that Christians call original sin, were detached from the celestial matrix and the endless spirit is incarnated in matter in order to enjoy it and suffer from it. They commenced a course that, after having brought them to the lowest point of materialization, was to enable them to climb back up from step to step through the organized hierarchies of beings, toward the primal source, the divine spirit from which they were detached.

That latter part of the course, that return to the divine, is operated by successive reincarnations in imperfect human bodies. It is our endeavors in each life, our capacity for detachment, that enables us to elevate ourselves more or less rapidly. The more desires we have, the more we yield to our passions, the more we love that which is material and the more we delay our arrival in the realm of the Spirit.

It is by virtue of an illusion that we place happiness in the satisfaction of our senses. All pleasure of the senses is limited to a counteraction of dolor. Every physical enjoyment is comparable to a backward step that a traveler makes, turning his back on his goal. The goal is the return to the spirit, in which one enjoys endless bliss. That is what the Hindus call Nirvana, which is not, as the ignorant claim, the annihilation of consciousness, but participation in the universal consciousness, or something more subtle and inexpressible, a kind of permanent state of love, which that divine word can scarcely characterize. The means by which that can be reached is the extraction of oneself from the illusory prison of our body, the producer of apparent pleasures.

The Albigensian wisdom, like the Buddhist wisdom, provides a method for annihilating the desire of life, of escaping the law of reincarnation, of reentering in a single existence into the unity of the Spirit. It is a method of renunciation like the one prescribed by the Buddha.

There were several degrees in the sect. Those who simply adhered to it recognized the verity of the enunciated principles, defending them according to their means, but nevertheless continuing to live the life of the world, being believers. They corresponded with those who follow "the middle way" recommended by the Buddha to ordinary people, to the human majority, to all those not animated by a determination for immediate deliverance. Above them were the perfecti. They had sacrificed the life of their body for that of their spirit. They had renounced magnificence of costume, the property of wealth, the joys of nourishment and even the joys of the possession of women.

The perfecti could transmit, by mans of the consolamentum, the sign of purity, to give the dying the invisible aid that permitted them to escape the chain of rebirth and open access to the spiritual realm. The consolamentum was only an external symbol. The Albigensian perfecti were the inheritors of a lost secret originating from the Orient, known to the Gnostics and the first Christians. That secret is based on the transmission of a force of love. The ritual gesture was the material and visible means of projecting the force. Behind it was hidden the gift of the soul, by which the soul was aided to traverse without suffering the narrow portico of death, escape the shadow, and identify with the light.

No other people, at any time, was ever as well-versed in the magical rites that concern death. The consolamentum must have had a power that we cannot suspect, a certain and proven power, so far as the living were concerned, for it could not have propagated with such rapidity otherwise, and it would not have become so popular. The illumination of those who died must have been visible for the observers. And they had, in order to aid one another in dying, procedures that science has lost forever.

In the Black Mountains not far from Carcassonne, a crypt full of skeletons dating from the Albigensian era has

269

been found. "They were laid out in a circle, the heads in the center and the feet at the circumference, like the spokes of a perfect wheel."[58] Those who have studied magic rediscover in that posture for death a very ancient rite serving to facilitate the emergence of the soul and to enable it to traverse the intermediary realms thanks to the boost that union gives.

The consequence of the Albigensian philosophy is that life is bad and that it is appropriate to escape the form that encloses us within it. The principle of creation, the creator God, is therefore evil, since he has engendered form, the cause of evil. He is the Jehovah of the Old Testament, the irascible exterminator, who takes pleasure in punishment and vengeance. The Albigensians saw in that terrible God the retrograde power of matter. Jesus Christ, the symbol of the Word, came to inform humans of the means to escape that God and return to the celestial fatherland. Some people claim that Jesus had no terrestrial existence and only came among humans clad in a spiritual body, and that the miracles recounted in the New Testament have a symbolic character, only being realized on the plane of the Spirit. The blind were only cured of a spiritual blindness because they were blinded by sin. The tomb from which Lazarus returned was the tenebrous abode in which humans imprison themselves voluntarily.

The veritable worship of the Albigensians was that of the Holy Spirit, the divine Paraclete—which is to say, the principle that permits the human spirit to attain the truly real world of which ours is only the inverse or the caricature: the invisible world, the world of pure light, "the permanent and unalterable city."

What was able to flow from that belief had effects that, in spite of their rigorous logic, appeared monstrous to the men of the twelfth century, just as they appear monstrous to the men of the twentieth century. Suicide, in order to escape the evils of life, aggravated by persecutions, was, if not recommended, at least permitted.

---

[58] Author's reference: "N. Peyrat, *Histoire des Albigeois*."

The Albigensians gave themselves willingly to death by opening their veins, like the ancient Romans. But it was prescribed not to terminate life thus until one had attained absolute calm and complete indifference, in order to avoid in the afterlife the anguish obtained by a death obtained in anguish. The executioners of the Inquisition often found the Albigensian perfecti exsanguinated in their dungeons and bearing in the pallor of their visages the reflection of the eternal light toward which they had lunched themselves.

Women play an unusual role among them. They are the equals of men, for the law of reincarnation is indifferent to the sexes. The sole restriction on that equality is that they are not allowed to preach. Marriage is hateful and its indissoluble bonds are not recognized. The union of man and woman ought to have no other sanction than that of their reciprocal love. That union is, however, forbidden to the perfecti, who ought not to propagate the human species and thus perpetuate dolor in the slavery of form. The simple believers who unite themselves with one another in the flesh ought not to lose sight of the effort toward the final liberation. One therefore sees in the Midi the sons of the nobles families espousing, without any sort of ritual, the most humble prostitutes, the daughters of the Toulousan or Bitterois suburbs, or camp-followers, in order to regenerate them, to enable their soul to take a forward step on the long road to perfection, for that fraternal aid is the most noble mission of human beings on earth.

They professed a horror of lying and they took as far as the Hindus the prohibition of killing an animal and eating its flesh. They had the injustice, however, of excepting snakes from that prohibition, for it was one of their superstitions to believe that evil willingly incarnates itself in reptiles, and that the bodies of those creatures cannot under any pretext serve as the temporary body of a soul condemned to penitence in an animal form.

What excited the greatest hatred against them, however, was their scorn for terrestrial wealth, their exaltation of poverty as an ideal. They did not recognize property and as far as human history goes back, one sees that anyone who renounces that essential attachment and despoils himself with love has been an object of execration, because of the social danger that he poses.

It was imitation of the Albigensians that Dominic waked barefoot along the roads and begged, was a fashion of combating them with their own weapons, those of disinterest and poverty. Saint Francis and his order were only following their example. But the asceticism that was permitted to the respectful monks of the Church was no longer tolerated if it was generalized among an independent people whose voice was loud enough to protest its indignation against Roman tyranny and royal cupidity. One had the right to raise oneself toward God by meditation and asceticism if one was an obscure member of a monastery whose other members levied tithes and extracted taxes in accord with seigneurs and the King; but if an entire people ceased to labor and give birth, no longer recognizing the authority of its masters, only to obey an interior authority, if it decided to converse directly with God, neglecting interested intermediaries, it was better to destroy that people. That was what was done.

The principal cause of the great Albigensian massacre, the hidden but true cause, was that the secret of the sanctuaries, the ancient teaching of mysteries so jealously guarded in all the temples of the world by all fraternities of priests, had been revealed. More than that: it had been revealed and understood. What happened at that time had never been seen before in the history of the world. While the ecclesiastical guardians of the secret stammered the Latin ritual of its formula, the meaning of which they had lost in the bottom of their heart, the divine secret had been brought to the comtés of the Languedoc by unknown messengers, along the clear waters of the Tarn and the Ariège. The humblest of men had been dazzled by it, and they had laid down the sword and abandoned the plow in order to respond to the appeal of God. For the universe they had just glimpsed was a thousand times more beautiful than their horizon of vines or their valleys covered with forests.

But then the masters of sentences, the faithless guardians, knew that the gold of tabernacles was about to be extinguished, that the sumptuousness of altars was about to fade. They shivered, as the Brahmins of India had shivered for a danger less great at the moment of the reform of Buddha, like the Persian priests of fire when the words of Zoroaster resounded.

Woe betide those who take possession of the secret and reveal it! The hierarchies of Greek and Roman priests, supported by republics and emperors, also punished with death the divulging of mysteries. Never had the mystery been so completely unveiled for humans. Never had organized society with its edifice of priests, seigneurs and kings been in such great danger. The slaves might liberate themselves from their servitude without destroying their masters' fortresses, without evolution and without effort, naturally, by the simple play of their intellect. Pope Innocent III and Philippe Auguste must have had a vague consciousness that their domination was compromised, that their thrones would henceforth repose on a void. The oppressed mass of the weak was escaping the strong by means of a portal to the afterlife that had been opened by no one knew whom.

The war of the Albigensians was the greatest turning point of human religious history. When the laborer understands the vanity of laboring, when the beggar refuses alms because he discovers that he is richer than the person who gives them, when the words of priests become devoid of meaning because everyone has a higher consolation within himself, then the social organization crumbles of its own accord.

The liberation that humankind nearly acquired was much greater than that of a vanquished people that rids itself of its conqueror. It was liberation from evil itself, from its crushing nature. It was communicated with the rapidity of fire among pine trees in summer. But those who hate the light were the

273

stronger. Not content with extinguishing the divine fire, they ran after every wisp of straw susceptible of giving heat and light, and they covered the slightest spark with ashes. They summoned to their aid their old ally, the friend of Darkness, invincible ignorance. They did not allow even a fragment of information to subsist, not a single page of a book or inscription on a wall.

No trace had to subsist of the Albigensian verity. Six centuries later, when people flatter themselves on knowing everything and learning everything, history has been able to by-pass that enlightenment without reigniting it. The Albigensian war is nothing but the birth and death of a heresy, a chapter added to the history of French unity.

The sublime secret of the consolamentum, which permits humans to die in delight because they identify by the illumination of love with their interior God is lost forever. No hill in the Lauragais, no Pyrenean mountain, has retained the trace of it in its stone. In any case, ignorance has obscured souls to such an extent that no one thinks of looking for it; no one even believes in the possibility of its existence.

Ferrocas' Hawthorn

Napoléon Peyrat recounts in his *Histoire des Albigeois* than on going to visit the village of shepherds called Montségur, which is situated at the foot of the ruins of the château, he was struck by the sight of a tomb to the right of the roadside surmounted by an iron cross, devoid of ornaments. Having interrogated the guide who had led him there, the latter replied to him that it was the tomb of a certain Ferrocas, buried a few years before.

Ferrocas, whom the guide had known, was a solitary old peasant, a sort of country philosopher, who had never wanted to go to mass throughout his life. The curé had reproached him for that vehemently, and had even denounced him publicly from the height of his pulpit. Ferrocas claimed to be the only man to practice the true religion, which as not that of the churches. He said, familiarly, that he bore Christ within himself, that he discovered him a little more every day but that he would only find him completely much later, in a subsequent life—words incomprehensible for those who listened to him, and caused him to be reckoned a madman.

When he died, the curé, although he was a worthy man, resolved to set an example and forbade Ferrocas' body to be carried to the cemetery. The inhabitants of Montségur dug a grave for the old philosopher by the roadside, as if for a dog. Nevertheless, they elected to place the grave under a large white hawthorn. The equitable grace of nature caused the hawthorn to flourish intensely and to spread out in a vault of flowers The curé died in his turn, but his successor, to whom the story of the impious individual was recounted, and who went past his floral monument every day, had the hawthorn cut down and planted in its place the rude cross that Napoléon Peyrat saw.

It was about 1860 when that historian, passionate about the Midi, visited Montségur and saw Ferrocas' cross.

275

Ferrocas was doubtless the last Albigensian, an Albigensian who must have carried semi-consciously within him the residues of the doctrine for which his forefathers had died. But it was written that, until the very last, the pure of southern France would be persecuted in their faith. It is because of the liberty of the century that Ferrocas' bones were not disinterred and dispersed. His white hawthorn was uprooted. He has still to endure over his mortal remains the weight of that cross, in the name of which he had once been made to suffer and die.

Poor Ferrocas of the Ariège! His fate is that of all the men of the Midi. When the great Albigensian movement was extinct, the grandchildren and the great-grandchildren of the heretics were obliged to bear on their garments, in front and behind, a yellow cross a foot long, in order that their heresy was known and that the malediction could be perpetuated over them. Civil employment and the right to engage in commerce were refused to them. Under the name of cagots they were assimilated to lepers in the villages of the mountains.[59] Like them, they had a special street or quarter in each town, they could only enter the church through a side door in a reserved chapel because the stones that their feet touched remained soiled.

Nowadays the descendants of the Albigensians no longer suffer the same treatment as lepers and no yellow cross is displayed on their chests. That is because they have become similar to common humankind. But they all bear a sign more redoubtable than the yellow cross, which is that of ignorance. They have forgotten. They no longer know. They have been detached from the woes of their forefathers. They learn the history of France, vaguely, but they do not know the history of their homeland. When the bell of the Church of San Salvi resonates in Albi, it does not awaken any echo. No one numbers

---

[59] By the time he wrote *Le Sang de Toulouse* Magre had obviously discovered that the *cagots* antedated the Albigensian crusade.

of the dead of the Pré-comtal near Toulouse. When foreigners wandering along the ramparts of Carcassonne carrying the mute Baedeker under their arms ask what dust is rising on the far horizon, no one replies that it is the phantom of Montfort's army.

When I was twenty years old, coming from my home-land of Toulouse, I went down the slopes of the Castellar of Pamiers, where Esclarmonde de Foix had lived, without emo-tion; I have seen Mirepoix and Lavelanet; I have walked on the roads where Esclarmonde d'Alion's horse whinnied with-out knowing the epic that had once unfolded in those places. All I knew about the Albigensians was what one can learn at school—which is to say, barely the name, the glory of Simon de Montfort and the defeat of Toulouse. I have advanced be-tween the peak of Bidorte and the forest of Bélesta, among the chestnut trees and the ferns, to the sound of sawmills and wa-ter splashing against rocks. I thought I saw in the distance the vague silhouette of a ruin, that of Montségur, and as the sun was about to set I measured the distance, my meager curiosity, and decided to retrace my steps.

It is the same for all those who have wanted to study Catharism and its sublime philosophy. They are put off by overly complicated documents, they have found the route too long. They have glimpsed from afar, veiled in clouds, the tow-er of Montségur, and they have renounced reaching it.

It is necessary for me to remember my walk of days gone by to explain to myself the forgetfulness into which an entire section of history has fallen. And I wonder sometimes whether there is not a more profound cause than the absence of clear texts that has distanced Occidental minds from the wisdom of the perfect sect. When I see cultivated southerners confound-ing their heroic ancestors with the Saracens, and even the Goths, and when I see those erudite in the history of philoso-phies and religions paying no attention to the Cathar doctrine, I think of a kind of conspiracy of silence, an organized effort to keep the dead truth silent.

It is true that verity is imperishable and when it is stifled here it is reborn elsewhere, a little later, in a more beautiful form. It is true that an iron cross beside a road still remains, the symbol of the spirit. But in place of the one that stands to the right, a little before arriving in Montségur, who will plant Ferrocas' hawthorn again?